$\mathcal{T}$he face-eating thorns lurked below, waiting for Angela to slip.

She eased one foot a millimeter off the rung.

"I don't suppose you need any help up there?"

The voice, deep in timbre and unabashedly male, startled Angela. Gripping the ladder with both hands, she found the next rung with her seeking toes. Only then did she dare to look down.

Her stomach lurched for a different reason. The man down there was *gorgeous*.

His dark blond hair was on the long side—a style Angela always appreciated, because it gave a girl more to grab hold of during sex. Blue eyes, as near as she could tell from here, a rough five o'clock shadow, and an easy smile. Possibly even a dimple.

Hot, hot, hot…

POSSESSED UNDRESSED

& in a mess

sophie mouette

LITTLE KISSES PRESS

POSSESSED, UNDRESSED, AND IN A MESS
Sophie Mouette

Print edition published 2014 by Little Kisses Press

ISBN-13: 978-0692251904 (trade paperback)
ISBN-10: 0692251901 (trade paperback)

Inquiries should be addressed to
Little Kisses Press
littlekissespress@gmail.com
http://www.littlekissespress.com

Cover image © iancucristi / Bigstockphoto.com
Little Kisses Press logo by Dayle Dermatis

For all lovers of Victoriana, hidden treasure,
and ghosts that ~~go bump~~ moan in the night—
and, as always, to Ken and Jeff,
who stole my heart like thieves in the night.

POSSESSED
UNDRESSED
& in a mess

Chapter 1

Angela balanced on the rickety ladder and prayed she wouldn't fall. The ladder wasn't actually rickety. It wasn't exactly new, and it wasn't fancy, but it wasn't old. But it *did* wobble a teeny bit. And she hated heights, even just ladder heights, and she couldn't shake the nagging sense that the ladder was about to collapse under her, or topple sideways and land her in a rosebush with a broken arm and a disfiguring gash across her cheek from a thorn.

The chill wind blowing in off the ocean, numbing her fingers, was no help at all.

Still, as she drove the nail cleanly into the wood with a single hammer blow, reinforcing the butter-yellow shingle that had come loose in the recent winds, she couldn't help but feel a level of contentment, too. Below her, the blustery breeze goosed the hotel's sign, causing it to swing back and forth on its chains.

Angelika

It still gave her a thrill of pride every time she saw it, thinking about the hard work she and Kari had put into restoring the place and making it into a swank spa and artists' retreat. Last year, their first, had been a bated-breath affair, but they'd gotten a good write-up in several magazines—from the *LA Times* to *Poets and Writers*—and taken off. Some solid Yelp reviews had boosted the signal. They hadn't turned much of a profit last year, but they'd broken even, which was stellar for a new small business. Now they were entering their second year, coming off the post-Valentine's Day lull with weekends, and many of the weeks, booked solid for the first six weeks of the summer.

Which was good and bad, because while the taste of success was thrilling, she and Kari were scrambling to make sure Angelika was ready for the onslaught—on a budget for which "tight" would be a compliment. All those bookings were great, but until the guests actually showed up, the hotel was strapped for ready cash.

With the shingle firmly attached to the house again, she could get off this Ladder of Certain Doom. Her stomach twisted. She had to climb down. She had to move her feet from her relatively safe, stable position.

The face-eating thorns lurked below, waiting for her to slip.

She eased one foot a millimeter off the rung.

"I don't suppose you need any help up there?"

The voice, deep in timbre and unabashedly male, startled her. Gripping the ladder with both hands, she found the next rung with her seeking toes. Only then did she dare to look down.

Her stomach lurched for a different reason. The man down there was *gorgeous.*

His dark blond hair was on the long side—a style Angela always appreciated, because it gave a girl more to grab hold of during sex. Blue eyes, as near as she could tell from here, a rough five o'clock shadow, and an easy smile. Possibly even a dimple.

Hot, hot, hot.

She took a deep breath. "Nope, I'm fine. What can I do for you? Looking for a room?"

"Actually, I'm here about the handyman job you advertised." He graced her with a slow, easy smile. "Although it looks like you're doing just fine on your own."

Somehow, he made that sound dirty. If she wasn't mistaken, those heavy-lidded eyes were appraising her ass.

She used that thought and his voice to distract her, and made it down the ladder without becoming intimate with the rosebush.

He had a very nice voice.

She gave a small, silent prayer when her feet hit the ground, then turned to face Mr. Gorgeous, their potential savior.

She was a tall woman—statuesque, a former lover had said, like the beautiful, imposing marble goddesses her Mediterranean ancestors had left behind—but he was a perfect couple of inches taller.

The potential handyman wore a fitted red T-shirt that had seen more vibrant days, although repeated washings had also softened the cotton so that it molded across his chest, arms, and stomach, revealing muscles more likely gained from healthy outdoor work than from reps in a gym. His faded jeans also clung to his body, not tight enough to reveal his religion, but enough to let the world know his side-dressing preference.

Left, in this case.

Angela resisted the urge to circle him and admire the view from behind. After all, he'd had the opportunity to do that to her already.

In the circular drive she saw a battered blue pickup with a shiny toolbox at the front end of the bed and a ladder across the top that was newer and fancier than hers. Probably less rickety, too.

"Glad you saw our ad," she said. "You come with references?" Oh, like *that* didn't sound like a double entendre.

His mouth twitched, and she had the distinct impression that he'd taken her words the wrong way. Or the right way, depending on how you looked at it.

"I do." He dug into his back pocket and retrieved a folded piece of paper. How he'd managed to get anything into those tight jeans was nothing short of a miracle. He smoothed out the paper and handed it to her.

"I'm impressed," she said after skimming the information. An understatement. He didn't just have work experience—he had training in restoration architecture and architectural history. Made her wonder just a bit why he was looking for work in historic, but isolated, San Sebastian, let alone at the salary she was offering.

But she shouldn't look a gift horse in the mouth as long as the references panned out. Especially when the mouth in question made her think wicked thoughts.

"Thank you," he said.

She looked up from the résumé. He was grinning. She suspected he was grinning because she was all too obviously impressed with more than his credentials.

And yes, there was a dimple. *Damn.*

She grinned back. She had no qualms about fooling around with employees. If everyone was an adult and in agreement, why not?

But she was getting ahead of herself. She needed a handyman more than she needed a hot, hard screw. At this rate, she'd screw him just to never have to go up that ladder herself ever again.

As if reading her mind, he said, "By the way, you've got another shingle loose up there." He pointed to a scallop-shaped piece of wood several feet higher than the one she'd just fixed, toward the end of the building where the rosebushes were particularly vicious.

Angela groaned.

"Tell you what," the gorgeous potential handyman said. "I'll go ahead and fix that one for you. And I'll rescue the hammer you left on top of your ladder."

"I still have to call a couple of your references," Angela warned.

"No problem. This one's on the house—so to speak. It's the least I can do to thank you for the view."

Angela glanced down, following his gaze. Thanks to the chilly spring wind, her nipples were clearly prominent beneath her silk-and-cotton burgundy Henley top.

He was a cheeky one, all right. Just for that, he could do the job. Maybe she could get him to do her, too. Maybe in exchange for figuring out what had gone all wonky with the plumbing in Bathhouse Three? Because the way he looked at her made her insides clench.

She stuck out her hand. "I'm Angela Georgenes, by the way. Co-owner of Angelika."

His hand was warm, surrounding hers in a firm grip, and he didn't let go right away. "Tyler Woodruff."

He went to get his own ladder, and she reluctantly pulled her gaze away from him, pausing before she went inside, as she always did, to admire the hotel.

Victorian houses of this type were called Painted Ladies, and the color scheme she and Kari had chosen, while garish, was nonetheless entirely correct for a late 1800s building: rose-pink, robin's-egg blue, and custard yellow picking out the fanciful shingling details, accenting the ornate gingerbread trim on the wraparound porch.

The wind brought with it the salty tang of the ocean. Angelika's gardens extended back to the cliff side; a short walk away was the path down to the beach. The northern California coast wasn't the warm, tropical paradise of the southern beaches, but it had a windswept, almost dangerous beauty about it, especially on overcast days like today. (They kept extra slickers and sweaters on hand because some of their guests, the artists especially, seemed most drawn to the beach in the worst possible weather.)

Indulging herself in one last glance at Tyler—who looked quite fine up there on the ladder, his biceps flexing as he hammered—she went inside.

She found Kari in the hotel office, on the phone.

Her friend and Angelika co-owner sitting on the floor in a lotus position, her hazel eyes closed. Her blond hair was pulled up into a plastic clip, wisps escaping every which way.

"No, Saturday. *This* Saturday. Not next week. No, not next Saturday. Two-days-from-now-Saturday." Kari lifted the pale pink receipt in her hand as if the person on the other end of the line could see it. Angela, who *could* see it, identified it as being from their towel delivery and laundry service. While Angela handled the hotel end of things, Kari, a massage therapist, ran the spa. Angelika featured natural hot springs baths, various types of massage, facials, manicures and pedicures, and even mud baths.

"Yes. Right," Kari said after a pause. "This Saturday. Read me the date again, please. Exactly! Thank you so much! We'll see you Saturday."

She hung up and pulled the headset off. "Why does everything go to hell in a handbasket the day before we open for the busy season?" she demanded. There was no real hostility in her voice, though. Kari was too mellow for that. Which was why she was such a good massage therapist: she was the most calm and grounded person Angela had ever met, and she was able to impart that serenity to others.

"Not everything," Angela said, doing a quick dance of triumph. "I think we've found our handyman."

"Where?" Kari asked.

It wasn't a strange question. San Sebastian wasn't big, and when their last handyman had buggered off to Kansas or Iowa or Missouri or somewhere to join his partner, the pickings had been slim. There were enough folks with basic carpentry or plumbing or drywall skills, but none who knew the vagaries of old houses. Well, there were a few, but they were busy keeping their own Victorian homes in one piece on top of their other jobs.

"Well, right now he's fixing shingles out front," Angela said. She glanced again at the résumé Tyler had handed her. "Down from Oregon, apparently. And he's gorgeous."

"Really?" Kari's hazel eyes lit up.

"I saw him first," Angela said.

"That's okay. I've got a feeling this one is meant for you."

"You haven't even met him yet."

Kari shrugged, her smile serene. "Doesn't matter. My intuition is telling me this guy's going to be important to you, and I know to listen to my intuition."

Angela shook her head, as always, at Kari's New Age outlook and called the references on Tyler's list. The second one didn't answer, but the first and third gave him such glowing reports that she didn't bother contacting more. Instead, she printed out the various employment forms, labeled a file folder with Tyler's name, stuck his résumé inside, and left the paperwork in a neat pile on her desk.

Kari was on the phone again when she passed, but seemed considerably less stressed than she had from her last call. Her smile and her more relaxed tone suggested she was talking with Cybelline, owner of the New

Age shop The Silver Stag, about the séance they were planning to celebrate Minerva's birthday.

Minerva May Fenwick: hedonist, world traveler, scholar, poet, forward thinker, artists' model, artist. She'd had the mansion built in 1893, not only as a home base when she wasn't spanning the globe in search of adventure, but also as a salon and hotel for the free expression of both thought and pleasure.

Angela and Kari had organized a "Minerva's birthday party" last year, with oysters on the half shell, asparagus, and plenty of the champagne Minerva had loved—as well as the legal version of the absinthe she'd also loved. But coffee with their new friend Cybelline, during which they'd mentioned a passage in one of Minerva's travelogues about attending a spiritualist gathering, had inspired a new idea.

Cybelline, in fact, had been the one to point out Minerva's birthday fell on a full moon and had urged them to follow through on the séance. Despite her classic New-Age-flake name and occupation, Cybelline was professional, methodical, and easy to work with—and she wouldn't take no for an answer when it came to organizing the séance. She'd taken over all the details, spending several evenings at the hotel after her shop was closed.

If the séance worked well, they might consider having one as a regular Halloween feature.

Angela grabbed a bottle of water from the industrial fridge in the kitchen, noting that Franklin, their cook, had been out shopping. A huge braided bunch of garlic heads on the butcher block workstation filled the room with glorious scent.

Outside, she found Tyler climbing down the ladder. Quite a few shingles looked more stable now. Now she also finally got the view he'd gotten of her. Damn, even the chamois-colored work belt he wore looked sexy, the way it slung low on his hips and outlined his ass, which was as lusciously firm as she'd imagined it would be.

"Good news," she said, tossing him the water. "You've got the job. We just have some paperwork to deal with."

"Fantastic," he said. "Mind if I leave the ladder for now?"

"Not a problem." No doubt there were even more loose shingles. Try as they might, there always were.

He left the tool belt at the base of the ladder and followed her inside. He gave a low whistle when he saw the lobby, and Angela flushed with pride.

The lobby alone had been featured in several upscale magazines. The pine beadboard, perfectly restored, was stained dark and gleamed with polish. Shield-back chairs with acanthus-leaf trim and matching occasional tables dotted the room. The entrance to the check-in area was framed with spoked trim, painted blue. A wide staircase went up the center to split into two halfway up, each then turning back and heading up to the second floor.

Even the plants were correct for the period: lush maidenhair ferns on delicate stands; a hulking, tropical-looking aspidistra in one corner; and, on the reception desk, small pots of fragrant amethyst heliotrope.

"Upstairs has two wings," Angela explained, seeing the curiosity and appreciation in his eyes. "One history of the building had said they'd been a men's wing and a women's wing—standard Victorian practice—but we know for a fact that the wings hadn't been separated by gender."

In fact, they had mixed as often as possible, except for the guests who preferred the company of their own sex, but Tyler didn't need to know that right now.

Angela, meanwhile, dragged her cursedly vivid imagination away from thoughts of mixing with Tyler. Repeatedly.

As they stood there, a lanky greyhound got to its feet and ambled up to them, toenails clicking on the oak flooring. Tyler held out his hand and the dog sniffed it carefully, then leaned against his leg, gazing adoringly up at him with liquid brown eyes.

"That seals the deal, then," Angela said. "Isabella's acceptance is the final test."

"She's a beautiful dog," he said, stroking the short, soft fur between Isabella's floppy ears. Isabella sighed in contentment and leaned harder into his thigh. To his credit, Tyler didn't have to readjust to brace himself.

"Thank you," Angela said. She hadn't been kidding about Isabella accepting him. She trusted the dog's judgment. "She's a rescue, after two years on the track. Kari found her, but she's definitely our dog. Or we're her people."

Isabella followed them into the office, circled once on a large bean-bag-like dog bed in the corner, and then lay down, thin legs splayed.

Angela passed the paperwork and a ballpoint pen across the desk, and he began filling out the information in bold handwriting.

"Do you have a place to stay?" she asked.

He glanced up. "I've rented a room from a Mrs. Parsons on Spring Street." He went back to writing, but added, "Although I might have to move if she makes another pass at me. Older women are wonderful, but I draw the line at someone old enough to be my great-grandmother."

Angela snorted. Adelle Parsons was known for her healthy interest in men of all ages as well as her complete lack of censure when it came to propositioning them. Apparently Minerva's decadent ways had rubbed off on her—unfortunately without Minerva's reported wit and style.

"Thankfully, you can outrun her," she said. "Just remember to keep your door locked at night, and you'll be safe."

Truth be told, she liked the quirky old biddy, who remembered the mansion as Fenwick House when Minerva May Fenwick was still running it. The more they'd heard about Minerva, from Adelle's tales as well as from the journal, the more affection Angela and Kari developed for Minerva.

Tyler handed the paperwork back to her, and she glanced over the forms before putting them in the file folder.

"Can you start tomorrow?" she asked.

He spread his hands. "I can start today if you've got something for me to do."

Oh, she did, all right. It involved her desk, her naked body, and those hands of his all over her. For starters.

Without looking down, she knew her nipples were hard again—she could feel the lovely, anxious ache—and this time it had nothing to do with the cold.

Still, it was better not to jump the help minutes after hiring them. Better professionally, anyway. Surely some etiquette book covered that.

"I think we're set for today," she said. "I'll sit down for a few minutes tonight and make up a list of things for you to look at tomorrow, though."

She stood and stuck out her hand again, wanting to feel his flesh against hers again, wanting to experience the touch of his hand again to fuel her fantasies later.

He didn't disappoint her. The warmth of his firm, calloused touch heated her blood. His eyes claimed hers as he said, "Don't stay up late on my account."

If he only knew. Actually, he probably guessed—and that thought made her wet.

"With a place this old, there's always something needing fixing," she said with a laugh. "You're the one who'll need a good night's sleep to keep your strength up."

He gave her hand a final squeeze before letting go. "Shouldn't be a problem, unless I forget to lock my door against Mrs. Parsons."

*

With a final pat on Isabella's head, because the dog had followed him to the front door, Tyler left Angelika. When he got in his truck, however, he didn't start it up immediately. Instead, he sat, contemplating the stunning, garish hotel before him.

His paperwork had checked out. He hadn't expected it not to, but there was always the risk that someone would dig too deep, catch a discrepancy he hadn't noticed.

He had a sense that the very tasty Angela Georgenes wasn't usually the type to miss discrepancies.

He shifted on the seat, not a little uncomfortably, as his thoughts about the attractive hotel owner went in a decidedly coarser direction. It had been a pleasure to stand there and watch her tight little ass in tight little jeans as she perched at the top of the ladder. Hell, watching the wind toy with her long, curly, dark hair had made him envy the wind.

Her lips and nails had been the same burgundy shade as the knit shirt that had clung nicely to her curves. The material had been light enough that it hadn't hidden the way her nipples had responded to the cold—and to him. He wondered if the tight buds were the same hue of dark red that she favored.

If he didn't stop thinking about that, driving was going to become rather difficult. He forced his thoughts to other things.

It was a pity, really, that he couldn't get to know her well. He really *did* have an interest in old houses—he didn't have to lie about that part—and it was refreshing to meet someone with a similar passion who wasn't gay, married, or approaching Mrs. Parsons' advanced age.

He'd do a good job for her. That was a matter of responsibility, and he took his responsibilities seriously. He never promised something he couldn't follow through on.

He was just very, very good at not mentioning certain things. Things like the real reason he'd come to San Sebastian, or his actual motivation for seeking out Angelika.

He started the truck. No, the sexy Ms. Georgenes wouldn't be happy at all if she found out about that.

Chapter 2

*I*t was a bad, bad day for the front desk clerk to call in sick.
Very bad.

Only one set of guests had been due to check in, but there were approximately eight-thousand six-hundred and eighty-three phone calls to be fielded (half of them to be transferred back to the spa, where at least Kari had someone to handle the booking requests) and questions to be answered and deliveries to be signed for, and Angela needed to be five other places.

Thank goodness for her Bluetooth headset and the ability to transfer incoming calls to her cell, or she'd have to clone herself.

Hm. That sounded like a tempting proposition. One of her could be handling the front desk, one of her could be doing her actual job, and one of her could be writing the e-mail she owed her parents about getting together in San Francisco in a few weeks (she didn't have time for a day off, but she was going to meet them anyway, because who knew when they'd be in the country again?). And one of her could be back in her room, alternately catching up on her sleep and pleasuring herself to naughty and occasionally perverse thoughts of Tyler.

Of course, if she could also clone Tyler...

Angela blinked, looking around the office. Other than a framed Victorian seaside print that was decidedly askew on the pumpkin-colored wall, everything seemed to be—for a second or two—actually in order.

Not only that, but there was blissful silence. No phones ringing, no questions…

With a whimper, Angela slumped back in the leather office chair and closed her eyes. Isabella stood with a jingle of her collar bell, and padded over to insinuate herself under Angela's dangling hand.

Rough greyhound fur and a few moments of blessed peace.

Peace was a relative term. But in a day full of frantic phone calls, and last-minute deliveries, and the extra housekeeping staff getting everything ready for the guests who'd be arriving tonight and tomorrow (and bombarding her with questions since they were still getting back into their seasonal groove), and Tyler popping in with updates, a minute or two when the phone wasn't ringing off the hook and no one but the dog needed her urgently (insofar as being petted was an urgent matter—it was to Isabella, at least) was a minor taste of paradise.

Now, if only Tyler would saunter in and say he needed her urgently—and her not having to tell him where the touch-up paint or the third fuse box was hiding or what items in the dining room (which needed the touch-up paint) were especially valuable and fragile—that would be a *real* taste of paradise.

Of course, even such mundane questions had their benefits. She'd take any excuse to look into his melting blue eyes while they talked and cock her head to ogle his tight buns while he walked away. She hadn't been distracted by a new acquaintance in so long she'd almost forgotten how much fun the dance was.

Feeling that erotic spark when a wickedly hot man walked in, and catching the glint in his eyes that said he was feeling it, too.

Flirting, and being teased right back. Testing the waters

Hmm…she'd love to test the waters with him, maybe in one of the bath houses. It wasn't fair that she was part-owner of the hotel and yet she'd never had the opportunity to enjoy the luxurious baths in the intimate way she guessed some of the guests did, or as Minerva described in her journal in loving detail.

Minerva once held a full-moon party that, after rivers of champagne and absinthe, ended with half the guests doing wildly carnal things in the baths and gardens. Which was certainly an interesting fantasy image, but Angela would settle for getting naked with just Tyler.

She was configuring him for her maximum imaginary pleasure when the bell on the front door jangled, announcing an entrance.

Angela jumped, dragging her mind out of the gutter. Isabella poked her head out around the desk, then settled back down, dismissing the two women who'd entered. They weren't Kari, and they didn't appear to have doggie treats, so they weren't worth getting excited for.

Angela didn't have the same luxury. Taking a deep breath, she rearranged her face into a welcoming smile, because smiling always made her feel a little more cheerful anyway, and stepped up to the counter.

Both women had what she deemed the Hollywood Executive Look: polished to glossiness and stressed to the breaking point.

The one on the left had a honey-blond chin-length bob and a full mouth bracketed with laugh lines, but that mouth was set so tensely now that they looked more like frown lines. She simply looked tired.

The slightly older one—mid-fifties, Angela pegged her, although a nipped and tucked and Botoxed mid-fifties that could pass for early forties if you didn't look too hard—was in worse straits. Her eyes were haunted, and she looked like she'd been running on nerves so long she'd forgotten there was another way.

A woman direly in need of being stripped out of her expensive power suit and pampered to within an inch of her life before she snapped in two.

Well, she was in the right place for pampering. Kari and her staff would take good care of her and her blond friend as well, get them massaged and scented and centered and ready to face the world again.

But who were they? No one else was due in today.

She scanned the register.

There they were: Carole van Horn and Barb Swain, a producer and… Angela couldn't remember the details, but maybe a potential investor? In any case, they were at Angelika to discuss a movie project. That would explain why the older one looked ready to snap. Hollywood ran on stress.

A second glance suggested another reason. The older woman had a pale circle on her ring finger, where a wedding ring obviously had been until recently. Definitely in need of Kari's spa-magic.

And at the moment, so was Angela. Angela stifled the urge to clutch her hair and wail. Carole and Barb weren't due to arrive until *tomorrow*. Gah!

There was no way in hell she could actually point that out to them. Bad customer service, and besides, the older woman would probably cry, if not just melt into a hysterical puddle that would necessitate refinishing the hardwood floor.

Deep breath. She could handle it. This was only a tiny crisis. Just a question of whether their rooms were ready or not. And how they'd react if the rooms weren't ready. And whether they planned to eat here tonight.

Okay, maybe a medium-sized crisis. On the other hand, at least she was here to take care of it, not the desk clerk, who'd have needed to track her down.

"Ms. van Horn and Ms. Swain? Welcome to Angelika. I'm Angela Georgenes."

"Thank God we're here!" the younger woman said. "We got so lost. I thought we'd never make it. Sorry about that, Carole," she added.

Okay. The blond was Barb. Angela made a mental note of that. Personal attention to guests was a matter of pride for her.

"No problem. It gave me time to catch up on my e-mail," Carole said in a tense voice that suggested it wasn't okay at all.

"You're right on time for tea." Angela punted in the only way she knew how: offer comfort food (chocolate could solve just about anything) and soothing, caffeinated beverages. "Let me show you into the parlor and I'll call over to the kitchen." Okay, they hadn't planned on serving tea today, but Franklin, their amazing chef, had been trying out a few new desserts and she had the utmost faith they'd be delicious.

Franklin was always prepared to feed a small army at a moment's notice, in any case, which meant the dinner crisis could probably be averted.

That would give her time to check on the rooms.

She got the wayward guests settled in the parlor enjoying some of Franklin's exquisite, caloric delicacies and a pot of Oolong.

Carol took one nibble and asked for a recipe. Barb made a laughing comment to the effect of "I can burn water, but for these I might try cooking again." She took another bite and said, though a mouthful of rich, chocolaty pastry, "Nah, I hate cooking. I'll just come back here."

Angela hedged about finding out if Franklin would disclose his recipes—she knew he wouldn't—and slipped away. Once she was out of their direct view, she raced up the stairs two at a time.

Thank the powers that be, Housekeeping had done their usual wonderful work a day ahead of schedule. The Cairo Room, with its pseudo-Egyptian kitsch, needed nothing more than straightening a picture of a voluptuous belly dancer balancing a sword on her head. (What was it with art being ajar today?)

Satisfied there, Angela passed to the adjoining room that would be Carole's.

A good choice for the stressed-out recent divorcée. Ocean Mists was all in calming shades of blue, with a sand-colored maple floor, grey-blue and pale jade linens on the bed, and drapes in the same seaside tones.

Drapes that were currently closed, obscuring the stunning sea view. Angela twitched them open.

And stared, transfixed, not at the ocean, but at something equally scenic that was much closer.

Kari had conscripted Tyler into hauling around some giant potted plants that had been in the greenhouse over the winter. They normally lined the walkway between the bath houses.

There were eight bath houses in all, little shack-like buildings decorated with gingerbread trim and painted the same colors as the hotel. Fancifully, Angela thought it looked as though the hotel had given birth to a litter. Inside, each one contained a brightly tiled square tub, sunk into the floor with steps leading down, so bathers could immerse themselves as deep as they wanted.

But that was the furthest thing from her mind right now.

Even from up here, Angela could see Tyler's biceps flex as he man-handled the enormous pot, his movements quick and efficient. She sighed. She felt like a schoolgirl with a crush—although when she'd been a schoolgirl, her crushes hadn't been accompanied by such detailed fantasies about how she wanted to be manhandled.

In a steamy bath house á là Minerva, hot water and hot hands and a hot mouth sluicing over her sensitive skin until she cried out in ecstasy. In the garden under a full moon, again á là Minerva. Or bent over the fainting couch in the parlor, her skirt bunched around her waist, thrusting back to meet the rhythmic assault of hard cock. Or in any of the big, luxurious beds in the hotel, with the space and freedom and time to indulge in drawn-out, teasing foreplay that made orgasms that much sweeter.

Hell, in all of them in succession. Maybe a little bondage in the sturdiest of the four-posters—and either of them being tied up could be equally fun. The mental image of Tyler, naked and stretched out, muscles taut against the restraints, hard and aching for her, made her catch her breath.

God, she'd been hot and bothered to begin with. Now she was smoking. Tonight she would definitely enjoy an extended masturbation session, with toys and fantasies and maybe a glass of wine to make it a real date with herself.

Of course she'd promised herself that last night, too, because ever since she'd met Tyler, she'd been awash in sexual fantasies. Alas, she'd been so tired by the time she dragged herself to bed last night that she'd had two sips of wine and fallen asleep with her hand between her legs and her favorite purple vibrator untouched and forlorn on the trunk that doubled as a bedside table.

Then she'd been woken out of a sound sleep at 6 a.m. by a potential guest from London who'd miscalculated the time difference, and she'd been off and running ever since.

Well, she didn't have time to do anything about her arousal now, not to mention it would be grossly inappropriate in the middle of the work day, with guests waiting for their rooms. But she could at least take a couple of minutes to breathe. Kari always said paying attention to your breath relieved stress and focused you, which she sorely needed. That's it, breathe deeply and enjoy the view out the window. And if the view happened to include a handsome handyman putting his muscles to good use, no harm in that.

Maybe the deep-breathing exercises and the inevitable naughty thoughts about Tyler would balance out, leaving her calmer and full of positive thoughts. Sexy thoughts, sure, but positive ones.

She leaned against the windowsill. It was a beautiful day. The gardens were shaping up nicely, though they'd probably never reflect the glory of Minerva's era. But Tyler's arms, even from a distance, were the best part of the view. God, she could almost feel those arms wrapped around her...

Watching Tyler's muscles flex as he placed planters along the walkway sent her into a dreamy fantasy, her vision hazing around the edges as she fell deeper under the spell of arousal. So deep that when he looked up, when their eyes met, at first she just thought it was part of her erotic daydream.

He wasn't looking at her in the same moony way she was watching him, though. As far as she could tell, he was just studying Angelika. That appealed, though, in its own right. He wasn't just insanely sexy, but genuinely interested in the home she was so proud of.

Angela realized with a start that she'd been rocking her hips against the windowsill to a sexy beat only she could hear. Good thing he hadn't been paying attention to her. Not that he'd probably be able to tell she'd been unconsciously rubbing up against the windowsill like a cat in heat, let alone that she'd been thinking about him while doing it, but *she'd* know. That kind of thing wasn't good in a professional relationship.

How would he react if he knew? Horribly unprofessional or not, it might turn him on knowing he was the object of her fantasies. She liked to think so. A fresh wave of desire skittered through her at the thought.

As if hearing her naughty contemplation, he raised his head and his gaze found her window—and her.

For a moment their eyes met, and neither moved.

How would Minerva have handled the situation? A smile curved the corner of Angela's mouth. Minerva would have leaned out the window, her breasts spilling from her loosened corset, crooked her finger, and throatily invited the sexy handyman up to the room. By the time he arrived, she'd be stripped down to her corset and knickers and wicked smile, lounging on the bed with her hand between her thighs.

Images flooded her mind, enflamed her senses. Tyler inside her, filling her, his lips at her collarbone. Tyler playing with himself, eyes dark and hooded as he watched her bring herself off. Wanton Minerva, long ago, luring the handyman to her bed of pleasure.

Deep breath. Take a deep breath in, hold it. Now let it out slowly. What was it Kari said? Try to make the exhale about twice as long as the inhale when you were feeling stressed, because it calmed the nervous system. (What Kari said was more complicated than that and involved a few Sanskrit terms, but that was the gist of it.) Angela didn't exactly feel stressed, except from rampaging desire she wasn't in a position to satisfy, but the deep breaths were soothing.

Down on the lawn, Tyler nodded his head and touched his fingers to the brim of the ball cap he wore to keep the sun out of his eyes.

Gallant. A little cheeky, even. God, that alone was enough to make her clench a little.

Great, just when she'd been starting to calm down.

Taking another deep breath, she waved back, and he returned to his work.

As she headed back to hers, she couldn't help wondering why that little exchange felt so significant. She felt like they were now co-conspirators. But at what?

Flirtation, maybe. And that could be both delicious and dangerous.

*

Tyler had shivered through a cold frisson of panic when he discovered Angela was watching him. How much had she seen?

Calm down. There had been nothing for her to see. He'd just been looking at the hotel. If she asked, he could say that he was scanning the roof for problems, or double-checking the shingles he'd repaired this morning.

Pulling off his cap, he swiped his wrist across his brow. It wasn't hot out, but the steady physical work had scared up a sweat on him.

The shingle repair had been something of a coup. He'd been able to take some measurements of the house and, on the ladder, peer into every one of the upstairs windows to get a sense of each room. Obviously, he'd check out every room from the inside as well, but it was important to get the lay of the land from all angles, and so far he'd been able to examine things unnoticed.

He mentally kicked himself for not checking out the rooms before the guests started arriving. But there simply hadn't been time, since he had to carry out his own investigations while doing his hotel-handyman best. After all, a building this beautiful deserved his best.

Not that it was the only beauty around here. Unbidden, his thoughts turned to Angela again. To distract himself, he heaved up the wheelbarrow again, replacing desire with the stretch and pull of physical labor.

He'd felt a prickle on his neck right before he noticed her watching him. From this distance, he hadn't been able to discern the expression in her eyes, but she'd been leaning on the windowsill as if to see him better, and smiling like they were sharing a special, sexy secret.

Screwing the boss was a dodgy proposition at best. Sex could get messy fast in a situation like that—and his plans would be shattered if he were fired.

Somehow, though, he had the sense that Angela, with her mysterious dark eyes and long, long legs, wasn't the type to cry foul at attention from anybody. If she didn't want it, she'd brush it off good-naturedly.

But if she did, she'd go for it, full throttle.

And if he wasn't misreading the undercurrent to her words and her body language (and that body of hers was fluent in several exotic languages), she wouldn't brush him off.

He shook his head and grinned ruefully. He was getting soft. (At least in one sense.) It used to be simple: get in, do the job, and get back out. No leftover untidiness, no entangled strings left behind.

Still, he couldn't deny that getting his hands on Angela would be a very nice perk indeed.

Chapter 3

"Thank you all for coming," Angela addressed the guests in the dining room. "Have you been enjoying the food?"

Murmurs of assent and a smattering of clapping answered the question—along with an antique cherry buffet mostly devoid of the tea sandwiches, hors d'oeuvres, and pastries that had covered it an hour before. Franklin had outdone himself again.

Of course, the liberally flowing champagne hadn't hurt anyone's appetites. Angela took a sip from her own glass. She shouldn't indulge too much, but she couldn't resist one glass.

"In a few minutes we'll go to the parlor to begin the séance," she continued. "But before we do that, Kari and I would like to give you some background on Angelika, or specifically on the house's original owner, whose birthday we celebrate tonight."

"Minerva May Fenwick was a woman ahead of her time," Kari took over the story.

The guests ranged from mildly interested (Carole and Barb, who at least looked less like they were going to explode into messy stressy bits on the dark-stained oak floor than they had yesterday) to the leaning-forward and rapt (Adelle, but then, she might have been looking at Tyler; and Tyler himself, which surprised Angela a little).

To Angela's amusement, Cybelline's date was one of the people who didn't look all that interested. Jill Hunter was a pretty black woman with what even Angela, straight as they came, agreed was an amazing body, but she looked a bit mainstream for Cyb's usual taste. Angela had assumed that was protective coloration since she taught at the local high school—they'd met when Cybelline did her gypsy fortuneteller shtick at a school fundraiser.

Maybe, though, Jill *was* kind of mainstream, in which case she'd be gone soon. Oh well, Cybelline had gone through four girlfriends in the six months or so since she moved to town, but it didn't seem to bother her all that much.

Most of the people currently at the hotel were sitting in, although Angela noted the author Margaret Blum, staying for a month to finish a project, hadn't joined the little group. (She hadn't come to any meals so far either, though she emerged occasionally to get more tea bags.) Her husband, a slender, quietly attractive grey-haired man named David Strauss, on the other hand, was one of those who seemed fascinated by the presentation. Not surprising; he'd been asking a lot of questions about the hotel's history whenever he could catch a staff member. Angela liked him already.

Rounding out the group was Satya Badal, here to write an article about Angelika. Satya had a contract with the *San Francisco Chronicle*'s travel section and was live-blogging her stay on a travel blog, but she also planned to include Angelika in a roundup of unusual boutique hotels she'd pitched to prestigious *Condé Nast Traveler*.

Angela could barely suppress a squee at so much publicity.

Kari finished the history of Minerva herself, and Angela picked up the story. "We know so much about Minerva because she kept meticulous, fascinating, and witty records of her travels and her ideas. Those were published in multiple volumes, which you can see in the library here at Angelika."

The beautifully leather-bound journals detailed Minerva's philosophies, her joie de vivre, even her refreshingly open attitudes toward pleasure.

But those tomes had only hinted at the variety and scope of Minerva's inventiveness and true, devious plans for her home.

"Little did we know, there was more." Angela lowered her voice a fraction, and the ruse worked: everyone leaned forward, intent on her words.

Still including, she couldn't help but notice, Tyler.

She'd already noticed that he cleaned up but *fine*.

They'd made it clear there was no dress code for the séance; those who wanted to gussy up in Victorian finery along with their hosts were encouraged to do so, but that wasn't a requirement. Tyler had paired his jeans with a button-down shirt and a brown blazer, and loosened his hair from the small ponytail he favored when he was working.

The top few buttons of the shirt—which was a shade of blue that made his eyes more vibrant—were open, and Angela had already lost herself in the fantasy of pressing her lips against the revealed flesh, then slowly, teasingly, popping each button and following the trail down as his breath quickened…

Focus.

"When we bought Angelika from Minerva's great-grandnephew, it was full of more than a hundred years of *stuff*—some of it valuable and beautiful, some of it junk," she said. "While cleaning out a wardrobe, we found a gorgeous diamond-and-sapphire earring—and we recognized it. Some of you have seen the portrait of Minerva in the parlor, yes? The earring matched the one she was wearing in that picture."

Minerva was wearing little else besides the magnificent earrings in that particular photograph, in fact. Just a corset and knickers, white with lace trim (or perhaps cream-colored—the picture was sepia-toned). She was sprawled on a fainting couch, lounging seductively. Her incredibly long, dark hair was braided, but hung down, thick and snaking around her arm and across her belly.

Adelle Parsons had known Minerva when Adelle was a young girl and Minerva was late middle-aged and running the hotel, and she'd hinted at Minerva's decadence. (Poor Adelle. They got the feeling she'd always wanted to be "decadent" but hadn't had the guts until she was a bit old to pull it off as anything other than bad comedy.)

Angela and Kari had put down her vague words as meaning maybe Minerva had worn flapper dresses or trousers before they were truly accepted, or that she'd hosted parties with alcohol during Prohibition. Or maybe that she'd traveled so much, and not just to the proper places like England and Europe, but also India, Africa, Asia, and South America; not merely seeing the sights, but living for a time among the locals.

The portrait had made them suspect that maybe Adelle's comments had been more than just wacky ramblings and off-kilter conjecture. Not that Minerva was decadent in a bad way, but hedonistic and fun-loving.

Decadent in a *good* way.

A woman after their own hearts, in other words.

"And then we found Minerva's very personal diary," Angela continued, "hidden in a false-backed drawer in the same wardrobe."

In the diary, Minerva spoke of commissioning a great house to be built before she even arrived back home. She wanted to create a space where artists could share their thoughts—simply put, a salon, for both men and women. But she also envisioned a place where people could be free to explore sexually, to experience the joys of passion.

Unsurprisingly, Minerva expected to be right in the thick of things.

"We knew there were salons and art colonies in the late 1800s—but not sex resorts." Angela paused and looked as coquettishly as she could beneath her lashes. Her audience leaned closer. Excellent. "Certainly not ones that catered to women as well as men."

Nudge, wink.

The diary had gone on to detail Minerva's plans, many of which they'd incorporated, as best they could, into the modern version of the hotel, making Angelika welcoming to artists of all types and a romantic retreat for lovers of all persuasions.

(The diary had also detailed escapades that would make a porn star blush—but they weren't going to talk about those stories tonight.)

"She also wrote about her interest in the occult," Angela went on. "Séances were a fad in her time, and she said in her diary that it would be lovely if someone tried to contact her after her death."

Satya raised a hand. "Do you believe that Minerva's spirit haunts the hotel?"

Angela laughed. "We've never seen her," she said, "but I like to think she's pleased we're carrying on her legacy."

"We're not making any promises that we'll be able to contact her tonight," Kari added. "We just think it'll be fun to try!"

Angela suspected Kari was staying neutral for the sake of the guests, because she knew Kari was open to the idea of spirits. Kari wasn't as hardcore as Cybelline, but admitted there it was a short step from believing in aromatherapy and energy work to believing in ghosts.

"On that note," Angela said, "if everyone would follow Kari, we'll go to the parlor, where Cybelline is waiting." She let them file past her, hanging back in the hopes of snagging the last of Franklin's delectable crab-and-scallop cakes. She should be sainted for refraining from diving into the mouthwatering spread of nibblies so the guests could enjoy their fill.

Oh, heaven. She almost moaned aloud, but settled for closing her eyes and just savoring.

When she opened them again, she saw that Tyler had hung back as well, lounging against the door jamb with his hands casually in his pockets. He had a knowing smile on his lips—he'd clearly enjoyed watching her pleasure—and a glint in his eyes that made her stomach go fluttery.

He slid into step with her as she headed after the guests. He leaned close. She caught the scent of aftershave, something subtle and musky and very *him*, and her stomach leapt with desire.

"So, I have a question for you," he said.

She shivered, wishing that low voice was growling sexy suggestions at her. He managed to make the most innocent remark sound dirty.

Her corset suddenly felt tighter, pressing against her breasts. Her nipples beaded with desire, and the combination of the silk against them and the rigid construction of the corset made the ache lusciously unbearable.

Minerva had usually eschewed the "proper" clothing of her time period, preferring to dress in the loose and relaxed—yet luxurious and hedonistic—Bohemian fashions. Tonight Kari had gone with that style, but Angela had opted for a more traditional outfit. After all, Minerva had

had her portrait done in a corset and knickers, so she must have sometimes worn the clothes that went with them.

Or maybe, like Angela, she occasionally enjoyed the sensation of wearing a corset for her own slightly perverted reasons. For Angela, wearing a corset was a sensual, even arousing experience. A properly made corset didn't pinch or bind; instead, it lovingly molded around your figure, a constant erotic caress.

Like the large, strong hands of a man bracketing your waist as he prepared to slide into you.

The hint of bondage, the whiff of perversion.

Outwardly proper and sedate, inwardly wanton and wanting.

Tyler, she suspected, would appreciate the dichotomy as much as she did.

Or maybe he'd just care about the swell of her breasts above the line of the corset and the fact that split knickers gave easy access.

She licked her lips. "And what would that be?"

His eyes definitely lingered on her cleavage as he spoke. "This diary… it sounds fascinating. Is it as lascivious as you implied?"

Oh God, that voice of his was made for saying wicked things in the dark.

A rush of heat to her face and her loins. "She could get pretty detailed about her experiences," she said. "Because she didn't intend to share the diary—except maybe with those very close to her—she felt free to be open."

"I'd love to read it." His breath rustled through the pin curls that dripped from her upswept hair, and they tickled her neck.

"We…we've agreed not to show it to anyone," she managed. "Minerva kept it hidden for a reason, and we don't feel right passing it around." She tried to remember what she was supposed to be doing before she went into the parlor? Besides trading innuendos with a hot man, that is. That's right. Nothing major—just snagging the last of Franklin's yummy treats before Housekeeping cleaned them away.

Oh no. *Yummy treats* led directly to images of licking Franklin's caramel-rum sauce off Tyler. Or him doing it to her.

Say something sensible. Say *anything*. "The journals touch on much of what she said in the diary, and you're welcome to read them when work is slow."

"I was really hoping for more of a…first-hand experience."

Did he mean for his words to sound so seductive? Probably. Damn him.

She tapped him coquettishly with her fan. "Play your cards right, and maybe I'll read you a few passages. But right now, if you're going to participate in the séance, you need to get yourself in there."

The look he gave her curled her toes inside her custom ecru leather granny boots, but he complied.

The round oak table was big enough to accommodate the twelve bodies required for a proper Victorian séance. They'd had to rearrange a fair amount of furniture to fit it in the parlor, but it was worth it. Right now, about half the guests were seated; the rest still milled about, admiring the painting of Minerva or perusing the leather-bound volumes and knickknacks that filled the shelves.

Angela took as deep a breath as she could in the corset. It was going well so far. The guests were intrigued, the hotel looked perfect, and she couldn't think of a detail she'd missed. There was ample food and drink, they were on schedule, and Isabella was safely ensconced in the tiny gardener's cottage Angela and Kari shared, just behind the hotel. (Isabella got nervous if too many people were around, plus she didn't like the patchouli essential oil Cybelline favored and could never completely get out of her clothes or hair.)

Cybelline, wafting that very patchouli scent, sidled up to Angela. "That's your new handyman? Kari said he was gorgeous, but whew!" She fanned herself.

"Angela's called dibs on him," Kari said, coming up on Angela's other side.

"Oh. Well, he doesn't have the body parts I'm interested in—and even if he did, he told me I reminded him of his sister." Cybelline rolled her eyes. "But tell me when was he born, and I'll read his chart and see if you're compatible."

"He's our employee, not my future baby-daddy," Angela said, pursing her lips in mock-primness. "Can we please focus?"

Whether or not Tyler was in the cards as anything more than a handyman was not the point right now. Okay, she *wanted* it to be the point, as her damp knickers could attest. But they had to concentrate on the business at hand.

At hand. Oh, bad, *bad* thoughts!

Then again, what was wrong with a few bad thoughts? A few good bad thoughts about a handsome handyman might work as a Minerva-magnet.

Not to mention the handyman in the flesh, pure temptation sprawled in a very improper, non-Victorian way in a formal Victorian straight-backed chair. God, his leanly muscled legs went on forever.

Kari touched her on the arm. "Distracted much, sweetie?"

Uh, yeah. Right. They had a séance to conduct. She started to sit down in the closest chair like a good hostess.

Then she saw Adelle heading for the chair nearest Tyler's.

Oh dear. She had to give the old woman credit for admitting senior citizens had sexual desires, but she knew Adelle's brazen flirting had reached the point of making Tyler uncomfortable.

She was just being a good boss by snagging that chair and protecting him. Right?

Muttering distracted "excuse me's" as her long skirts brushed people, Angela made her way to the chair next to Tyler's.

Almost as soon as Angela sat down, Kari turned off the electric lights on Cybelline's signal, leaving the room lit by two flickering oil lamps, before making her way to the table. On cue, the rest of the guests sat as well. Angela glanced at Tyler. The dim light didn't hurt the view.

Just made it good in a different way. The flickering light and shadow did interesting things to Tyler's cheekbones.

Way too easy to let her mind wander from the parlor to the bedroom (Minerva's, of course) and imagine them undressing each other in soft, flattering Victorian lamplight. He'd help her with all the hooks and eyes and buttons on the dress, making a teasing game out of the necessary fussing. Then when she was down to corset and knickers, she'd help him out of his shirt and jeans.

She might have to kneel down to work the jeans off. And of course (yay, fantasy!) he wouldn't be wearing underwear. Once she was on her knees in front of him, she'd take his cock into her mouth for a teasing taste.

Half-consciously, she licked her lips.

And was rewarded by a smile that suggested he knew what she was thinking. Or at least that his thoughts were equally deep in the gutter.

The smile incited little undulating tremors as if he'd dropped a rock in a pond.

She forced herself to look away.

Focus, drat it! Cybelline had been working for a while now, energizing the space or clearing negative energy or something—she'd explained it to Angela and Kari beforehand and it sounded like a lot of what Cybelline said: perfectly sensible, if you believed a lot of stuff that Angela only half-bought but thought was fascinating.

She'd better pay attention. Not that she expected anything would happen except a spooky/silly good time with some theatrics courtesy of Cybelline, but it would suck to have Minerva turn up and be so lost in sexual fantasy that she missed it.

"At this time, I'd like you to take the hand of the people next to you," Cybelline said.

Tyler's hand, hard and work-callused, closed over Angela's. He gave her a little squeeze.

He might as well have pinched her nipple, considering how it jolted through her.

It was going to be a long night. But potentially a very interesting one.

Cybelline stood. This was part of the Victorian tradition. She'd said, when they were planning the evening, that it was to prove she wasn't knocking on the table herself or doing any of the other things shifty mediums did, but it had to be at least partly theater. Tall and rail-thin and exotic, she looked like a sorceress from a pre-Raphaelite painting in a flowing black silk robe embroidered with green and gold and scarlet swirls.

The oil lamps backlit her mass of flaming red hair (which Angela knew was a wig, hiding shoulder-length black locks currently tipped with electric blue) and made her already big green eyes appear unnaturally huge.

Cybelline spread her hands, tilted her head back, and intoned, eyes closed, "Minerva May Fenwick, I invite you to join us on this night, the anniversary of your birth, in this house that you built!"

Tyler stroked Angela's palm with one finger, sending new shivers down her spine, straight to her core.

For a blissful millisecond, nothing seemed to exist except Tyler and her and the places they were touching.

Then came the tapping. Angela remembered Cybelline saying this was typical: once everyone had their hands clasped, who could be making the sound? Angela assumed Cybelline had set something up. She and Kari had specifically asked that they not be told about those details.

Maybe it was her imagination, but she swore Tyler took advantage of the distraction to inch closer. Not that she was complaining.

The chill breeze that snaked through the room didn't do much to cool her …until one of the oil lamps flared, illuminating the room in a startling way, then just as abruptly went out.

Holdonaminute. *That* couldn't be easily faked.

Someone female—Angela couldn't tell who—gasped. Hell, she wanted to gasp herself and she knew how drafty even a well-maintained Victorian house could be when it was windy.

Except it wasn't windy tonight.

The room went very quiet then, as if everyone held their breaths. She shivered. Fear and excitement smashed to pieces the concern that the séance would be a bust.

Across the table, Satya looked as though she wanted to twitch free of the hands she held so she could take notes. Please, oh please, let her be wanting to note how awesome this was, not that it was cheesy or overdone.

Tyler's face looked angular and devilish in the weird light. He grinned at her, a cocky grin with a hint of uncertainty behind it, and the hint of vulnerability (not to mention the wicked grin) made her breath catch in her throat and a pulse pound between her legs.

He drew his tongue slowly across his lower lip. Maybe it was unconscious—if there was ever a time for nervous fidgeting, this was it—but she swore she felt that tongue of his swirling around her nipples and, at the same time, on her throbbing clit.

My God, at this rate she'd come in about two seconds from any kind of direct stimulation.

"Minerva? Is that you?" Cybelline called in a Big Radio Voice. "If a spirit is present among us, give us a sign to let us know who you are."

For about fifteen seconds, the room was still, expectant.

Nothing.

It could have been the wind. Must have been. Coastal weather could be erratic.

Angela shivered with a sudden, creepy chill, then just as quickly felt overheated. No, not exactly overheated, just warm and pleasantly confined, like someone wrapped her in a friendly hug.

Someone laughed.

A throaty feminine laugh that belonged to a woman of worldliness and experience, a laugh that out-Dietriched Dietrich.

Only no one was laughing. Everyone seemed frozen, waiting for the next spooky fun. Angela could hear Adelle's slight wheeze from the other end of the table.

Angela still heard that sexy chuckle, though.

And this time it was obvious: it was in her head.

Whatever the hell was going on, it wasn't a special effect.

She squeezed Tyler's hand a little harder, and he gripped it in response.

Not only that, he took it as a cue to move his thigh against hers.

Heat seared her. Way more than made sense. Majorly sexy guy she lusted after or not, that contact shouldn't have pushed her from pleasantly aroused to painfully horny.

And then things, which were already weird enough to top both the Regrettable-College-'Shroom-Experiment and the High-Fever-in-the-Nepali-Temple-Incident at age twelve, took an abrupt left turn to Surreal Land.

Angela's vision skewed, so she was seeing the room in double-exposure, two images imperfectly aligned. Then the room snapped back into focus—but now she felt out of sync with it, like some of the things she was seeing were new to her, vivid and in some cases odd.

Like someone else was looking out through her eyes. Someone, maybe, who hadn't had a chance to see anything since when Minerva May Fenwick died. Someone who seemed to be checking out all the changes she and Kari had made to the house.

Luckily, the someone seemed to approve. At least Angela sensed goodwill. Happiness, even.

Note to self: be careful what you wish for. Hadn't she been hoping for some proof that Cybelline's and Kari's New Age beliefs were true?

And now she seemed to be sharing brain space with a ghost.

It tickled the inside of her skull. Not unpleasant, but not exactly comfortable, either.

And it tickled even more when, through Angela's eyes, whatever was in her head took a good look at Tyler.

An appreciative look. Definite sense that her guest was enjoying the view. What woman wouldn't, assuming she enjoyed good-looking men? And they knew from Minerva's own words that she enjoyed men. Every chance she got. Occasionally more than one at a time.

The tickling in Angela's skull let up, and for a second she thought things might be returning to normal.

Then Tyler yelped and jumped in his seat. "All right," he said. "Goosing me was *not* funny." He was barely managing not to chuckle as he said it. "Okay, okay, it was funny." Then he looked around. "But who…"

His eyes got wider when he realized that the only people who could have reached him were holding his hands.

Thank…lovely party, Angela heard dimly. The cultured, seductive voice in her head matched the throaty chuckle, but it was coming through broken and staticky, like a radio that was losing the station.

Without consciously meaning to, Angela looked at Tyler.

No, she *shot a sultry glance* at Tyler, like a bad-girl character in an old movie. She couldn't have pulled off that kind of femme-fatale routine if she'd been trying, but she could practically hear the smoky, sexy soundtrack. Unfortunately, Tyler was still distracted by the ghostly goosing. But he stroked her palm again with one finger, and though it seemed absent-minded, it was all she needed.

Angela's body clenched, trembled. She clasped her thighs together. Once, twice, three times, each time putting pressure on her swollen, sensitive clit.

Only…only she wasn't doing it. Her legs seemed to be moving of their own accord.

What in the name of all that was freaky?

She trembled so much she could barely breathe.

But it wasn't all fear. Her silky drawers were wetter than before… almost as if the ghost was touching her damp pussy.

In her head, Minerva moaned softly, like a woman anticipating a pleasure she'd been craving for a long time.

Chapter 4

*A*ngela's blood roared. The room went red. She bit her lip, trying to distract herself.

A champagne glass leapt off the sideboard, hit the floor, and shattered.

Uh-oh, she heard over the pounding of her own heart. *Are you a screamer?*

Unfortunately, she was. And that would be bad. *Very* bad.

Think about filing quarterly taxes. About root canals. About the pile of overdue bills on her desk.

If she did come, she'd look crazy at worst, or like someone staging a really tacky PR stunt at best. Any negative PR at this point could hurt their fledgling business.

Could even ruin them.

There was no way she was going to put Angelika on the line just because a ghost seemed to be horny.

Or because she was, for that matter.

The thought of risking her beloved hotel—and the home she and Kari had made there—was a more effective buzz-kill than a cold shower.

No way in *hell*. She was keeping this place, no matter what. Economic vagaries might challenge them; the slate roof might need repairs that would stretch the budget until it groaned; aliens could invade tomorrow (after tonight, she wouldn't write that off as impossible), but she'd be damned if she lost her aspirations. Her sanctuary. Her home.

Breathe. Think about *home* and breathe.

The tremors of approaching orgasm stopped, leaving her aching with a combination of frustration and relief. Her clit pulsed in rhythm with her panicked heart, while her body, not in line with her brain's program, grumbled, but she was in control of herself again, alone in her head. Her palms were as damp as her knickers.

She forced herself to look at the assembled guests, glancing from face to face, meeting everyone's eyes as brazenly and calmly as she could manage.

As far as she could tell, no one had noticed the little fiasco. A ghost had just goosed Tyler, which might be enough to make the person next to him jump and twitch, too.

"Well," she said, calling upon acting skills she'd never known she had to sound unruffled and pleased with the way the séance was going, "I'd say we had a live one tonight—or rather a dead one—and I'm sure it was Minerva. Cybelline, what do you think?"

Cybelline chuckled, her light laugh a refreshing contrast to the throaty, sensual Minerva-laugh Angela knew would haunt her forever. "Normally I'd caution you to speak more respectfully of spirits among us, but whoever it was seems to have a good sense of humor. That makes me think it was Minerva—that and the fact it was an unusually vivid presence."

"Tell me about it." Tyler's smooth, sexy voice held a hint of amusement. "I think she left a bruise."

Carole and Barb sucked in simultaneous breaths. David Strauss looked like he was considering whether to flee the room—or maybe whether to be insulted the ghost hadn't goosed *him*. Angela choked down a bubble of hysterical laughter. And Jill definitely didn't look bored anymore. More like awed. The way she was looking at Cybelline suggested that Cyb, at least, would be getting lucky tonight.

"I believe, all right," Adelle agreed, leaning forward eagerly, enthusiasm revitalizing her face. "Minerva was larger than life. Even when she was older than I am now, she treated every day like an adventure. She loved her champagne—and good-looking men like our friend Tyler."

Everyone laughed.

"Minerva," Cybelline intoned, "is there anything else you'd like to share with us tonight?"

There was no response. Cybelline added, "Then we thank you for honoring us with your presence," and instructed everyone to release each other's hands. As she blew out the candle on the table, Angela twitched.

Right now the Laphroaig on the sideboard looked more tempting than Tyler.

The lights went up, and with them voices raised from murmurs to excited chatter filling the room.

Surely it was obvious. Angela's face felt flushed, any exposed inch of skin tingling, hypersensitive. She was light-headed—just a little, in that way where sounds are sharper and clearer—and she was sure her eyes were glassy.

Kari wasn't rushing over, and Kari would have been the first to notice, right? Tyler, though, was another problem altogether.

A big, looming, tasty-enough-to-nibble problem.

She'd never been good at denying herself. Getting that close to coming without the benefit of the orgasm made her cranky, an emotional state she certainly couldn't share with anyone right now.

If she got too close to Tyler, though, things were going to go wrong in the other direction. One hot breath against her neck, one resting of his strong hand at her waist, or worse yet, that husky voice purring in her ear, and she'd pitch right over the edge.

She had to get away. Right. Now. Not to bring herself off—although that was a tempting proposition—but to pull herself together. Be able to mingle and bid goodnight to the guests.

She had to make sure the party goers enjoyed the rest of their evening before they headed to their rooms or homes, make sure the dining room and parlor got cleaned out and prepped for the next day. All without letting on to anyone that she was both rattled and horny as hell.

She was edging toward the doorway out of the parlor when Adelle sidled up to her.

"Adelle, I—"

"So, was it good for you?" Adelle cocked her head, her eyes glittering as she smiled through a visage of wrinkles.

For a moment, Angela couldn't even draw in a breath. "What?" she managed.

"Meeting Minerva!" Adelle chirped. "I know you've been so interested in her since you bought the manor."

She went limp again. "Adelle," she said. "It was just in fun. Séances aren't real. This was just a show."

"You don't have to lie to me." Adelle dropped her voice to a whisper. "You say what you want to everyone else. We'll talk later."

No, we won't.

But Angela knew they probably would. Adelle, for all her dottiness, had the stubbornness of a limpet, and she had been a wonderful (if potentially dodgy) resource for all things Minerva.

Right now, thought, Angela just had to…

Tyler, right next to her. Dammit. She smelled his aftershave first, and it made her shiver right down to her still-sensitized core.

The blood-filled heat didn't just rise in her cheeks. Now it spread below, warming her belly, pooling with a heavy ache in her groin.

It took everything she had to step away from him. She remembered how he'd licked his lips, how she'd imagined it on her clit. If he touched her, she'd be gone.

She felt—heard?—a purr in her head. A commentary that wasn't entirely her own.

Handsome specimen…surely…creative bedmate.

La la la la dinosaur! Angela dragged her gaze away from Tyler's bedroom eyes, reaching out to lean on the polished door molding.

He wasn't worth risking everything for.

A tryst in private was one thing. Pitching over the edge right now was another.

"It's been quite an evening," she said. Was that really her voice, all husky and sensual? She cleared her throat. "I hope Minerva didn't injure you too badly."

"Well, you know what they say." Tyler's lips curved in a wicked grin. "It's not really fun until someone gets bruised."

Oh. Oh, she'd never heard that one before, and the image raced to mind of love bites, tender and hidden beneath a fall of hair or a well-placed scarf. Or having to pull down your sleeves to hide the marks on your wrist that happened when he'd held you down. She swallowed.

"I just need to nip to the bathroom…"

Tyler stepped back, but his eyes never left hers, as tangible as a caress. "Go on, then," he said, and she wondered from his tone if he believed her excuse. "Is it all right if the hired help indulges in a finger of Scotch?"

"Knock yourself out," she said, managing a smile. "You've earned it. Save one for me."

She turned away. One step closer to the doorway…

A hand rested itself on her forearm, warm and soft and caressing, and she nearly exploded like a cat who'd been poked in the ass by a wet dog nose.

"Are you okay?" Kari asked. "You—"

"No, *you*," Angela said, poking Kari, "and you," she pointed at Cybelline. "Ladies' room. *Now*."

Once in the bathroom, she leaned her head against the cool subway tiles—original to the house—on the wall. Even in her flustered state, she couldn't help but stop and appreciate this corner of Angelika. It was just part of the whole that made her home, the home she'd worked toward all her life.

The walls and original hexagonal floor tiles, patterned white with a smattering of black, had been lost under layers of grime and let's-not-think-about-what-else. They'd managed to salvage the sink fixtures and lights with only minor compromises.

With painstaking care (and nearly coming to blows with the contractors on at least one occasion) they'd had two stalls installed without appreciably harming the nature or original structure of the room.

Angela didn't take the time to pop into one of those stalls and, erm, adjust herself. Instead, once the outer door closed, she flipped the lock and demanded, "What—what the hell happened out there?"

Kari's hazel eyes widened. "I could ask you the same question."

"We contacted Minerva!" Cybelline clapped her hand together. "It was amazing! I've never experienced such a clean channeling."

Angela clenched her hands into fists in an attempt not to lock her fingers around Cybelline's willowy neck. "What do you mean, 'clean channeling'?"

Cybelline blinked kohl-rimmed eyes, apparently unaware of Angela's murderous tension. "You channeled Minerva. It was brilliant! Oh, shit." She gathered Angela's hands in her own. Her flesh was cool, which helped. Marginally. "You don't remember, do you? Hosts rarely are aware when they're taken over. I'm sorry, I'm jumping ahead. It's just that this—"

"No, the problem is, I do remember," Angela said, yanking her hands free. "And it's not so much memory, as…" Fuck, what *was* it?

Just accept it, as crazy as it sounds.

"Minerva was there," she said. "With me. Inside me, or something. She was *talking to me*."

"Ooh!" Both Cybelline's and Kari's eyes were wide. "What did she say?"

"She's hot for Tyler," Angela said between gritted teeth. "Get. Her. Out. Of. Me."

Both Kari and Cybelline took a cautious step back.

"Honey," Cybelline said, "that's just not possible."

"What do you mean?" Angela demanded.

"A spirit can only manifest during the séance itself. When we broke the circle of hands, Minerva had to leave. She would need the conditions found during the séance to stick around."

Angela closed her eyes. Okay. She was exhausted, stressed, and apparently had developed a hair-trigger libido. Maybe she'd imagined the whole thing. She'd never really believed in the hocus-pocus—oh, she liked the idea of it, believed in keeping an open mind, but possession? Really?

"Are you sure?" she asked, opening her eyes.

"Did you not hire me for my expertise?" Cybelline arched an eyebrow.

"Of course we did," she said, unable to keep back a smile. "That bit with the oil lamp was inspired, by the way. But breaking the glass was going a little far. Especially since there was still champagne in it."

"Um, that wasn't me, either time," Cybelline said. "That really was Minerva." She sounded both excited and nervous.

God. Angela didn't know what to believe anymore. Even if she was going to accept that Minerva had actually spoken through her, she had to trust Cybelline when she said Minerva's spirit had left as soon as the séance formally ended. The stuff afterward had just been her imagination.

Right? Please?

That didn't explain—or help with—the subsiding tremors between her thighs or the must-be-suppressed desire to slap anyone who spoke to her.

But it was a start. And it would have to be enough to get her through the rest of the evening.

*

Tyler set the last parlor chair back in place, noticing one of the walnut spindles that made up the seat back was loose and making a mental note to see if he could fix it. Since it was hand carved, getting a replacement would be difficult and costly.

Rearranging the furniture post-séance had probably taken longer than it should have, but first he hadn't wanted to shoo the guests out, and then he'd lingered, using the time in the parlor to check out the room more carefully. He didn't feel any unusual changes in the floorboards under the reproduction Victorian throw rug—nothing other than the usual settling and shifting of hundred-plus-year-old beams—but he itched to explore every inch of the paneling around the fireplace.

That, however, would have to wait until the house was empty. Tapping on the wall could be considered suspicious behavior. Or crazy behavior. He didn't want to look suspicious or crazy or anything other than a competent handyman.

Angela had told him he could leave once things were back in place, so he didn't have to let her know he was headed out. Which was a pity, because she'd looked utterly delectable in that Victorian outfit of hers, all curves and lace and buttons just begging to be undone.

Down, boy. Focus on the long job, not the short-lived temptations.

He headed out to his truck, shivering in the chill night air and hoping that Adelle was safely home in bed and wouldn't waylay him on the stairs of the boarding house. He was tired and looking forward to a hot shower and—

His cell phone buzzed in his pocket.

He swung up into the truck, started it, and eased down the driveway a ways so the engine noise wouldn't bother anyone at Angelika. He cranked the heater, and warm air whooshed into the cab. Then he dug out his phone, curious who was contacting him so late.

He frowned when saw that an unknown sender had contacted him at an e-mail address only a few select, trusted people had access to.

The truck's heater couldn't dispel the adrenaline chill that hit him when he read the message.

I know who you are and why you're here. So unless you want your past shared with the police, you work for me now.

*

With a sigh, Angela shut her bedroom door. It resisted, the wood not fitting neatly into the frame, but a punt from her hip and it snicked closed.

Finally, she could stop being in control. She'd give anything to flop down on her old futon on its rickety frame and pass out.

She knew that just wasn't going to be an option. She was just too wired—and just too horny.

She and Kari had used bedrooms in the hotel when they were renovating, but once Angelika opened for business, they'd chosen to vacate to ensure all the rooms could be moneymakers. The little gardener's cottage out back was a decent-enough alternative: two bedrooms barely big enough to house a bed each, a miniscule bathroom, and a combination living/dining room with a postage-stamp-sized kitchen tucked in the corner.

They'd sunk every spare cent they had into the hotel, so the cottage was a hodgepodge of college relics, mismatched dishware, and furniture that didn't fit in the hotel, including a hideous, aqua, nubbly polyester sofa that they'd tossed an antique candlewick bedspread over.

The bedspread had only a couple of small holes in it.

The shower spat hot water only when it felt so inclined (thank goodness for owners' access to the spa) and thanks to some hole they'd never been able to locate, they often shared said shower with an indignant tree frog.

Kari had gotten excited when the tree frog moved it, saying it must be a totem, since frogs signified good luck, opportunities, and renewal, like the renewal Angelika had undergone.

Angela had nothing against wildlife; she just preferred it outdoors.

They hoped to have enough disposable income to fix the heating before next winter. And maybe an electrical system that didn't buzz them when they touched a faucet at the same time as reaching for the light switch.

Or that rotted-through patch in the hardwood floor, artfully covered by a piece of plywood, a threadbare Deco rug, and a battered wrought iron plant stand from the 1950s.

It was a place to sleep, to retreat to when needed. The hotel, though, was *home*…the home Angela had never had.

She'd been so tempted to drag that bottle of Laphroaig back with her, but she needed to be awake and alert tomorrow. She was also loath to release herself from her corset and trappings just yet, if only because that sensual confinement could add so much to her pleasure.

But she needed to fall into bed as soon as possible—and, she suspected, it wouldn't take her long to achieve release and then blissful unconsciousness. The trappings weren't necessary. They were like the difference between a quickie and a…longie: sometimes you took what you could get, and it was still pretty damn satisfying.

Still, she couldn't resist making the disrobing part of the process, rather than shucking the outfit and tossing it in the corner. (Okay, she would never toss the exquisite Victorian costume anywhere, but still.) If she could take the time to undress, she could take a few extra moments to do it properly.

The fantasy was easy to conjure. Tyler, of course. She'd been watching his hands: they were large, strong, capable. A worker's hands, but not overly rough. Nails trimmed and clean. Fingers equally at home wielding a wrench or typing on a keyboard…or coaxing pleasure from a woman's body.

He'd take his time with the tiny buttons that ran from cleavage to waistline. He'd pluck each one from its corresponding loop, murmuring in appreciation as each parting revealed another sliver of pale silk chemise and pale slice of flesh.

Not just murmuring. Tyler, she guessed, was a vocal man. Sure of himself, sure of his needs and desires, sure of his abilities when it came to sex. God knew he had the voice to go with that. He was like a male Siren.

Part of it was the confidence, obviously. He knew exactly how his words affected a women—he made that clear by following up with those sultry, bedroom blue eyes that held the wickedest promises she'd ever seen.

You couldn't trust some men's promises. Angela already trusted Tyler's.

Her corset laced up the back for proper fitting, but hooks down the front allowed for easy removal. Still, she took it nice and slow.

One hook at a time, savoring how the comfortable, erotic confinement lessened, just a little. Her cleavage diminished, yes, but her breasts eased to their natural shape—and her nipples, previously and constantly hard against the rigid garment, peaked even tighter in the cool air.

She sucked in her breath at the sensation. She hadn't even touched them, and they were already begging.

She'd probably be begging by this point, although she wouldn't make it so obvious. She'd make breathy suggestions, arch her back to make her breasts more prominent, available. A blatant invitation to feast.

Tyler would laugh softly, she suspected. Went along with that wickedness. He'd accept the invitation…but on his own terms.

He'd cup his palms around the fullest part of her breasts, fingers caressing the curving sides. He'd heft them, ever so slightly; they'd still be on display, but on *his* display.

She'd bite her lip to keep herself from pleading aloud. She'd turn that into a coy look, up from beneath her lashes, playing the game, pretending she was letting him have control.

By the time he'd brush his thumbs lightly across her nipples, she'd be so ready that the flare of desire would make her knees buckle.

Of course she was mimicking what she imagined, and her legs did wobble at the thrill of need.

Screw *slow*. She popped the rest of the hooks, and with shaking hands folded the corset over the discarded dress and chemise on the straight chair by the bed. In her mind she could hear Tyler laughing, but at the same time she could see his gaze flare in intensity, taking in her mostly naked form as she sprawled across the not-very-comfortable (but-it-was-fine-for-now) futon.

She left on the split drawers, the sheer silken stockings. He'd like that.

She liked it, too. Liked sliding her hand up along the silk against her thigh before dipping her fingers between. She knew she was already wet, already thrumming with arousal.

"Taste yourself," he'd say, bringing his fingers to her lips so she could suck on them, making desire flare in his dark blue eyes. Or maybe he'd taste them himself, in preparation.

Screw it. She licked her fingers, shuddered at the scent, and went down for the kill. After everything that had happened tonight, after how on edge she'd been for so long, it would take only a few seconds to find blessed release.

One hand tweaking a nipple, one flicking against her clit, and—

—a buzzing rose in her mind—but she assumed it was just lust—but then—

Thank goodness…far too long.

It wasn't Tyler's imagined voice in her head, no matter how much she wanted it to be.

It was feminine. It was *Minerva*.

Angela snapped.

There was no pitching over the crest into sweet relief.

There was no illusion of being in control anymore.

The scream she let out wasn't of release, but of pure frustration laced with a healthy dollop of completely freaking out.

Chapter 5

*H*er bedroom door slammed open.

"Are you okay?" Kari demanded. "That wasn't your happy scream." She glanced around, seemingly unperturbed by Angela's state of near undress. "You usually don't scream when you're by yourself—you're more of a moaner—and there's no place to hide Tyler in here."

"No, I'm not okay." Angela hauled herself up into a sitting position propped up against the pillows, and ran shaking hands through her half-unpinned hair. The rest of the pins tumbled every-bloody-where. Crap. She'd never find them all and one would end up lodged in her foot years from now.

"Cyb was wrong," she went on. "Minerva's still with me. She's all too happy to be here, too." She grabbed her cell phone from the battered steamer trunk that doubled as a night table and clothing storage unit, found the psychic's number.

"I don't do house calls," Cybelline said instead of hello.

"You do now," Angela said. "Don't make me come over there and go all possessed on your ass."

*

Angela shucked the final Victorian undergarments and dragged on a lipstick-red kimono. The silk lingerie made her feel vulnerable, reminded her too much of the voyeur in her head.

Could Minerva be a voyeur if she was experiencing Angela *through* Angela? She groaned. Not a question she was anywhere near capable of thinking about.

The kimono gave her a sort of armor, comfortable in its familiarity. It was silky and sensual, sure, but her *parents* had sent it to her from Japan, and it covered her, and it had nothing to do with Tyler or Minerva.

Except hadn't Minerva visited the Orient on one of her world treks? Angela firmly squashed that thought and pulled the robe tighter around her.

Cybelline, meanwhile, sported smudged mascara and obviously hastily donned leather pants and a torn Styx T-shirt hanging off one shoulder. "I was *busy*," she announced without shame, collapsing onto the sofa next to Angela. "Jill is *talented*."

"Will she be there when you get back?" Kari asked.

Cybelline shot a glare. "That's not the point." She turned to Angela, who'd tucked herself up against the arm of the sofa (the secure arm, not the wobbly one, otherwise she'd likely pitch backward onto the floor and give them both an eyeful and herself a concussion). "This better be important."

"Minerva is still in me," Angela said. "Possessing me. Whatever you want to call it. I can hear her in my head, and I want her out, and it's your job to get her out." She leaned forward, held out her hands. "Do it."

"Um," Cybelline said, suddenly looking just the tiniest bit freaked. "I'm going to need a little time."

"What do you mean?" Angela demanded.

"Well. You see, like I said, I've never had such a clean channeling before. Usually the bulk of the séance is smoke-and-mirrors on my part: table rapping, swooning, voices. Whenever I've actually made contact with a spirit during a séance, I've been the medium. The ghost has always spoken through me." She stopped and peered at Angela, smeared raccoony eyes narrowed. "Have you ever done this before?"

Angela pressed back against the sofa arm. Now this one wobbled, just a little. Crap. "No! I mean, no formal séances. I played with a Ouija board with friends when I was younger, but we never actually *spoke* to anyone."

"And she's still with you?" Cybelline went on. "While I *have* had spirits speak through me, I've always embellished—and I've never known one to latch on to someone else, certainly not for this long or outside of the circle. If you could tell me more about what she's telling you…"

Angela shook her head, wishing the gesture would knock something loose. "I don't hear her all the time. I get snippets, fragments. Some impressions. Mostly I can just *feel* that she's with me, but I get the sense she doesn't have the capability or strength to communicate 24/7."

It was like a low static, a barely audible buzzing. The untuned radio metaphor made a lot of sense.

Assuming any of this made sense, that was.

"Is there a particular time or set of circumstances where it's easier for her to come through?" Kari asked. "I'd think when you're relaxed and centered, you're more likely to be open to her."

Relaxed wasn't the way Angela would have described her state of being when Minerva was most clear. No, Miranda seemed to be boosting herself on the state of Angela's—cough—tension…

Despite her long-time, tell-all friendship with Kari and her growing closeness with Cybelline, Angela had to struggle to bring herself to admit the truth that she feared.

Just too personal.

Or was it personal, if Minerva was invading at Angela's most crucial, private moment?

She took a deep breath. "Well. Yes, yes, there is a particular time when she's most…when I can hear her clearly." God, did they have to stare at her with such eager intensity? Just. Say. It. "It's when I'm about to come."

Two pairs of eyes blinked slowly, then widened in comprehension.

"Angela Georgenes," Kari said. "Were you masturbating during the *séance*?"

"*My* séance?" Cybelline demanded.

"Wait," Kari said. "You were holding hands with Tyler and me during the séance. Were you wearing a *vibrator*?"

"*During* my *séance*?" Cybelline looked seriously steamed.

"No!" Angela held up her hands to forestall more of the insanity. "No, I wasn't doing that! At least, not on purpose." Both of her friends opened their mouths to protest further, so she raced on, damn the consequences and full steam ahead. "I was aroused—you know how the Victorian clothing gets me, and being around Tyler didn't help—but I wasn't doing anything on purpose. When Minerva first entered me—"

She stopped. Realized what she'd said.

Dissolved into laughter at the same time Kari and Cybelline did.

When they could breathe again, she wiped her streaming eyes on her kimono sleeve. "You know what I meant. You do. Stop it. Stop. When Minerva…" She almost said "came," but stopped herself in time. "When Cybelline raised Minerva, I channeled her. It seemed like Minerva chose me. And that's when I got even more turned on than I'd been, almost to the point of coming, and that's when I could really hear Minerva's voice in my head. But it was still just in little pieces."

"So, in your bedroom earlier…?" Kari asked.

"I was still horny," Angela confessed. "Please. I'm only human."

"Well, that's certainly understandable." Kari leaned over and patted her hand. "I would've done the same thing."

"Well, Minerva's presence seems to be heightening things for me, too," Angela said. "Which could be a very serious problem. We have a hotel to run, not to mention a reviewer to court." She pointed at Kari. "You, be my wingman. If I start to…if anything happens to me, take over. Redirect people's attention, or get me out of there, or whatever it takes.

"You," she said to Cybelline, "go home and research this. As much as I love Minerva in the conceptual sense, I can't have her possessing me at random. We need to find out what she wants, ASAP.

"I want her out of me—*now*."

*

Being interviewed wasn't exactly on Angela's top ten list for things to do this morning. She was so fried that numbers one through nine would be "get more sleep," with "figure out what to do about the friendly Victorian pervert in my head" making it onto the list only after the nice long nap, and "molest Tyler's manly form" relegated all the way down to the second tier.

Plus there was the possibility that at any moment, she might think too hard about Tyler's manly form, get a sweet tingle, and suddenly have Minerva answering the questions through her. Since Angela suspected Minerva didn't have very good filters, that meant Satya's hair was likely to catch on fire.

But at least answering Satya's questions mostly kept her mind off ghosts, not to mention more mundane and even less appealing problems like bills and the mysterious leak in Bathhouse Three.

The parlor was one of her favorite rooms, even if now it reminded her of the séance and the attendant craziness that surrounded it. Tyler had done a good job of putting everything back where it ought to be, which was comforting.

In fact, it was fun waxing lyrical about their vision for Angelika. *That* was something she had no problem getting enthusiastic about—and, in fact, sometimes she had to be aware she was babbling and rein herself in before the listener perished of boredom.

Not everyone shared her level of interest in Anaglypta versus Lincrusta wall coverings. In fact, almost no one did.

Thus, Angela had a good time until Satya asked, "Before we wrap up, do you think we actually encountered Minerva's spirit last night?" The writer smiled, but her dark eyes, though good-humored, were sharply observant.

Too damn observant. She'd probably pick up that Angela was hedging, but her readers—and especially the readers of *Condé Nast Traveler*—so did not need to hear, "Yeah, and she's still in my head, and she has an unwholesome interest in my sex life, especially when it come to my frustrated desires for my handyman."

In the light of day, Angela could almost convince herself she'd dozed off mid-fantasy and dreamed Minerva's voice last night. She'd been tired and tipsy and rattled from the séance, and that made a lot more sense than Minerva hanging out without Cybelline doing her New Age shtick to attract her.

Angela refreshed Satya's teacup from the etched silver teapot to give herself a few seconds to regroup. She pasted on her best hospitality-industry smile and tried to come up with a suitably ambiguous statement that would back off from the supernatural while still hinting at mysteries fascinating enough that Satya's readers could buy into a ghost story if they wanted to.

After all, it might be good PR. She might be a lousy liar, but she could beat around the bush with the best of them.

"I know everyone had fun and a few chills last night, including me. I couldn't say whether it was something real or our imaginations and the atmosphere getting us going—and Cybelline did a wonderful job setting the scene so our imaginations could run free."

Getting us going might not have been the best word choice, because, exhausted as Angela was, it still led her to think about Tyler getting *her* going. She forced back several lovely images and tried to concentrate….

Saved by the bell—or, at least, the ringtone. Angela had never been so glad to hear her phone ring.

So glad that she murmured, "I should take this," and tapped the button on her earpiece without checking the caller ID.

"I have an idea," Cybelline said without so much as a hello. "Minerva is linked to the house, obviously, but we need to figure out why she chose you to possess."

Angela made a noncommittal noise. She'd love to pursue this line of thought, or any other that would get rid of her charming but still annoying passenger—but this was so not the time. Angela bit back a curse and stood up, retreating to the far corner of the parlor. Ignoring the burgundy-and-gold-cushioned seat beneath the oriel window, she paced. "What now?"

"We need to rummage through Angelika for clues," Cybelline continued. "Nothing in the public rooms resonates, but maybe something in the attic…"

"There could be an elephant up there, for all I know!" Angela and Kari had made several passes through the attic and barely made a dent.

Satya, who'd been thumbing through the *San Sebastian Weekly News* and politely trying not to listen, perked up, but when she realized Angela had noticed, she hastily looked back at the newspaper as if it were the latest Nora Roberts. They probably taught that look of nonchalantly not paying attention while actually listening in journalism school. It might have worked if Satya been a hair quicker to glance away.

Angela dropped her voice low. "The journal, maybe?" It was a wild guess, but since the journal was so intimate it seemed as logical as anything did at this point.

"I doubt it. Otherwise she'd be possessing Kari, too, since you found it together. Maybe it's something archeology-related, because of your family, or something Greek. Maybe even a photograph of someone who looks like Tyler; maybe she's interested in you because you're both attracted to him. I'll know it when I see it. When would be a good time?"

There wasn't one, unfortunately, not during such a busy week. But she'd have to figure something out. "I'll call you and set something up," she murmured, and hung up.

Photos of someone who looked like Tyler? There were definitely a lot of old photographs around; they'd framed the most interesting, but a lot remained in boxes in the attic, especially ones of people they couldn't identify, and there were probably a lot they hadn't unearthed.

Might as well get started, because the sooner she got Minerva out of her head, the sooner her life would get back to its normal level of chaos.

"Satya, I'm sorry. Something's come up that I need to take care of, so we'll have to make this quick," she said, using all her control to sound calm. "I think you should ask Cybelline, or maybe Kari, if you're interested in ghost-lore; I'm no expert. But I *am* a bit of an expert on food, and I think you need to speak with our chef, Franklin, and hear about his menu innovations for this season." Let the nice reporter be Franklin's problem for a while.

Franklin was perfect for the job. He was so devoted to Angelika that he would die in that very kitchen, a grumpy yet charming old man, trying to roll out one more incredibly flaky crust before he keeled face first into his homemade apple-raspberry filling. And a little of said apple-raspberry filling along with his orgasmic chocolate ganache would go a long way toward winning Satya's heart—and the coveted good review.

That would give Angela a chance to make her escape, such as it was, for the attic.

*

After a little while, she wanted nothing more than to escape *from* the attic.

When she'd told Cybelline there could be an elephant hiding up here, she'd been only half-kidding.

The Fenwicks, both Minerva and her brother's descendants who'd inherited the house, had been packrats of the first order. She and Kari had already done a very basic comb-through of the attic, replacing Victoriana where it belonged and selling obviously-collectible-but-non-Victorian items to people who'd treasure them.

The Dadaist sculpture made of found objects had been hideous, but worth enough to someone to buy a functional commercial range and dishwasher to replace the '80s household models that had come with the house.

But that was just furniture and larger, obvious objects...in an attic that ran pretty much the length and width of the entire damn hotel.

They'd hardly made a dent in the mountains of junk, and it was daunting to figure out where she might find something as small as one photograph of some old lover of Minerva's that might or might not even exist. Never mind the other vague ideas Cybelline had spouted; if she found no picture, she'd turn Cybelline loose sometime to see if anything "resonated."

Normally Angela would be fascinated by rooting through a family's past like this—just not when she was on a deadline. Not when she had guests downstairs, and bills to pay, a nap to take (oh, only if she had time!), a menu plan to discuss with Franklin, e-mail to answer, and an ad to discuss with the *Contra Costa Times*.

So far, she'd unearthed everything from tacky souvenirs Minerva had acquired on her travels (Minerva had collected exquisite items, of course, which were now displayed around the hotel, but the contents of this box was so appalling Angela figured Minerva must have been flirting with particularly charming vendors, or perhaps helping out particularly tattered, hungry-looking ones) to fifty years of Christmas cards from a woman named Hanna to a box full of faded but still vomit-inducing psychedelic-swirl-patterned sheets from the '70s.

Angela put that last box in a pile mentally labeled Hazardous: Dispose With Care.

Plus, it was hot up here; the ventilation was nonexistent and the afternoon sun slashed like a seraphim's fiery sword through the old windows. She shucked her raspberry cardigan, draped it carefully over a dress form after blowing away the dust. Normally she wouldn't wander around during work hours in a satin camisole, even one as pretty as this one, dusky rose edged with lace that looked antique and tea-stained. But no one was going to see her up here.

She piled her hair on top of her head and secured it with a pair of plastic chopsticks from the Tacky Box, wished she'd thought to bring up a bottle of water, and dove back in.

One more box in this corner and then she'd try another section of attic. Not that the boxes were in any kind of logical order, let alone labeled, but if she chose another random spot and opened another random box, maybe it would invoke some random kind of magic.

One more box…

This one looked relatively recent, but she'd found some Minerva-era items in newer boxes, where a later inhabitant of the house had stowed things away when they stopped being useful.

Ooh, clearing out dear departed Auntie Minerva's old photos could fall into that category, right?

Here went nothing.

Pictures, all right, but not the kind Angela hoped for.

Instead, it was a box full of crayon artwork and little-kid schoolwork on that greenish, wide-lined paper with room for a picture on top.

"We live in Auntie Minerva's house. It is very old. It is very big. There are many places to hide."

Report cards from kindergarten to twelfth grade for the Minerva-great-grandnephew who'd sold her and Kari the house, and his sister. A couple of newspaper clippings showing the girl on the honor roll at San Sebastian High.

A prom picture, the kind that the now forty-something people in it would be glad to know was lost in an attic (those hair styles! those shoes! that polyester dress and weirdly colored tux!).

A few toys, tucked in among the papers—nothing fancy or collectible, just the ordinary artifacts of a late-1970s childhood.

Little treasures. The evidence of a childhood spent in a settled home.

Angela's eyes welled.

She flapped her hands around and sniffled and laughed at her own sentimentality, but the tears started before she could hold them back, and between exhaustion and fifty-seven flavors of stress, they didn't seem to want to stop.

Thank goodness for a handy psychedelic pillowcase. She wiped her eyes, blew her nose, didn't give a whit of care about the damage to the pillowcase.

A good cry helped clear a woman's head sometimes, and between opening-week craziness and ghosts and not enough damn sleep, by God she'd earned it. It wasn't like anyone was around to witness....

A warm hand rested on her shoulder.

A deep, sexy voice asked, "Hey, you okay?"

Cue "shriek like a girl" time.

Chapter 6

*A*ngela pressed a hand to her chest. She could feel her heart slamming against her palm, she was sure of it. Her ears rang from the adrenaline rush.

Here was the thing, though: Tyler's hand was still on her bare shoulder. And that kept her heart skipping merrily along and the adrenaline buzzing merrily in her system.

Somewhere in there, he'd moved close enough that Angela could feel his body heat through her thin camisole. Good heat, as opposed to stuffy-attic heat. Her body reacted, despite her mental state and despite her best intentions. Hel-*lo*, inappropriate nipples.

Inappropriate, but already tingling. Her libido never listened to logic, dammit.

She tried to do the sensible, adult thing: lie like a rug. She had something under her contact lenses, that was a good one. Except she didn't wear contacts, and no doubt he'd learn that somewhere down the line. Not that it mattered, because he worked for her, for goodness sake.

It mattered to her, though, which put a wrinkle in things.

Okay, think. She'd say she'd breathed in too much dust and was all allergic, thankyouverymuch, and then change the subject. Good one.

That was what she opened her mouth to say, honest.

Instead she found herself shaking her head and saying "Yes. Sort of. Not really. No. Shit."

When Tyler's arms went around her, she didn't resist. And if some little part of her lizard brain was cheering because any contact with Mr. Überhottie was good, most of her registered only strong arms holding her close, a warm, spicy fragrance—not a cologne, but him, maybe augmented with good soap—and a sense of comfort and safety.

Had to be some primitive nervous-system thing that it felt so damn good to lean on a solid man and let go of all her tension.

Only for a moment, though. A few more sobs, a few deep breaths, and she was able to get herself together again.

She had to. Leaning on Tyler and melting was tempting—and a bad idea. She didn't know Tyler well enough to feel this safe and comfortable with him; flirtation or not, they were barely acquainted with each other.

Probably some hormone-driven instinct that was useful to Cro-Magnon woman but not so much now.

Not to mention that now that she wasn't distracted by weeping, her hormones were kicking in big-time, prompting the reminder that Tyler had uses far more entertaining than tear-absorption.

"Uh, thanks," she said, forcing herself to pull away from that comforting touch, not to mention that appealingly hard body. To his credit—and her disappointment—he didn't try to stop her. In fact, he rocked back on his heels, increasing the distance between them. "But if you tell anyone you saw me like this, I'll have to kill you and bury your body in the back garden."

"I'd deserve it. What can I do to help?"

She hesitated, thinking of the right way to put it. Telling him about Minerva was right out. "Nothing, thanks. I'm just over-tired and over-stressed, I guess, and some stupid things I found hit my gloomy button."

The damnable box was still sitting on the floor next to her. Inevitably, he glanced in. His brow furrowed. "Your childhood stuff?"

The unexpectedness of the question startled a laugh from her. "It's more like a box full of the childhood I didn't have."

Now his frown was more along the lines of saying *Maybe she's lost it and I should back away slowly*.

Well, she deserved that. Say something cryptic and of course you're going to get a look that implies your marbles have rolled into cracks between the floorboards.

"My parents are archeologists," she explained. "By the time I was twelve, I'd been in more countries than Indiana Jones. I actually went to school in Mongolia for a semester."

"Sounds fascinating."

Brick by brick, she was building up the wall around those emotions. "It might have been an adventure if it'd been a vacation, but it was a crappy way to grow up. We didn't have time to make friends—if we weren't being home-schooled, that is. We never stayed in one place for very long, so personal effects were limited." She picked up a battered Barbie, its hair half ripped out and its nose smushed, and fingered it. "My brother and I got to keep whatever we could stuff in a backpack on a moment's notice. A few books, a toy or two, the rest was clothes. No room for school papers, memorabilia."

She tossed the doll back in, slapped down the flaps of the box and firmly pushed it away from her. "Oh well, it's just *stuff*, right? All of it is." She waved a hand to indicate the entire attic. "Sometimes I think I should just dump it all on the front lawn and torch it. Except there might be something worth money that I can hock to help keep this place running."

There. She felt better already.

"Because it's home as well your business?"

Damn, perceptive as well as studly. She was in deep trouble.

"Yeah, and because the house deserves it. Kari and I found this place when she was coming up to interview for a spa job here. We saw the For Sale sign at the end of the drive and decided we had to detour and take a look."

"Let me guess. You decided and Kari went along with it."

"She was curious, too," Angela admitted, "but it was my idea." She stared at the floor rather than look at Tyler. Telling this story felt intimate, though it was hardly a deep, dark secret. Adelle knew it, for one, so probably half the town did. But that felt different from telling Tyler. Telling him like this, after he'd caught her in a moment of weakness and comforted her. "It was all boarded up and battered, but I took one look and wanted to put my arms around it and promise I'd make it all better."

"And you've done a great job so far." He laughed. "Including hiring me."

He sounded so deliberately egotistical that she chuckled, too, letting the last of the melancholy go.

She turned, started to get up, but Tyler said, "Hang on, if you don't want anyone to know about the meltdown, you need to clean up." Then he reached out, and it was if she were watching his hand in slow motion. His nice, big, competent hand. She'd never been one to fetishize body parts, but sweet Jesus, the fantasies she could conjure just thinking about what that hand could do to her…

He cupped her face, stroked away a tear with his thumb.

A tear that maybe he'd invented, but it didn't matter because as soon as he touched her face, she forgot painful memories and regrets, and remembered only the way her body reacted when he touched her.

Her skin came alive where he stroked it, sending shivers to places that weren't normally connected to her cheek.

She turned, pressed her lips into his palm, then flicked her tongue, kitten-like, at his thumb, tasting away the salt.

They both froze.

His face was so close that she was almost overwhelmed by the sharp lines of his cheekbones, the faint stubble along his jaw, the denim blue of his eyes that wouldn't leave her gaze.

Time dilated like a scene from a bad movie. They probably held the pose for less than a second, but it felt like hours. It was certainly enough time for Angela to review and discard all the reasons why jumping her employee was a poor plan, yet she had just enough time to draw in a breath, but not to release it.

Before they were kissing like there was no tomorrow.

And for a few moments, there *was* no tomorrow. Nothing but this moment, and Angela didn't even know where this moment was, because it didn't matter. The frustrated desire that had been building in her since

Tyler had sauntered up her front walk was finally culminating, and that's all that there was.

No flirting, no brief touches that could be explained away by accident or everyday occurrence.

No solitary masturbation while imagining what it would feel like to touch and be touched by him.

Finally. Oh God yes.

His lips were soft but his mouth was hard, confident. Boy howdy, did he know how to kiss. His tongue stroked the inside of her lip and all she could imagine was how that would feel on other parts of her body.

The hollow of her throat. The dip of her navel. The damp folds between her legs, as he circled in, tantalizingly slowly, on her swollen clit.

Thought was gone, only sensation left in its wake. Tyler's hands stroked along her upper arms, his fingers biting in just a little. His grip kept her upright even as her bones melted.

She moaned, a low noise in her throat, and pressed closer to him, until she was half-sitting on his lap. He caught his own breath as she settled onto him, and when she felt the hard length of his cock straining against his jeans, she understood why.

He snaked an arm around her and used his free hand to explore her body. His fingers brushed the nape of her neck and she shivered. Was that a whimper? Had she just *whimpered*? Oh God, she had, because that was such a trigger spot for her and with her hair piled up, it was like he'd found a damn bull's-eye.

From the way he murmured something unintelligible, it was clear he was pleased with himself.

He skimmed his hand down her bare arm, the faint roughness of his calluses raising goose bumps of pleasure. Then up again, and he swept across her nipple, vulnerable and needy against the thin silk of her camisole. She arched her back, seeking more pressure, even as the light touch sent a shockwave through her.

Her stretch-lace panties felt like a vise, as if her lips and clit had swelled against them. She knew she was slippery, ready. Definitely beyond ready.

Her breasts ached, begging for more. She'd always like rough play there, the sensitive pleasure teetering into pleasurable pain. He laughed softly against her mouth, pulled away just long enough to murmur, "Oh, you like that, do you?"

The low sound of his voice was like another added touch on her skin. Too much sensation…she spun on a current of desire and lust and the growing need to come.

When she felt the low buzzing start in her head, at least it didn't shock her this time. Didn't surprise her. It unnerved her, but only because she didn't want distractions. She wanted to stay lost, uncaring about the fact that in another point-oh-two seconds she was going to grab Tyler's hand—now moving less languidly on her nipple, but still not the sharp pleasure she craved, and she knew he knew it and was enjoying her frustration—and shove it under her skirt.

And if *that* wasn't enough of a blatant invitation for him, she was going to dive down into her panties herself and let him enjoy watching her bring herself off.

That's the spirit, Minerva's voice whispered, and then she heard peals of tinkling laughter as Minerva got her own joke.

Angela couldn't stop the bubble of amusement (only slightly hysterical) that rose in her own throat, but she half-caught it and it came out as another moan. She didn't want to pull away from Tyler's exploring tongue, but she did long enough to say "Tyler, hold on, I—"

She hadn't wanted to tell him to stop. She really, truly hadn't. But Minerva's damn commentary was enough to bring her back to the here and now, and the fact of the here and now was that she was crawling all over her handyman.

Which wasn't the best idea she'd ever had—although she had to concede it was far from the worst.

Tyler grinned as he said, "I promise I won't accuse you of sexual harassment as long as you don't accuse me," but the smile, Angela thought, was charged with regret.

"I don't think it's harassment when we hit on each other simultaneously."

"But I suppose it's not a good idea, since I'm working for you?"

Angela sighed and pushed her hair out of her eyes. "Probably not." *Though I'd probably forget about that angle if I actually had time to spend a leisurely hour or so being seduced by the handyman.*

"Damn." Tyler smiled lazily as he said, half regret and half further sedition. "Unfortunately, it makes sense. I guess I should get back to what I was doing, which was looking for the broken chair that matches the ones in the parlor, so I can steal one of the spindles to fix the wobbly chair downstairs."

Angela pointed in the right direction. "I found that right away, but I still haven't been able to find what I needed, and I think I'll have to come back another time. Thanks for short-circuiting my doldrums, though."

And her brain, but that was another story. One she suspected Tyler knew already.

*

Tyler turned off the water and stepped out of the tiny shower. The poorly ventilated communal bathroom, an appalling shade of 1980s turquoise, was clogged with steam. He dried off enough to pull his jeans on, not bothering with underwear or even with buttoning the jeans all the way up.

He opened the door a crack and peered out, then made a dash for his room, towel around his neck.

He was in the room for only a few moments, toweling off his hair, when the knock came. He paid the pizza delivery girl, who'd obviously been sent up by Mrs. Parsons, and locked the door after the kid left. That way Mrs. Parsons was less likely to drop in unannounced, as she had the first night he was here, beaming and bearing a plate of stale macaroons on a paper-doilied tray.

Even the memory of the cookies (he'd had to eat one out of politeness) didn't dim his appetite now. The smell of tomato sauce and oregano were already making his stomach growl. He threw the box on the bed and opened it, tearing off a slice and pretty much inhaling it.

The disturbingly named Carnal Carnivore ("sink your teeth into our sausage") wasn't half bad, really, especially given that it was layered with pepperoni, sausage, linguiça, and ground beef.

He could have eaten at the hotel—employees were welcome to gather at the table at one end of the kitchen and take meals as part of their pay—but tonight he had work to do.

Real work.

After he'd devoured several slices, he wiped his hands on the T-shirt he'd stripped off before he'd showered, then threw the shirt in the general direction of the pile of dirty clothes in the corner. Sort of in the corner. He shoved the pizza box onto the doily-topped bureau, then turned to spread the paperwork out on the bed.

The main document was slightly yellowed, and the creases where it had been folded numerous times over the years were starting to thin and separate, tiny holes flashing light through as he unfolded it before laying it out. It took up half the bed.

The faded blue lines on the old paper depicted architectural drawings of Angelika, formerly Fenwick House.

They weren't the original plans, unfortunately; those he hadn't been able to get his hands on, and by all reports they'd been lost or destroyed years ago. These had been done in 1923 after the Cape Mendocino earth-quake that had rattled San Sebastian.

Tyler believed they weren't accurate.

At least, he hoped they weren't. He had reason to believe they weren't, and if they weren't, it meant his entire purpose for being here was legit.

His laptop was on the wobbly pressed-board nightstand, already open. He woke it up so he could look at the photos he'd taken of the hotel. He grabbed a battered manila envelope and dumped out the rest of the paper-work he'd accumulated so far: the sketches and notes he'd made of Angelika over the past few days, based on what he'd actually been able to see so far.

The bed was surprisingly comfortable, but the bedspread was a weird polyester-nylon blend that made his skin crawl. He normally stayed at higher quality establishments, but Mrs. Ancient Parsons's rent-a-room was the expected type of place for a handyman to stay. The swanky B&B down the street would be suspect, and it would certainly look bizarre if he could afford to stay at Angelika.

He'd considered that angle, actually—make a reservation and stay at the hotel as a guest. But he did have the background in historic restoration, and it was a better way of getting into the hotel for a longer period of time than most guests would stay. As the handyman, he could go anywhere, even other guests' rooms, and it wouldn't take much of a story if he was caught poking holes in the wall or crawling around in the attic.

Well, he could see Angela or Kari having an issue if he poked a hole in a wall without a damn good excuse. And to be honest, he truly didn't want to cause any sort of permanent damage to Angelika. She was a beautiful building, with a sweet resonance.

Not unlike one of her owners. Kari was a cute thing, but it was Angela who attracted him. Something about her mane of ebony curls and those dark, mysterious eyes. A guy could get lost in those depthless pools.

Not to mention the way her nipples perked against that silky camisole she'd been wearing that afternoon, so responsive when he touched them.

How she'd moaned, shifted against him, met him kiss for desperate, wild kiss.

His jeans were getting uncomfortably tight. Tyler shook his head, trying to dislodge the distracting thoughts of the alluring Angela.

He had a job to do.

But no matter how hard he tried to concentrate, his mind—and body—kept circling back to images of her. The feel and taste and smell of her.

Okay. Fine. He knew the drill. If you couldn't focus because someone was distracting you, you took care of the distraction.

He stood and popped the buttons of his jeans. His cock sprang free from its confines, and he sighed with relief. He wiggled out of the jeans and kicked them in the general direction of the sort-of laundry corner.

There was a bottle of lotion on the bureau, lime green and shaped like a woman in a floor-length, poofy skirt. He winced before he even opened it, imagining the scent. It was, as expected, cloyingly flowery, but oh, well. Short of heading back into the shower (which would involve stuffing himself back in his jeans, a prospect that, despite the sickly-sweet lotion, was growing increasingly unlikely), this was his only option.

Tyler moved the paperwork to the floor in careful stacks, lay back on the bed, and covered his palm with lotion. He pressed his hands together for a moment, warming the cream, and thought of Angela.

His cock jumped before he even touched it.

Her hair, he thought as he began to stroke, would trail across him, silken strands slithering across his chest and belly. She'd skip over his cock to tease him, brushing against his thighs, before taking pity on him and moving up to twine her locks around his shaft, the ends tickling his balls. When she pulled away, there'd be a drop of pre-come glistening at his tip, and she'd swipe it up with her tongue.

Closing his eyes, he imagined her pink tongue darting out to lick him, and he smeared his thumb over the pre-come at the head of his cock.

She'd already be wet, because they would have been playing for a while. Her juices would be drying on his chin, their scent still lingering, adding to his arousal.

A sultry smile would play on her red, lush lips as she straddled him. Promise would sparkle in her midnight eyes. She'd tease again—she'd be like that—rubbing her wet pussy against the crown of his cock.

Tyler followed suit with his own fingers, lost in the fantasy.

She'd slowly sink down on him, and when she reached the bottom, her eyes would flutter shut. He'd reach up and play with her nipples, lightly at first, then harder, tweaking them and toying with them as she got closer to orgasm. She'd post up and down, faster, and as her climax washed over her she'd grind down, clenching and fluttering against him.

He squeezed himself harder, his fist moving faster as he cupped his balls in his other hand, feeling them tighten as he got closer himself.

She'd lean over then, rubbing her nipples into his chest as she kissed him. She'd try to tease him some more, but he'd be having none of that. He was too close. He'd urge her back up, orchestrate her movements with his hands firmly on her hips.

When she felt him swell, just before his release, her eyes would widen and her mouth would open, and she'd cry out and come again, writhing against him as he shot into her.

He must have blacked out for a second, because the next thing he was aware of was knocking at the door.

"Mr. Woodruff? Everything all right in there?"

His tongue was dry, and it took him a moment to call out, "I'm fine, Mrs. Parsons."

"All right then. Sleep well."

"Thanks."

He found his discarded towel and cleaned himself up, grabbed another slice of pizza, and arranged the paperwork back on the bed.

As he compared the drawings to the photos and sketches, searching for some out-of-place detail, some elusive, hard-to-spot clue, his mind still wasn't totally on his work.

The hotel obviously meant more to Angela than just a business, he got that. She hadn't enjoyed being dragged all over creation when she was growing up, had wanted a place to put down roots and create memories. She didn't have the wanderlust gene.

He, on the other hand, would have reveled in it. Angela had idealized the things she couldn't have, had no idea how mind-numbingly boring a "normal" life in an average town could be.

He'd ditched it to go backpacking around Europe and Asia as soon as he'd been able, and he'd never looked back.

Still, if she'd even joke about torching the contents of the attic—or was willing to sell whatever she found that was worth a few bucks—then she didn't deserve what was hidden somewhere in Angelika.

And he felt no qualms about liberating it from her.

Get in, do the job, leave before Angela—or the blackmailer, for that matter—created further complications.

With a growl, he scooped everything back up and tucked it away between the mattress and box spring, and got dressed. He needed a cold beer. Maybe two.

He'd better find what he was looking for soon, because he wasn't entirely convinced he'd done away with the distraction of Angela Georgenes.

Chapter 7

Angela peeked out from under the covers. The red, glowing numbers on the alarm clock glared balefully back at her.

3:13 a.m. A whole two minutes from the last time she'd checked.

She groaned. The pulsing crimson display of pure evil matched her burning, bloodshot eyes. The gods of irony had decided to make her imaginary allergic reaction in the attic real, and several days of sleep deprivation weren't helping.

Angela to Universe: the insomnia could stop at any time. It was getting old.

She'd had bouts of it before when her stress reached nuclear-detonation levels—the weeks before they'd first opened, not to mention waiting to get the mortgage approved in the first place—but always before, she'd had one surefire way of relaxing enough that she could at least cat-nap.

And her voyeuristic resident ghost had eliminated that option.

Thanks a lot, Minerva. I always figured if we met, we'd be *friends*.

She swore she heard a soft, rueful chuckle, but since she was about as far from being turned on as it was possible for a healthy thirty-year-old woman to be, she suspected it was her brain trying to get in some REM time, with sleep or without it.

Fine.

If she wasn't going to sleep anyway, she might as well cross a few of the more rote tasks off her to-do list. If she could actually find the top of her desk, it would help her stress level.

And the choice of hot beverages and snacks in the hotel was far better than in the meager cottage kitchen. Franklin had mentioned peach cobbler…

She grumped out of bed and into something resembling clothes—okay, yoga pants and a worn T-shirt featuring the Painted Ladies of San Francisco weren't exactly professional attire, but who cared at 3 AM?—and made her way out of the cottage as quietly as she could.

Not that it mattered, because Kari, damn her, could—and, in fact, had—sleep through earthquakes, let alone minor restless-roommate-type noises. Must be all the yoga.

The night air was bracing enough to really perk Angela up (and it definitely perked her nipples up, bringing back a sharp memory of Tyler's fingers), and by the time she'd gotten halfway through the garden, she felt a bit less like Zombie Angela in Search of Brains.

And less inclined to go catch up on nice, soporific paperwork.

Instead, she sat on a shiver-inducingly damp cedar bench to survey her domain as best she could in the dim light from solar-powered garden lanterns.

The garden wasn't anything like a restoration of what it had been in Minerva's day—Minerva had had a small army of gardeners, while she and Kari were lucky to have one perma-stoned aging hippie who'd work two afternoons a week cheap so he could get the occasional Franklin care package—but it looked and smelled good at this time of year. Spring bulbs were easy.

Maybe just sitting here would relax her enough to…

What the hell?

She levitated to roof-level and hovered—or, at least, that's what it felt like.

Whatever was moving around near the hotel was too big to be an animal. At least any animal she'd expect to see in San Sebastian. And Isabella had been safely asleep at the foot of Angela's bed when she left the cottage, so it probably wasn't a greyhound magnified by nerves to immense proportions.

Could be a burglar.

Could be a mountain lion.

Hell, it could be Bigfoot. They already had a ghost, so why not Bigfoot?

Common sense told her to sneak back to the cottage and call for help. She wasn't exactly equipped to deal with any of them.

Especially not Bigfoot. She had a dim idea of what you were supposed to do about criminals and cougars, but mythical beings were another question.

She took two steps back toward the cottage. Then she heard—or thought she heard—the sound of someone poking around in one of the sheds.

In one of *her* sheds. Filled with her things, things she needed to keep Angelika running and make her guests comfortable. Some of those things were artifacts from Minerva's time—precious garden ornaments they hadn't put out yet; a marble bench that Tyler would need help to move; even ancient, sturdy shovels and rakes that their gardener swore were still better than anything you could buy today.

And no burglar would steal them and no marauding animal would damage them. Dammit.

So naturally she ended up creeping on her belly through the damp grass like Angelina Jolie in an action movie toward where she'd thought she'd seen or heard something.

More likely than not, it was a guest—or guests. She'd hate to have cops sweeping down on Carole trying to walk off her angst, or worse yet, Margaret and David enjoying a private moment in the garden. (Angela had heard intriguing moans and bed-creaks as she passed the older couple's room that afternoon, thus proving that it was the quiet ones you have to watch out for.)

That might account for the funny sound she thought she'd heard. But if it wasn't a guest and it was a threat in any way, she'd kill it.

With her bare hands.

Even if it was a cougar.

Or Bigfoot.

Every night sound magnified. Generic birds. A car passing in the distance. The soft shushing of the surf. The guest-or-not doing whatever it was they were doing.

Unfortunately, mixed in with all that was the sound of one hotel-owner trying to make like an action hero.

The low crawl was a silent thing in the movies, but not so much in real life. Lots of snapping twigs and grunting and stuff, though she was trying to not even breathe. Her target, be it guests with a hankering for love under the stars or a misplaced yeti, must be able to hear her.

Probably the neighbors could hear her, and the nearest neighbors were a quarter mile away and no doubt fast asleep.

This was so stupid.

Another hint of motion, and this time it looked like it was heading toward the porch.

As if the intruder (or not) was planning to break into the hotel.

No way in hell.

But she wanted to get a little closer, because if it was a guest (and that was still the most likely option), she'd prefer to slink back into the shadows and not be seen looking like a grass-stained, mud-streaked lunatic.

She'd had no idea you could do a low crawl so damn fast. She was pretty sure she'd ripped the knee of her yoga pants, and the shirt would never be the same again, but she was almost there.

Just in time to hear the door open.

An indistinct figure—female, she thought, but it could have been Margaret's husband, who wasn't a big guy—entered and closed the door behind her/him/it. It looked like the person was pocketing a key.

Which would mean it had a key.

Which meant it belonged there.

And wasn't a burglar or a wild animal, real or legendary.

Still, she'd want to check. Look for signs of forced entry or damage, stuff like that.

She scrambled to her feet and groaned as various muscles she couldn't name protested their ill-treatment. No wonder action heroes were always so buff—it was hard work.

It wasn't that far to the back door, but by the time she got there, whoever it was was out of sight, leaving nothing behind but a few muddy sneaker prints on the steps and porch.

No damage done. Not even a scratch on the polished brass lock fittings.

And once Angela got inside, only the faintest traces of mud in the hallway.

That settled it. Definitely a guest having a pre-dawn stroll for some private reason.

A burglar wouldn't wipe his feet.

Too many worries and not enough sleep make Angela an idiot.

And the noises in the shed must have been her imagination.

All the adrenaline drained from Angela's body so abruptly that her legs buckled and she had to fight not to catch herself on the wall. (She'd leave muddy streaks on the precious vintage wallpaper, and even in her current state, she knew better.)

Sighing, she dragged herself back to the cottage, where she fell into bed still in her ruined clothes.

Her last thought, before fading into much-needed sleep, was to be careful what she wished for. Her embarrassing adventure seemed to have helped the insomnia, but she wasn't about to try that particular cure again anytime soon.

*

By morning—morning-morning, the morning that involved sunshine and coffee and a buttery scone with marionberry jam and the blessed sensation of having actually slept, if only for a few hours—Angela could see the incident for the slapstick comedy it was. Someday, after an appropriate amount of adult beverage, she'd tell Kari about it and they'd share a good laugh.

She might even tell her parents about it when she met up with them in San Francisco in…less than two weeks, oh my God. Might help them worry less that her life was too dull.

Caught up in the crises du jour, she'd almost forgotten the whole thing except for a few twingy muscles.

Until Stella, the head of housekeeping, stuck her head into the office and said, "Angela, can I ask you something?"

And then shut the door behind her when Angela absently said, "Sure."

"Have you or Kari been rearranging things in the library? I went in to dust this morning and there were a bunch of books pulled out. And

I know the guests don't always put them back so I figured it wasn't a big deal. But then I saw the Chinese statues on the mantel were switched around and the little painted box was open and a couple of other things were in different places. If that's where you want those things now, I'll remember it."

Her tone was definitely one of "Someone's been messing with my precious order," but that was Stella for you. The head of housekeeping was the head of housekeeping because it allowed her to channel her OCD in useful ways and not end up washing her hands sixty times a day or something.

Although for all Angela knew, Stella did wash her hands sixty times a day.

At any other time, Angela would have politely dismissed Stella's concern. Guests often liked to take a closer look at the decorative objects and didn't always note exactly where something belonged. Not everyone had Stella's meticulous memory for minor details.

But the memory of last night—and of that niggling sense that whoever was outside, guest or not, seemed to be sneaking and snooping, not just wandering—made Angela nod thoughtfully. "I think it was just a thoughtless guest. But do me a favor and let me know if it happens again."

Great. Now she had something else to worry it. And even though common sense told her it was nothing, that she was only considering it at all because of money problems, ghosts, and every other damn thing making her paranoid, common sense wasn't entirely helping.

What would help was another cup of coffee—she swiveled her chair around to refill her cup, because getting up might have disturbed Isabella, who was sleeping under the desk—and focusing on something else. Like one of those dull but necessary jobs she'd meant to do last night before getting distracted by playing commando.

As opposed to going commando, which might be distracting in a good way if, for instance, a certain hunkalious handyman had to dislodge the dog and crawl under her desk to figure out why the outlet wasn't working. Which fortunately it was because in real life she'd be too busy being annoyed by one more damn minor snafu to enjoy any clichéd-but-fun porn-movie adventures with Tyler....

Paying bills was one of her usual Monday tasks. It wasn't as dull as she hoped it would become someday—some weeks, juggling what got paid when was a little more exciting than writing checks ought to be—but there was a modestly decent chunk of money in the bank this week and only a couple of bills that had the red second-notice stamp on them.

Piece of cake.

Or it would have been if Tyler hadn't sauntered into the office, propped his hip on the corner of her desk (stretching the faded denim of his jeans across the taut muscle of his thigh), and said, "Mornin', Boss Lady."

Chapter 8

*A*ngela looked tired, Tyler mused. In the glow of her computer screen, the skin beneath her eyes had a fragile, bruised quality, apparent despite her dusky complexion and an attempt to minimize the issue with makeup.

Tyler had once heard that Italians considered dark circles under the eyes sexy, because it implied the person had been up half the night doing delightfully risqué things.

As an avowed enthusiast of delightfully risqué things—night *or* day— he gave that theory a hearty thumbs-up.

What he wouldn't give to whisk Angela back to her cottage, slowly lift her form-fitting turquoise top over her head while paying great attention to every patch of skin that was revealed. He'd trap her arms in the sweater and run his fingers over the curve of her breasts where they swelled out from her bra, which had to be some sort of slick material, like satin or silk, to not show lines beneath her clothes.

He wondered if she was wearing another one of those amazing pencil skirts she seemed fond of, which hugged her temptingly curvy ass and had a slit that showed off just enough leg to make him think about…

Tyler cleared his throat and slid into the chair across from Angela's desk before he took that thought too far and needed a glass of ice water thrown on his crotch.

Angela was staring at him, head cocked curiously to one side. "What can I do for you, Tyler?" she asked.

She was all business, as if they hadn't made out in the attic the day before. It reminded him that he needed to be all business, too. Focus on the prize—which was *not* Angela. He couldn't afford that kind of distraction.

But damn if she just didn't make him want to fuck her soundly. Or maybe just force her to take a long nap.

Then again, the former might relax her enough to make the latter happen.

Normally he'd just think about the former, which was exactly the problem here. Angela was already getting under his skin in ways other than sex.

She'd been fine before he got here. He had to keep reminding himself of that. She'd be fine after he left, despite what he intended to leave with. The sooner that happened, the better for both of them.

Especially with the added complication of a blackmailer butting into his business.

"I noticed some dry rot in the fifth bath house," he said. "It's not crucial right now, but you'll want to deal with it at some point."

She sighed and opened the spreadsheet on her computer where she kept notes on upkeep and repair. Her normally tidy desk (some would say obsessively tidy, but he refrained from such judgments) seemed messier than usual, an odd counterpoint to the stress she seemed to be carrying.

He'd trained himself to read people. She presented more of a challenge than he was used to.

Before she could finish recording the information—and, thankfully, before he could let his train of thought derail dangerously further—Franklin poked his head in. A moment later his solid form filled the doorway.

"It's Monday," he said. "Any requests?"

"As long as we're well stocked with Ghirardelli and that fabulous brand of Kona coffee, I'm good," she said. "Need some cash?"

"A hundred should do it." He glanced at Tyler. "Hey, Tyler."

"Hey." He liked Franklin, who seemed like a decent guy and was obviously a god in the kitchen. How those big hands could deftly create delicate pastries and gorgeous hand-cut raviolis was beyond him. He just appreciated that the help had the option of taking meals at the hotel.

The local pizza joint was surprisingly decent in a pinch, but it turned out they didn't like to deliver orders to Adelle Parson's unless they had a female delivery person available.

Big surprise.

Angela went to the safe in the corner and crouched down to open it. Mm, yes, a narrow, formfitting little skirt, brown with tiny vertical stripes in the same turquoise hue as her top and her chunky earrings.

He waited until she'd just finished dialing the combination before he stood, knowing he shouldn't be too obvious. He eased up as if needing to find a new, comfortable seating position. If it also gave him a better view of Angela's delectable bottom, well, that was an excuse that could make him look innocent.

So to speak.

He glanced at Franklin, who grinned as if he understood and then made a notation in the small Moleskine notebook he held.

Tyler couldn't see anything obvious in the safe besides some files and a metal cash box, which Angela was currently accessing.

Angela swung the safe shut and spun the dial, then stood and handed Franklin some bills.

When he was gone, Tyler asked, "What's so special about Mondays?"

"What?" Angela settled back into her office chair, which wobbled more than just a little. He suspected it was one of the many ways she'd cut corners to hoist Angelika in the black. "Oh, the farmer's market is today. We like to get our produce local and organic whenever we can."

"A wise choice." He turned to leave, then, because he couldn't resist, said over his shoulder, "If you need anything, call me."

He looked away before he saw her response, but he smiled at her indrawn breath.

The smile faded as he headed toward the kitchen. He didn't know how long Franklin was going to be gone, so he needed to be in and out of there before anyone caught wind of what he was doing.

*

By the time he made it to the kitchen, he had his story in place just in case someone caught him. He was interested in old houses; he wanted to catch a peek at the fixtures here, to see which ones were original, at a time when he wouldn't be in the way.

He said hello to one of the maids, who doubled as a waitress during meals, as he passed through the dining room. Pausing in her layout of the luncheon china, the petite brunette flashed him a smile—a smile of pure invitation. If he wasn't so taken with Angela…

But that was the thing. He *was* so taken with Angela, a fact which still surprised him.

Angelika's original kitchen had seen some modifications since it was first built. Old kitchens had been designed to take advantage of natural light, so one wall here had housed a bank of south-facing windows. Those windows had originally looked out on an airy breakfast porch.

Now the windows were fewer, and the breakfast porch beyond had been expanded to be a larger space for guests to enjoy a cocktail and hors d'oeuvres before dinner.

The appliances were all new—new at the time Angelika had opened as a hotel, Tyler estimated—and all were industrial-capacity to handle the demands of an ever-rotating slate of modern guests.

That was the extent to which Angela and Kari had invested in upgrades here, apparently. The lighting, while perfectly adequate, dated from the 1970s (although the bulbs were energy efficient), and the walls could've used a fresh coat of white paint.

Since the area was off-limits to guests, returning the kitchen to its original Victorian glory wasn't high on their priorities, he guessed. As long as the work area was clean and up to code, the period details didn't matter.

The fact that the kitchen wasn't accessible to guests didn't mean that what he sought wasn't hidden here, somewhere.

This was one of the few areas that he couldn't explore with impunity. He had to have an excuse to be poking around in the kitchen.

So he had to create that excuse. As much as his palms itched to dig in and explore, he just didn't have the time now. San Sebastian wasn't a large town, and there was no telling how efficiently Franklin could cut a swath through the farmer's market and make it back to the hotel.

If he stayed in here longer than it took to grab a snack, the maid (for all her flirtation) might snitch on him, possibly without even realizing what she was doing.

Get in and get out. That was his personal credo.

So. The question was, what could he do here now that would allow him a decent amount of access later? Nothing that would cause serious physical harm to anyone—that was a line he wouldn't cross. But other than that…

Ah. Of course. He smiled and reached into his pocket.

*

Angela raised her martini glass. "To the start of a successful second year!"

"I'll totally drink to that," Kari said.

"Sláinte," Cybelline said as they all clinked glasses.

MacGowan's was nondescript and off the beaten path, which meant it didn't have to spiff itself up to cater to tourists. The sound system occasionally crackled out, the floor was sticky, and the lighting was dim, not for ambiance but because of just being tired, apparently.

It was a locals' bar, and Angela liked the camaraderie of being accepted as a local.

"Do you really think it's going okay?" Kari asked after taking a sip of her merlot. "I mean, we had some rocky moments there. This past year hasn't been easy, and we have the debts from the restoration…"

Angela reached across the table and made sure Kari couldn't continue. "Hush. We're not going to talk about work tonight," she said. "We're here for a positive, relaxing drink. Okay?"

"Okay," Kari said from behind the muffling hand over her mouth.

"Pinky swear?" Angela pulled her hand off Kari's face and held it up, little finger crooked.

"Pinky swear?" Cybelline echoed. "What are you—nine?"

"Angela didn't have a normal childhood." Kari laughed and hooked her pinky around her friend's. "She sometimes forgets what's appropriate."

"Shut up," Angela said cheerfully and crunched down one of the tiny pickled onions in her drink. It was too easy to get stuck at Angelika—the place was big, and the grounds bigger, but sometimes she needed to get away. Even when "away" meant three miles into San Sebastian's town center, a cheap taxi ride away so they could indulge without guilt.

Not that San Sebastian was all that big. It was too far away from the city—either Sacramento or San Francisco—to get regular traffic, but its old-world charm and plethora of stately, sometimes gaudy Victorian homes made it a popular tourist attraction. Main Street was lined with antique shops and boutiques and eateries.

Which was why they were sequestered in MacGowan's.

Sure, they could have essentially had a few drinks for free at Angelika (insofar as Angela paid wholesale for the alcohol), but that whole getting-away thing was the point. No guests, no paperwork, no renovations.

Plus they could chat freely, without worrying that a guest—or, God forbid, Satya—would see or overhear something they shouldn't.

"Okay, okay," Cybelline said. Tonight she was wearing a bombshell-blond wig in a '50s style and green cats' eye glasses, also retro-looking (and totally for show, since her eyes were fine). She'd changed up her look, she'd explained, so if any tourists did find their favorite bar, they wouldn't spot her and do something annoying like ask for an on-the-spot Tarot reading. "I get that you don't want to talk shop, but I have to ask: has Minerva been active?"

"Hey, no fair," Angela said.

"*I* didn't pinky swear," Cybelline pointed out. "Now, just answer the question."

Angela sighed. "She's still…here. Wherever 'here' is. Inside me."

"I still need to rummage through the house with you. Somewhere, there's got to be a key to why she latched onto you. And I'll know it when I see it."

"In my copious spare time."

"Make time. It's important." Cybelline leaned forward, her green eyes intent behind her faux spectacles. "So anyway, tell me more. What's Minerva up to?"

"Most of the time, she's not really awake, if that's the right word. I can almost forget she's there. But anytime I get the slightest bit, um, aroused…"

"Angela's like a guy," Kari said, holding up her wine glass to avoid repercussions. "They think about sex, what, every fifteen seconds?"

"Every seven seconds, actually," Angela said.

"Of course, you *would* know that," Kari said.

"It's my parents and their research," Angela said. "It's a curse."

"But a useful one. We wouldn't have balanced books or an authentic restoration without it."

Cybelline waved her hands. "Hey, hey, back to the subject. You get horny, and what happens?"

Angela narrowed her eyes. "Why are you so interested in this?"

"Trying to figure out ways to help, but it's also a professional interest." Cybelline tried to look respectable and failed, mostly thanks to the wig. "I was thinking, you know, that it would make a great case study. Maybe even a book."

"You are not writing a book about me," Angela said.

"I'd change your name, and any identifying details," Cybelline said.

"Kari," Angela said, "frisk her for any audio or visual recording devices."

"Stop, stop!" Cybelline managed through her laughter. "I'd make you sign a release first anyway."

Angela pursed her lips and stared at her martini. "Didn't you buy this round? You could've slipped something into my drink, and then you'll get me to sign your evil release while I'm not in my right mind."

"I could say something about how often you're in your right mind, but I won't," Kari said.

"And you're supposed to be my friends," Angela said without rancor. It was good to get away, be comfortable and silly. She *could* trust them. She and Kari had been together since college and put their financial futures on the line together, going deep into debt with Angelika. Cybelline, although they hadn't known her nearly as long, seemed like the missing piece of their puzzle.

The music changed to some generic pop song that many of the patrons perked up and sang along to, at least the first few lines. Angela wasn't surprised she didn't recognize it; she hadn't been exposed to the latest music growing up. Her parents played late '60s and early '70s music when they had access to a boom box on a dig, so she was well versed in the complete Led Zeppelin catalogue as well as everything early by Tom Waits and Lou Reed—or she'd picked up on the local music of whatever culture they'd been in at the time.

She could pick out a zither from an oud at thirty paces, but no matter how many times Kari tried to explain it to her, she kept confusing New Kids on the Block with Kid Rock.

She went on. "As I was saying, any time I feel a little horny, I can sense Minerva more clearly. It's hard to explain. It's almost as if that opens up a channel to her. Sometimes it's very clear, but other times I can only pick up a word or two."

"I've never heard of a ghost haunting someone during sexy moments before, but there's a first time for everything," Cybelline said.

Kari said solemnly, "I've been doing a little research of my own." At Cybelline's startled look, she said, "I know this is more up your alley, Cyb, but it's fascinating stuff and I was curious. Anyway, some ghosts are really predictable and consistent—the theory is they're more like fragments of memories repeating themselves, rather than full personalities. But ones that are more like the original person aren't always consistent from one appearance to the next, and are stronger or weaker in ways that don't seem logical."

Cyb nodded. "Makes sense that stronger ghosts can behave unpredictably, just like living people. Good job, Kari."

"Although I haven't found anything yet about ghosts that are drawn to sex or arousal," Kari added.

"Maybe Angela's more relaxed, or otherwise more open to her then," Cybelline said.

"But I'm relaxed when I get a massage—" Mal, their other massage therapist, had given Angela a half-hour neck-and-shoulders job just before they'd headed out "—and when I'm sleeping. Although I haven't been sleeping well."

She went on to relate her midnight wanderings, complete with James Bond-worthy ground stalking, and had the other two in tears of laughter.

When her cell rang, she could barely gasp out her "Hello?"

"It's Franklin," the cook said unnecessarily, since his name had come up on the screen. "We have a problem."

As if she'd been dumped in the still-frigid Northern California ocean, Angela sobered and sat up straight. "What is it?"

"The industrial dishwasher," he said. "It's hemorrhaging water. I've turned it off, but the kitchen floor is a lake and I don't know what happened. And I don't have Tyler's phone number."

Brilliant chef, useless handyman. It was a trade-off Angela was willing to take.

"I'll call Tyler and we'll head back," she said. "Don't worry, we'll get it all fixed up. Grab a mop and we'll pitch in when we get there."

Franklin hated anything amiss in his kitchen. She wouldn't say he was close to tears, but he certainly sounded rattled, bless his big heart.

She hung up and, while she scrolled for Tyler's number, briefly updated Kari and Cyb on the situation. When Tyler answered, she repeated the information, adding, "I hope you have a working knowledge of industrial dishwashers."

"I know my way around them," he said, his voice giving her that little tingle she just didn't need right now. The stirring down low in her belly was probably just arousal, but she couldn't help but wonder if it was Minerva waking up. Or whatever.

She gritted her teeth and mentally recited the architectural styles of Victorian houses from Gothic Revival through Queen Anne.

"Meet you there, then," she said, and hung up.

In fact, his truck was already parked to the side of Angelika when she and Kari arrived.

"Damn," Kari said. "He got here fast. Are you sure he didn't have any speeding violations on his record?"

"Nope, he was squeaky clean."

She told Kari she didn't have to stay; no sense both of them staying up half the night with the problem. If things sorted themselves out in a reasonable time frame, they could share a nightcap in their cottage before they both collapsed.

Kari headed around the hotel to their cottage. Angela took a deep breath.

Squeaky clean. That might be Tyler's police record, but she had every reason to fantasize that in bed, he'd be as dirty as they come. And if he talked dirty to her, all the better.

Mmm…

Wait. Was that her, or Minerva?

Damn. It was going to be another long night.

She headed back to the kitchen.

Chapter 9

Tyler couldn't help but stare when Angela walked through the kitchen door.

When she wasn't around, he could get lost in thoughts of a beautiful woman with sweet lips and soft curves and a potent sensuality—but she was also the boss, the co-owner of Angelika, and the way she'd strode in and assessed the damage reminded him of that.

Stood there, hands on hips, like she owned the place—because she did.

That she was wearing a wine-colored stretch lace shirt paired with soft, well-worn (and sweet-curve-hugging) Levis and a necklace of bright, chunky beads, possibly African, somehow seemed to highlight that she was the authority around here. It was one thing to convey "I'm in charge" in I'm-in-charge suits, but when you were dressed for a night out with friends and could still project that aura, that said something.

He tried not to see it as a challenge to find where her in-charge persona broke down in the bedroom. At what point would she capitulate beneath his hands and mouth, begging him not to stop?

"Not as bad as I'd feared, thanks to you guys," she said, her glance taking in soapy puddles, piles of sodden towels, and a disgruntled-looking Franklin using the wringer on the ginormous string mop he was wielding.

A disgruntled Franklin looked like someone you wouldn't want to meet in a dark alley, but Angela's words made him beam and brought out his inner teddy bear.

"Thanks for getting here so fast, Tyler," she went on. "How did you…?"

Thankfully he'd already planned his excuse, because right now his brain was too busy trying to reclaim needed blood that had drained southward.

"I was out picking up a late night sub when I got the call."

Which, like all the best lies, had the benefit of being more or less true. He had grabbed a sub and the remains were in the truck to prove it. "Anyway, I was just about to double-check that Franklin turned off the water just to the kitchen and not the guest rooms."

"I'm pretty sure I did the right thing, but you know me." Franklin shrugged. "If it's not attached to a stove…"

"Why don't you go with him?" Angela suggested to the cook. "That way, if there's ever a problem again, you'll be sure. I'll take over mopping."

As they left, Tyler stole a wistful glance back at Angela. She was bent over, wringing out the mop, and the pose accented her ass nicely. He really didn't want to leave that alluring view, but he reluctantly followed Franklin toward the stairs.

The basement was cool stone, minimally finished. The original coal furnace was still in place, though its function had been taken over by a modern heating system. He saw what looked like a root cellar entrance and itched with curiosity. Who knew what could be stowed in that out-of-the-way place?

No, if Franklin accidentally killed the water to the whole complex, he needed to fix it as quickly as possible. Besides, the root cellar could be full of roots. For all technology had advanced, it was still the best place to store certain vegetables. (He'd read an article about restoring old root cellars for modern use.)

He asked Franklin about that, casually, and Franklin, shining a flashlight at the main pipes because the single bulb above barely illuminated the room, distractedly answered that it was empty.

Damn.

He joined the other man and was relieved to discover Franklin had indeed chosen the right shut-off lever.

"I'll get labels on them when I have a chance," Tyler promised. The former handyman had a laminated diagram posted on the wall, but the system was complex, allowing water for the various parts of the hotel to be shut off separately, and said former handyman had apparently created his own secret code for it all.

Tyler could suss it out, but it wouldn't hurt to make it clear for staff people who didn't understand plumbing, which was probably most of them. A small effort to protect a building he'd grown fond of.

Or help out a woman he'd grown unexpectedly and disturbingly fond of?

Dangerous line of thought, that. "All set here. Let's get that dishwasher fixed. I don't know about you, Franklin, but I hate doing dishes."

*

Angela had her sleeves pushed up when they got back. Her dark hair was pulled back in a disheveled ponytail, not in a cute, I'm-getting-my-hair-out-of-the-way-in-preparation-for-giving-a-blowjob way, and the hems of her jeans were soaked. But the floor was mostly dry and she looked curiously content, as if a bit of down-and-dirty physical labor relaxed her.

Which was a notion he could get behind. Or under. Or on top of. Or next to.

He hunkered down next to the dishwater to hide his thoughts. If his eyes didn't give him away, his crotch would in a few minutes. Their flirtation was mutual—okay, it had gone a little farther than flirtation, even if she'd turned all sensible before things got really interesting the other day in the attic—but he suspected she wasn't the type to flaunt it in front of a third party.

Plus, mutual attraction or no, she was still in Boss Lady Damage Control mode.

The five-paneled kitchen door swung open, but Tyler didn't look up. Probably someone from housekeeping coming to get a room service order or maybe get a snack themselves. Not his business.

He did look up, though, at the tone in Angela's voice. It was polite, even gracious, but it wasn't her normal genuine friendliness.

"Ms. Swain, how can we help you?"

Barb Swain was dressed in yoga pants and a blue hoodie that looked like any other yoga pants and hoodie, but he was willing to bet were über-expensive. Decent body, though nothing like Angela's. But he didn't care much for women who sported full makeup, including red lipstick, at 11 p.m. when they were dressed for curling up with a good book.

Unless she was here to flirt with the chef. She *was* standing awfully close to him. She wasn't a tiny thing, but she had to look up at Franklin, and to Tyler's jaundiced eyes, she appeared to be working it.

"I wanted another piece of that wonderful berry pie we had with dinner," Barb said, putting a hand on Franklin's arm as she said "wonderful."

"Room service would be glad to bring you some." Angela's voice was patient. "But I'm afraid guests aren't allowed in the kitchen."

"Really? Franklin's kitchen seemed like it would be such an *inviting* place." Yup, she was batting her eyes.

And Franklin was falling for it, or maybe he was just being polite to a guest. "I'd be glad to show you around if you want to make an appointment, Ms. Swain, but there are some silly Health Department rules about people just popping in, especially when I'm in the middle of baking for breakfast tomorrow. But since you're here…" He'd eased away from her as he spoke, and now he opened the industrial stainless-steel fridge and pulled out the pie.

Barb, abandoned, now seemed to notice the rest of the kitchen: Tyler on the floor, Angela with her sleeves rolled up, the mop bucket and film of water drying on the floor. "Looks more like you're in the middle of fixing something. Is there a problem?"

Angela obviously thought fast. "I was talking with Franklin and dropped my coffee cup. I wouldn't be setting a very good example for my staff if I didn't clean up after myself."

"And a piece of the cup ended up under the dishwasher," Tyler took Angela's ball and ran with it. Lame explanation, but the guest's eyes were back on Franklin's huge hands, or maybe on the pie he was plating for her, so apparently it worked.

It was clear that Barb wanted to stay and talk—make that flirt—but Angela took control of the situation. "You know what goes perfectly with this pie? Chambord and cognac. Would you like one?"

"Well, I really shouldn't." Barb patted her flat tummy and Tyler guessed she was the type who'd wait for someone, ideally Franklin, to swiftly assure her about how thin she was.

The clock on the wall ticked into the silence. Bingo.

The smile on Barb's face never wavered as she finally said, "But what are vacations for, in not indulgence? How about one for Carole, too?"

When the two women were safely out of earshot, Tyler said, "I don't think pie was the snack she had in mind, my man. I think she was hoping for chocolate."

Franklin laughed, a deep, hearty belly laugh of pure amusement. "Wouldn't be the first time, but why is it always skinny, Botoxed white women? She's not bad looking, but I'd break a scrawny lady like her. Why couldn't that reporter be the one hitting on me? Skin like honey, and she's…" He searched for the right word and instead described a voluptuous hourglass in the air.

Satya had only vaguely registered on Tyler—full figure and a pretty enough face, he thought, but nothing compared to Angela. Still, he made appropriate male-bonding noises of agreement and got back to work.

Angela had mopped up the worst of the mess on the main floor, but hadn't been able to get to the dark red and peach linoleum down here. As Tyler lay on his side to squeeze between the dishwasher and the wall, the water sucked into his T-shirt and jeans. He could still smell the sweet scent of soap and see a few bubbles along the floorboard.

He could also see where the linoleum—which he'd already pegged as a more recent addition rather than the original, although whoever had chosen it had done an excellent job of finding one that looked period for the house—ended and a line of old black-and-white hexagonal tiles extended along the edge of the wall.

Out of curiosity, he rapped lightly on the wall with his knuckles, gauging the material and thickness. Not original, either. Hm.

He didn't ask about it, not just yet. His job was to figure out the problem with the dishwasher, and if he was obviously distracted, that might look funny.

"I see what happened," he said, pitching his voice loud so Franklin could hear him behind the looming steel contraption. Briefly, he wondered how strong an earthquake would have to be to make the heavy machine shift, pinning him down here. "There's a split in the drain hose."

He wormed his way back out to see Franklin's brow furrowed.

"Is it going to be hard to fix?" the chef asked. "I mean, we can get extra staff in to do dishes by hand, but…"

"It's an easy fix for now—I just need to cut the split section off and attached the undamaged part back in. I probably have a hose cutter in my truck," Tyler said, because he knew he did. "Let me take off the hose clamp and then I'll double-check."

"What would cause that?" Franklin asked.

"Could be an older hose. This'll fix it for now, but the next time I'm at a hardware store I'll pick up another. Won't be more than five bucks."

He selected a screwdriver from his tool belt, which he'd had to remove in order to squirm into the tight space, and squeezed his way back in to attack the hose clamp.

"This wall back here," he said. "It's not original, is it?"

"Which one?" Franklin asked, which was a valid question because the dishwasher was in a corner.

"The back one." Tyler tapped it with the heel of his boot.

"I don't think it is," Franklin said. "A lot of the renovation was done in the forties, and the work Angela and Kari did was mostly before they hired me. But I'm pretty sure that wall was changed at some point. There used to be a breakfast nook there, with access from the kitchen, but it was closed off and now it's just part of the porch. The porch there has a view of the ocean. A lot of guests like to take tea there when the weather's nice."

Tyler could imagine the original layout. The kitchen probably would have been open to the nook, or had a half-wall with windows, and the nook itself would have been largely glass to accommodate the incredible view. The sunsets beyond the ocean cliff were breathtaking.

Angelika was situated on an amazing spot. Minerva May Fenwick had chosen well.

He finished removing the hose clamp and tossed the metal piece out ahead of him before sliding back out. "So a lot of the kitchen was renovated in the forties or at some other point," he echoed, trying to urge Franklin to continue revealing what he knew without making the man suspicious with a lot of questions.

Franklin raised a massive shoulder. "Not my area of expertise," he said. "It's a gorgeous house, but architecture isn't my thing. As long as the kitchen's laid out the way I need it, and everything works, that's all I care about. Angela knows this place inside and out, including what changes were made when. She's researched everything. You should ask her."

"He should ask who what?" Angela strolled into the kitchen as Tyler was getting to his feet. Her face looked a little pinched; Tyler knew she'd been reining in her annoyance with Barb. Too bad, because when she'd first arrived back from wherever she'd been—he'd surmised a bar, given the background music when she'd called him—she'd seemed more relaxed than she'd been earlier today, despite this setback.

"Tyler was asking about the changes made to the kitchen over the years," Franklin said.

Well, technically, he hadn't really been *asking*, but Tyler didn't bother to correct the statement.

"I can usually tell what's new and what isn't," he said, "but it helps to know a little of the history of changes when I'm working." He held up the hose clamp. "Obviously the dishwasher is modern, and the plumbing attached to it is reasonably so. But what about the internal plumbing? I can tell that wall isn't original, and Franklin told me it used to open on the breakfast nook."

"He's right," Angela said. "In 1943, the owners made a lot of changes to 'update' things." The way she said "update" made it sound like a dirty word, and not a sexy dirty word, either. "They decided to extend the porch—which, in and of itself, wasn't a bad idea—but they made the nook part of it, and wanted more counter space in the kitchen."

"Convenience over style," Tyler said.

Angela made a moue of disgust, which he found utterly charming. "William Morris might have said you should have nothing in your house that you don't know to be useful or believe to be beautiful, but I always felt he believed the two things could—and should—exist in the same objects," she said.

"Now, over here," she went on, taking a few steps toward the center of the room and gesturing toward the stove area, "there used to be a wall with a beautiful arch, where the original stove was, with a copper vent over it. We've found pictures. I know Franklin wouldn't be able to cook on a period stove, even a retrofitted one, but those monstrosities were about the size of this industrial one. Behind the nook was the butler's pantry, which had storage, a prep sink, all that. Someone ripped out the whole wall to make the room bigger."

She put her hands on her hips, staring at the current stove as if imagining how it used to be. "I'd put a bullet in their head if I ever had the chance."

Tyler knew she wasn't serious, but he agreed with the sentiment. Plus her passion for the hotel and its history made her dark eyes flash, and he liked that. Liked it a lot.

She looked pretty tonight, he mused. In a different way than usual. Distracted, he tried to figure out why. If, indeed, she'd been at a bar, she'd been relaxing with friends, and maybe that was it. It looked like she'd had her nails done at the spa; although they were trimmed short by necessity, they looked especially groomed and bore a faint sheen of iridescent polish.

He tried not to think about those nails digging into his back as he drove into her and made her come over and over.

Maybe it was just her vehemence over what had been done to "her" hotel, even if those things had been done in the past, well before she'd ever seen Angelika.

He remembered her telling how she'd found the place, how she'd wanted to put her arms around it and tell it everything would be all right.

Kind of like Tyler was itching to do with Angela, except in a much more naked and sweaty fashion, with as many creative positions as she could bend her body into.

"The plumbing," Tyler prompted, because those thoughts led to madness, and because he was expected to ask, given the part he was holding in his hand.

"Oh, right." Angela turned back, toyed with her ponytail as she thought. "We had copper pipes run to the kitchen and spa. Everything else was upgraded in the seventies and is holding on so far, thank God."

"Thanks, that'll help. Let me check my truck for parts and see if I can't get this fixed tonight, so nobody has to be up to their armpits in dishwater tomorrow."

Like Angela herself. Tyler didn't doubt she'd try to save money by pitching in rather than paying staff overtime, just like she'd pushed up the sleeves of that curve-hugging burgundy stretch lace top and mopped the kitchen.

It alarmed him a bit that he found Angela mopping to be as erotic as anything he'd ever seen. He had it far, far too bad under the circumstances.

*

Tyler returned, smiling triumphantly and brandishing what had to be a hose cutter.

"I don't believe you had one." Angela resisted—barely—the urge to hug him. Once again, he proved to be her knight in a shining pickup.

"Be prepared. It's the Boy Scout motto. I was an Eagle Scout, so I'm always thoroughly prepared. For anything."

The words themselves weren't suggestive, but the little lift to his eyebrows and the sultry pitch to his voice made her imagine him being prepared for a hot date, with candles and rose petals on the sheets and a bottle of chilled champagne and a few toys.

She swore she heard Minerva's sultry laugh, somewhere far away and yet in her head.

She blamed her overheated imagination for the images (if not, alas, for the Minerva moment) until Franklin, who'd been continuing his clean-up efforts and starting to line up ingredients for the morning's cinnamon rolls as they talked, growled, "I'll 'prepare' your ass with a side dish of risotto if you don't stop flirting and fix the damn dishwasher," and shook a wooden spoon in mock menace.

"Right. Don't piss off the guy who's a pro with knives. This should only take a few minutes." Tyler lay back down on the slightly damp floor and continued his work.

Flirting. Oh God, had they been flirting? Had it been obvious to Franklin?

That was just plain *bad*. Her attraction to Tyler wasn't supposed to be serious, much less be plain to everyone else. It was one thing to joke with Kari or Cybelline; it was another for the staff, the guests, or Satya to think some sort of unprofessional hanky-panky was going on.

At this point she wasn't so sure she was still against the concept of unprofessional hanky-panky. But maybe that was the stress talking.

She considered going to bed. (Alone. Dammit.) Things were clearly in hand here. But her brain was still buzzing too much to let her sleep anyway. She could try a glass of wine, but she'd been doing that a lot lately.

Better to hang out and chat with the guys as Tyler worked and Franklin put the finishing touches on the cinnamon rolls that would rise overnight—until she started yawning.

She enjoyed spending time with Tyler, and not just because he was made of The Sexy. Not many people could keep up with her when she geeked about Victorian architecture, and he not only kept up, but could sometimes surprise her with new information.

Damn it.

It was one thing to lust after a near-stranger who happened to be working for her. That was hormones. The guy looked like a slightly scruffy Greek god.

But she was starting to really like him, and that could get awkward.

Chapter 10

Franklin, as it turned out, was almost done for the night. He finished shaping the rolls and set them to rise in the warming oven and said his good nights.

"I half hoped I'd find a secret passage when I moved the dishwasher," Tyler commented. "This seems like the kind of place that should have secret passages. And I keep hoping I'll finally work on a house that has some." The incongruity of the statement was more pronounced with everything above Tyler's waist obscured by the dishwasher.

But maybe it wasn't so incongruous, if he loved old houses. "I admit Kari and I checked when we were doing renovations. It's a crazy romantic idea, isn't it?"

"Like priests' holes and tunnels for the Underground Railway. Only in this house, it would be probably be for sneaking from bedroom to bedroom."

Angela laughed, reflecting that it was easier to have a serious conversation with someone's face, but the view was certainly nice. "Apparently that was Minerva's one rule for her guests where sex was concerned: if you have to sneak around to do it, take it somewhere else. She was all about free love, but not keen on cheating."

"I approve," Tyler said. "But secret passages would have been so fun."

"Or a secret room where voyeurs could watch exhibitionists," Angela blurted out before she could stop herself, "both pretending they didn't know what was going on. We looked for those, too, after we found her journal." Oh well, at least Tyler couldn't see her blush.

"That sounds like Minerva's style." His voice had dropped to a sexy low burr that seemed to ask *and is it yours?*

Which it wasn't, really. She understood why people might like it, but she liked privacy for her sexy times.

Quickly, she changed the subject to a house she'd visited during her childhood travels that did have secret passages.

Before long, as predicted, Tyler reemerged, a few cobwebs in his damp hair, wiped his hands on his jeans, and proclaimed victory.

"Thanks again for taking care of this so quickly," she said, handing him a dishtowel. "It could have been a disaster if Franklin hadn't noticed it so soon, or if you hadn't been free to come back right away."

Like if he'd had a date. She knew nothing about his personal life, other than he filed his taxes as single and he was new to town. And that he certainly seemed to be attracted to women.

Make that attracted to *her*—no point in false modesty—but that didn't mean he wasn't hot and heavy with half a dozen other women, and for all she knew, a man or two.

Damn, didn't *that* bring a series of distracting images to mind of what he might have been doing tonight instead of fixing the dishwasher?

He shrugged and the way the shrug made his muscles move under his wet, light blue T-shirt brought her back to reality. Sort of. "Glad I could. It's a lot easier to repair a leak than fix water damage."

He'd managed to get himself thoroughly soaked while crawling around the leaky dishwater, but on him, wet clothes looked good. Or maybe anything looked good on him.

Or nothing.

That notion robbed her of whatever practical thing she'd been about to say. *Practicality is over-rated…impressive torso* popped into her head, in a voice not her own.

Since she was inclined to agree on both counts, she barely fought back a grin at her resident ghost's commentary. Still, she really didn't need encouragement from a dead woman.

"Well," he said, "guess I should head back to Adelle's. My jeans are soaked, and it's getting uncomfortable."

She'd go to her grave swearing she had no ulterior motives for saying "Why don't we dry them here?"

Busily packing up his tools, he shook his head. "Don't worry. I have other clothes. I promise not show up naked tomorrow."

Glitch. Major brain glitch.

No matter how casually he'd said it, it brought too many good mental pictures for her sanity.

A naked Tyler would make the workday *much* more interesting, and probably garner big tips from some of the guests, including the darling older gay couple she'd checked in earlier.

She cleared her throat, trying to clear out her brain long enough to handle the situation and get herself to bed, because at this point she didn't care if Minerva did come along for a ride.

"Seriously," she managed. "It'll only take a few minutes in the industrial dryer and there's a cold wind off the ocean tonight."

"No, really, I'll be…" He opened the outside door and a blast of that chill wind burst in. He shut the door. "Holy crap, you weren't kidding. Guess I'll take you up on that offer."

She directed Tyler to the laundry room, then rummaged in the pantry for a set of Franklin's chef's whites.

Unfortunately, Franklin's idea of "whites" had a virulently kitschy pattern of steaks, rib roasts, and sausages, which meant they verged on being clown pants.

Both the pants and the (thankfully white) jacket were also huge. Tyler wasn't a small guy, but anyone who wasn't an NFL linebacker looked small next to Franklin. (Linebackers were the really big guys, right? She must have been out of the country during some critical period of development that would allow her to understand football.)

"Here you g—" She stopped in the laundry room doorway as her tongue glued itself to the top of her mouth and she swore her clit cheered a little "hurray!" in her panties.

Tyler hadn't waited for her to return. He'd started without her.

He'd already shucked off his jeans—and that must have taken some doing, because wet jeans were a bitch to peel away from your flesh—and was pulling the T-shirt over his head.

He tossed the shirt on the folding table next to the jeans and twisted half-around, just his torso, holding out his hand. "Thanks," he said, sounding impossibly casual.

Because apparently he hadn't been wearing anything beneath his jeans, and Angela simply wasn't used to naked men—certainly not naked men with asses like those found on statues from her ancestral home-land—being quite so blasé in her presence.

She managed to hand him the whites, feeling ridiculous when she averted her eyes. She'd spent some of her formative years in countries that were far less prudish than the U.S. Co-ed saunas in Finland. Nude beaches in the Mediterranean.

She sensed, rather than felt, a stirring in her head, and sensed, rather than heard, a murmur of approval.

You and me both, Minerva.

Still, she busied herself throwing the wet towels used for sopping up the dishwater into the washer, giving him time to slip into the whites.

That went too fast. She snuck a look.

It should have looked stupid. Maybe it did look stupid, but the way the oversized pants barely clung to his hipbones more than made up for the lack of fashion statement. In fact, he could wear goofy pants anytime and no heterosexual female would notice because the top half of him was so fine.

He hadn't bothered with the jacket.

She'd already known his arms were works of art, and the rest matched. Nice chest, even better than she'd imagined, barely dusted with dark hair. Definitely a working man's muscles, although he must have helped out that six-pack a little. All long and lean and good enough to eat.

"These pants are…really something," he commented.

"It's weird. I never noticed them on Franklin before, and not noticing someone as big as Franklin wrapped in fabric that hides us is like not noticing an elephant."

"A tacky elephant."

"I think my brain went numb from horror. That's the only explanation." Now her brain was going numb from lust.

He tossed his shirt in the dryer, then cleaned out his jeans pockets in preparation for doing the same.

Angela watched. Nosy, maybe, but you could tell a lot about a person by what they thought was must-carry stuff. Not that she expected him to be like her parents, who always kept their passports handy in case of a last-minute chance to dash off on another archaeological expedition.

A sleek brown wallet, not fancy, but well cared for. Change, which didn't tell her much. A few receipts—she recognized the distinctive canary color used by Yellowbird Hardware in town. She resisted the anal-retentive urge to pluck it up, because he was supposed to turn in all his work receipts, but she refrained. Let him fill out a reimbursement form.

An elaborate Swiss Army knife, the kind that contained everything from a corkscrew and nail clippers to a pocket-sized nuclear reactor.

And a condom. A very obvious condom.

A number of bad jokes harking back to his early comment about being prepared sprang to mind, but they'd all sound too blatant if she actually let them of her mouth. Or too nosy, like she was trying to ferret out if the plumbing emergency had interrupted hot plans for the night.

Which she *did* want to know, but also didn't. Not to mention that it would be inappropriate to ask.

Tyler, apparently noticing her noticing the condom, chuckled. "Damn thing has been in my wallet so long I'd forgotten about it, so of course it had to fall out now. The plumbing emergency only interrupted a wild night with Daniel Craig and Judi Dench. Somehow I've missed all the Daniel Craig Bonds." He turned and leaned casually on the washer, facing her.

"I'm still not sure about Daniel Craig as Bond," Angela said. "Don't get me wrong. He's great for the part, but destroys way too many historic buildings. And he doesn't take his clothes off nearly enough to make up for it, although that probably wouldn't disappoint you the way it does Kari and me." A shirtless Tyler more than made up for lack of shirtless Daniel Craig, since he had the benefit of actually being in the room with her.

Close enough to touch, if she had the nerve.

"I confess that while I can appreciate Daniel Craig's assets, in the end, I just don't swing that way." He grinned that cocky grin of his, and dropped his voice to that smoke-and-whisky pitch again, and her stomach quivered. "Mind if I stare shamelessly at you instead?" His smile could have let it be a joke if she wanted to make it one.

But with that voice tickling her in all sorts of interesting places, she didn't want it to be a joke. "Look all you want." Her own voice sounded throaty and breathy.

His blue gaze burned into her until she was sure her clothes were melting. She wanted them to melt. Taking them off seemed a little bit too nervy, although she was having trouble remembering right now why she wasn't supposed to jump staff members.

If, purely theoretically, she were to jump someone she'd known only a few days, an employee would be a good choice. Tyler had glowing references (no, not for *that*!) so she knew he wasn't an ax murderer or something equally nefarious.

But she wasn't going to. Really.

It didn't sound as convincing as it had only a little while ago.

And it sounded even less convincing when Tyler said softly, "The only problem with looking is I want to touch. Maybe right here would be safe."

As if in slow motion, she watched his hand rise, move toward her. She didn't know whether to laugh or cry when she realized its target: her face.

Gently—too gently, or not gently enough—he brushed a curl of sweaty hair off her forehead.

He barely made contact with her skin, but her hair impossibly grew nerve endings that connected directly to her nipples and clit. Her body grew heavy, weighted with lust. Her hips swayed forward, magnetized toward Tyler.

"No," Tyler whispered. "Not safe. Not safe at all. Stroking someone's hair shouldn't feel that good. Now I want to touch you everywhere and I know I shouldn't."

That was a cue for both of them to be smart and mature and step away from each other. They recognized the cue for one frozen second, maybe less. Angela engaged in an epic battle of lust versus common sense.

Common sense lost spectacularly. *Flamed out* might be the exact phrase to describe its demise.

She breathed—or, at least, tried to. "Touch me," she managed, and put her hands on Tyler's hips, on the lovely line of bone and muscle revealed by the oversized pants. "Please."

"I thought you'd never ask." His mouth closed on hers, and there was nothing sweet or tentative or gentlemanly about it, and Angela's body sang halleluiah and returned the assault.

He smelled like hard work, which she liked in a man, and his skin felt like sueded silk on top of catlike muscles and she couldn't stop kissing him, couldn't stop stroking his back and cupping his ass and running her hand across his chest or down the plane of his stomach. And his hands were just as busy.

She imagined Minerva making a soft, pleased sound. At least she told herself she imagined it and refused to speculate otherwise. The ghost could watch all she wanted. Hell, she could set up ghostly scorecards just as long she kept her mouth shut this time.

Angela hoped she was doing nearly as good a job as he was, because what he was doing felt incredible, and he hadn't even reached the really sensitive areas. Her cheekbones and collarbone came alive as he stroked them. Her belly quivered again as he slid his hands under the lace shirt to run down her sides, then over her denim-clad hips.

Finally, when she was ready to scream from a combination of arousal and frustration, he snaked his hands back up to tease her breasts. As he did, and she started writhing at the wonderful heat passing from his hands to her nipples, he slipped his thigh between her legs.

Now *that* was contact with sensitive areas. Even through jeans, it was almost enough to make her lose her mind.

If they didn't get naked soon, her jeans would need a ride in the industrial dryer along with his.

She ground against him, enjoying the tease.

The damn staticky radio crackled in her head. Minerva was waking up.

Oh no you don't, Minerva May Fenwick. I don't do threesomes with dead people. Even fun dead people.

Maybe it would be easier to block Minerva out when she wasn't flying solo. She couldn't count how many times she'd let overdue bills or questions about the menu intrude on precious moments between her and her vibrator, but that never happened when she had someone to focus on, someone else focusing on her.

Surely that would help.

Please, make it help.

Angela changed tactic, started kissing her way down Tyler's body. As she nibbled his neck and licked his collarbone, she needed to make a conscious effort to shut Minerva out. The farther she got, though, the more she stopped worrying about ghostly intrusions and focused on yummy man.

He tasted faintly like dishwasher foam, but underneath was a hint of salt and the tang of male sweat. He yipped when she nipped at his pec, but it didn't sound like a complaint so she did it again and was rewarded with "If you're going to bite, leave marks I'll enjoy in the morning."

With a rush, she remembered how much fun finding a nice bruise or bite from a night of wild sex could be, the way it could make you hot and bothered for days. And some primitive part of her brain reveled in the idea of marking him. They weren't in a relationship and she didn't have any claim on him except a paycheck, but to her hindbrain that was a great reason to make sure he didn't forget her.

Even if nipping and sucking at him wasn't exciting in its own right, and oh my God it was, the way he moaned while she marked him and ran her hands over his skin was making her giddy with lust.

Not quite as good as the noises he made when, after regarding the nice purple bite she'd left, she swirled her tongue over his hard little nipples. Gotta love a man with sensitive nipples, and the keening, lust-frenzied note in his voice melted her.

But really, a girl could only tease for so long. She kissed her way down the plane of his belly, enjoying how the muscles jumped under her lips.

Tempting to hurry it, but also tempting to rest her head here, breathe in his musky scent, and enjoy the way he was making the meat pants jut.

Decisions, decisions.

He gave her an answer by moaning "Please."

Good thing those stupid pants were so loose on him. Made her job easier. They conveniently slid to the ground.

Cocks weren't inherently elegant, but this one came close, long and lean like Tyler—but not too lean. Nice and thick, in fact. It made her mouth water. Maybe she was even hornier than she thought, because she wasn't usually what her fabulous gay hairdresser would call a size queen. Still, if a great guy happened to have a great cock, why not appreciate it?

Why not show her appreciation of it in the best possible way?

She knelt and wrapped her hand around the base of that delectable cock. Tyler let loose with another delicious moan. "God, yes."

His voice was sexy enough to slay her when he was talking business. It was apparently designed, however, for inarticulate sex-noises. The sounds he was making reverberated right down to her clit.

He repeated the "Oh God, yes," when she took him into her mouth, and her own enjoyment of the feel of a hard, sweet cock in her mouth was intensified because he just kept talking.

"Angela, you…that feels incredible. Your mouth is so hot, so wet. So good wrapped around me."

The reverberations intensified. Something about his voice—the tone, the huskiness, the…oh, who cared?—had the same effect as her favorite vibrator humming against her. She was rapidly approaching critical mass, and she hadn't had anything more than admittedly steamy kisses and some over-the-clothes groping.

She'd had some pretty fast orgasms before, but they'd always involved direct stimulation to crucial body parts.

Yet right now, she was as close to coming as she'd be if she had his talented tongue whispering sweet nothings on her clit.

Of course, that *would* be when Minerva took that moment to chime in with a crackly *About time*.

Although it dampened her own ardor—at least to the degree that she wasn't teetering on the edge—Angela couldn't argue with the sentiment. Besides, she was too busy tasting and licking and moving her mouth and hands along Tyler's shaft to pay too much attention to voices in her head.

The sounds coming out of Tyler's mouth devolved into a mixture of groans and hot, if not terribly articulate, words along the lines of "Yes" and "Oh my God, so good," yet they were far more interesting than what Minerva had to say.

Just when she was really getting into it, Tyler pulled away. "Too much." His eyes looked dazed. "Been dreaming about that since like ten minutes after I met you. Dreamed about fucking you after five, though, so that wins."

Under other circumstances, the bluntness might not have gone over so well, but Angela had been riding the hot-fantasy express right along with him since Minute Five. Maybe Minute Four. "In that case, I'm over-dressed for this party."

She was glad she'd worn simple flats tonight. Her trembling fingers couldn't have handled the buttons and laces on her favorite reproduction Victorian boots. She was having enough trouble with the zipper on her jeans.

Luckily, Tyler was there to help her. The shirt and bra went a little more smoothly, although she was afraid the shirt ended up in the cart with the last load of unwashed bed linens.

Tyler stared appreciatively, wide dark pupils almost overtaking the blue in his eyes. The tip of his tongue flicked his lips. She imagined how that would feel on her clit, and shuddered.

"You are so beautiful," he breathed, and the deep whiskey voice sounded shaken and sexier for it. "I want to taste you now. Will you let me do that, Angela?"

She'd never been one to succumb so easily to flattery. But Tyler's voice brought her closer to the edge again.

You'd best, dear. Life's short.

Thank you for that opinion from the dead-person peanut gallery. It wasn't as though Angela needed further encouragement.

She turned to the dryer...and realized, oops, they'd been so busy turning each other on they'd forgotten to turn it on. With a shaking hand, she twisted the dial, mortified that she'd even noticed, much less that she was rectifying the situation.

"Has anyone ever told you you're a workaholic?"

"Many times—but this time I'm all play." She clambered onto the whirring dryer, positioned herself strategically at the corner with one leg to each side.

He didn't need to know when exactly she'd thought of that.

"Extra vibrations? Greedy. I like that in a woman."

"Good, because that's what you've got." She wasn't going to be able to talk coherently much longer, and that was just from the way the dryer's movements sent shock waves into all sorts of interesting places. Once Tyler got in on the action, she'd be doomed.

"I've wanted to do this from the first time I saw you," he said, and his sultry voice danced over her clit. "At least once you got down from the stupid ladder and I saw the rest of you matched your ass. So less than five minutes. Wanted to touch you. Wanted to taste you."

Not exactly Shakespeare, but she'd bet Shakespeare didn't talk in iambic pentameter in the sack (or the laundry room), not unless he was quoting himself, and in that voice, in this moment, Tyler could have recited nursery rhymes and it would have turned her on.

Then he dipped his head and swirled his tongue over her clit.

She'd thought he had a golden tongue. Now she knew it. Oh my God, what that man could do.

Between his tongue and the magic of the dryer and the long tease—days of tease, really—fire built to explosion almost too fast. She thought she heard a husky female chuckle and a by-now familiar mental voice saying *That man…wicked plans.* She didn't let it throw her, though she did appreciate the voice-from-beyond hinting Tyler might have further lecherous ideas. Goodness knows she did.

She was screaming in seconds, screaming shamelessly and burying her fingers in his hair and spreading her legs and bucking her hips to grant him better access. The voice in her head turned to snaps and pops.

And Tyler didn't stop.

Angela had gone completely boneless by the time Tyler helped her slide down. On her own, her legs might have buckled.

Which is why she appreciated it so much when he carefully spun her around so she could cling to the dryer. Well, that and the way she could still take advantage of its warm, vibrating magic.

She turned her head to watch him put the condom on. Some men did that job briskly and efficiently. He made a show of it, knowing she looked, stroking it down into place with loving, teasing care. It was so hot watching a guy touch himself, even in this utilitarian context. A few moments of watching that and her pussy was already dripping.

She should be sated, or at least have the edge taken off her need, but she ached for more.

Ached to have him inside her.

"Hey," she finally said, "looking's nice, but feeling's much better. And I want to feel you in me."

Knowing Tyler, she half expected a cleverly naughty response, more verbal foreplay. The "hell yeah" she received though, packed a lot of erotic heat into two short words, maybe because of the sexy growl in which he delivered them. She couldn't help hoping he'd be able to tease her verbally later on—she did love the way he talked. On the other hand, if Tyler was at a loss for words, she must be doing something right.

He leaned over her, the weight of his body pressing into her, his hard cock teasing at the mouth of her sex. He kissed her ear, nibbled his way down her neck and shoulder. She arched back, opened her legs, squirmed.

And finally, when she was about ready to explode from wanting it so badly, he entered her.

He tried to make it slow. She wouldn't let him. "Hard," she gasped and pushed back, taking in more of him. "Fuck me hard."

"You don't need to ask twice," he said, and grabbed her hips. "Want you so much."

Okay, maybe it had been way too long (she didn't want to think how long, because it might depress her enough to distract from the current wonderful situation—but hey, she'd been *busy*) because she swore every cell in her body started dancing around and shouting "Whee!" Places inside her throbbed with bliss and sobbed with relief that someone was finally paying attention to them again.

After a few more thrusts, she wondered if her G-spot—and maybe the F- and H-spots, too—had ever had as much attention paid to them as they were enjoying from Tyler's cock. She'd had plenty of sex in her life, if maybe not the past year, and a lot of it had been damn fun. But maybe it was the prolonged teasing, or too many months with no time for dates with anyone except herself, or maybe Tyler was just that good, because she couldn't remember being this aroused, this close to completely losing her mind, with any past lover.

Lava pooled in her pelvis, boiling and bubbling, ready to explode. She clenched around Tyler, bucked back.

The sound of a warning cough in her head barely slowed her down.

Hi, Minerva, she thought. *Enjoy the ride.* It was weird being in a threesome with someone who wasn't there in any normal sense of the word, but she was too far gone to let a ghostly voyeur stop her.

Dangerous… she heard, and *thief.*

Some dim part of her brain said she should try to listen, but her body had its own ideas and so did Tyler.

"Come for me," he whispered huskily, half-begging and half-commanding. "I want to you to come on my cock. Now."

The volcano in her body erupted.

Tyler didn't let up. Didn't slow down. Didn't relent until she babbled and sobbed and called out his name. Then he thrust into her one last time and came with a wordless shout.

Once her brain recongealed (and Tyler didn't let that happen right away), it dimly dawned on her that Minerva had been trying to tell her something.

Dangerous. Thief.

If it was that Tyler was dangerously hot and might steal her heart, it was a risk she was willing to take.

Chapter 11

*D*ammit.

Tyler stared out the window. His room at Adelle's overlooked the back garden, surprisingly spacious for being in the center of town. It was late, and he was grateful that he'd stashed a six-pack in his truck earlier, because he really, really needed this beer.

He had to confess all to Angela.

He might have questionable ethics when it came to his job, but he had a strong moral code when it came to relationships. You never lie to a woman you're in a relationship with.

He shook his head and took a long swig of beer. One romp in the hay did not a relationship make, and yet…

And yet he had a sneaking suspicion his feelings for Angela already went beyond a casual encounter. He wasn't sure when or how that had happened, but he'd realized it when he'd kissed her, and then it had been too late to back away, emotionally or physically.

"Touch me," she'd begged. Was there anything more arousing than a woman being upfront and clear about what she wanted? He could still remember the taste of her lips, the feeling of her wrapped around him, her arms and legs pulling him close and her pussy welcoming him in. Her skin had been soft, and the rest of her had been hot and wet, oh God…

How could anyone walk away from that?

If he told her the truth, of course, he knew she was likely to end things right there. Maybe call the authorities, turn him in. He might be able to talk her out of that, or, short of her restraining him, might be able to get down the road. He had other identities, other vehicles; he'd beaten hasty retreats before.

That was a chance he'd have to take. He wasn't sure he was willing to lie to her anymore, not after tonight.

But if he did confess, would he be putting her in danger? Would it make her a de facto accomplice in the eyes of the law? Or at least make her lose some credibility professionally if word got out? He'd hate to do that when she'd worked so hard to build this business.

He tapped the beer bottle against his lower lip, took another swallow.

His actual work, the real reason he was here, skirted the edges of the law. He didn't do what he did solely for personal profit. Mostly he worked with museums; occasionally with private collectors who he knew truly understood the value beyond money of what he offered.

And this time he was working for a blackmailer, at least until he figured out how to get out of it. (Well, he'd been working for himself up until the point the blackmailer contacted him…) It was one thing to come clean to Angela. Quite another to have the police poking around.

Speaking of skirting legalities, he was pretty sure that herb growing in the far corner of Adelle's garden was not one used for cooking.

No wonder the garden walls were so high. Former pet was a high-jumping Jack Russell terrier, his ass.

He drained the beer, popped the cap off a second. He didn't want to get drunk, just take the edge off, help himself relax and sleep. Thinking about Angela had made him half-hard again, his body responding to the memories and the smell of her and them and sex that still lingered.

He turned away from the window, shoved random crap off the bed (he'd deal with laundry and receipts in the morning), and stretched, crossing his ankles and leaning back against the pillows, which, he'd been delighted to learn when he first rented the room, were plump and comfortable. Mrs. Parsons might be many things, but she ran a decent establishment.

Okay. New plan. Get his focus back on the job—the real job, the one he'd come here to do—and try his damnedest to stay away from the luscious and fascinating Angela Georgenes.

Because if he didn't, and he confessed the truth to her, he mostly likely would lose the girl, the job, and a whole lot more.

*

"For someone who barely has her eyes open after three cups of coffee, you look pretty relaxed," Kari commented over breakfast.

Angela yawned exaggeratedly in an attempt to hide a smug, sated grin. "I'm relaxed because I'm still asleep. Shut up, morning person." Kari had already taught a 6:30 yoga class—few guests attended, but the commuters in town loved it.

Kari passed the cream without being asked. "What time did Tyler get done last night anyway? I didn't hear you come in."

"Uh. Late. Really late. Not sure when." The birds had been making their dawn racket when she finally crawled home. After the sex, they'd raided the kitchen for the rest of the pie and talked for a few more hours (pausing to neck occasionally) over pie and tea.

At this point, she couldn't have said what all they'd talked about: old houses, awful renovations they'd seen, childhood memories (she found his suburban Des Moines upbringing almost as exotic as he found her nomadic one), favorite desserts. Still, it had been…nice.

She sighed dreamily and slumped forward, sniffing the coffee like it was the nectar of the gods. (It wasn't. Franklin's coffee was, but to get that she had to go into the hotel, and she was in no shape to run into guests at this hour.) "But the dishwasher's working now," she remembered. Kari would want to know that, would think it weird if she didn't mention it.

Kari knew her way too well for her own good sometimes. "You didn't! Angela, tell me you didn't sleep with Tyler."

"If sleep had been involved," Angela said with all the dignity she could muster when her curly hair was sticking out in all directions, "would I be this zoned right now?"

"If what you did before you slept was *really, really* good, maybe." Kari sounded like she wanted to ask for details. Instead she did her best to look stern. Her perky, round face wasn't suited to the job, but Angela got the message. "But Angela, it's a bad idea to sleep with employees and you know it."

Angela snorted. "Guess you better stop the booty calls to Mal."

Kari threw up her hands. "But that's different. I've known him forever. We went to massage school together. I trust him. Whereas you've known Tyler for, like, four days. He seems like a great guy. My intuition still thinks he's good for you. But who really knows?"

"Uh, he has terrific references?" It wasn't like Kari was saying anything Angela hadn't thought of herself—and decided to ignore in the heat of the moment.

With any luck, Kari would pick on up the lame double entendre, say something like "And just how great *are* his references, nudge wink," and they could move on.

Instead, Kari said, "Remember that old Demi Moore movie? *Disclosure*?"

Angela must have looked blank, which wasn't hard at this hour, because Kari went on, "Of course you don't. You were probably in a tent in Backassistan when it came out. Anyway, she and this guy have an affair, and then she sues him for sexual harassment so she could get his job or something, even though she looked like she was all into him, and things get awful. Or maybe it was the other way around and he sued her. It was a pretty terrible movie. But the point is, it's risky to sleep with someone you work with."

She stopped. "Okay, it's not really the same situation and I can't imagine Tyler doing something so slimy, and if he tries, Cyb and I will be all, 'oh, trust me, he was flirting with her big time' and so will Mal and Franklin even if they haven't noticed if you guys were flirting." She panted slightly because she'd forgotten to take a breath while she ranted.

For someone who was so serene and New Agey most of the time, Kari could get awfully vehement.

Angela raised a weary eyebrow. "Are you through, hon?"

"I'm happy for you, really. Tyler is super-sexy and your life's been lacking in the hot guy department for way too long. Just be careful, okay?" Kari flung her arms around Angela, and after a second—not because she didn't want to, but because her arms were sore from dryer-pushups—Angela hugged her back.

Men were great. Men were fun. But girlfriends were always there to take care of you, even if you didn't need it.

*

Angela was strangely in a good mood. She was *humming*, for crying out loud, as she fired up the computer in the office.

No, it wasn't really all that strange. Just amazing how a round of romping-good sex could change your entire outlook on life.

Oh, she was still pretty much sleep deprived—more so than she'd expected, even for the first busy week of the year—and she still had a mound of paperwork and various issues to worry about (juggling bills until a few more weeks of paying guests restocked their accounts, making sure Satya had every reason to write a kick-ass positive review, and exorcising her resident ghost—the latter being something she'd never expected to add to her To Do list).

But she was humming, and right now, it all seemed do-able.

"Mornin', Boss Lady."

Her insides clenched at the sound of his voice before she even looked up to see him standing at the entrance to the office. He leaned casually against the wall, arms folded across the chest she now knew was indeed just as fabulous as his work tees had always hinted.

Unbidden, Kari's warnings popped into her head. She searched Tyler's face for any indication that he was planning to sue her ass into the next millennium for inappropriate office behavior.

What she saw was, thankfully, the exact opposite. He stared at her with something like hunger—as in, if she only said the word, he'd have her stripped and naked on top of the desk and shrieking in ecstasy in five seconds flat.

Except with more self-control. He might *look* like he wanted to achieve all that in five seconds, but in reality he was more likely to go excruciatingly slowly, and get off on how she begged for more.

Now her insides were *really* clenching, with a wonderful, puffy ache that reminded her that she'd been thoroughly fucked last night—and if she played her cards right, it would happen again soon.

"Good morning, Tyler," she managed. "What can I do for you?"

He grinned either at the huskiness in her voice, thanks to last night's shrieking, or at the fact that thanks to last night, just about anything she said was going to sound like a double entendre.

"Dishwasher's working fine, and I'm caught up on everything else," he said. "Unless you have something specific in mind for me today—" and everything he said was going to sound like a double entendre, too "—I figured I'd get started repairing the dry rot in Bathhouse Five."

"That sounds like a perfect plan," she said.

"I'll need to pick up some lumber and other materials." Now he hesitated. "It could get a little pricey. I know you've got some petty cash…"

Ah. "No problem." She went to the safe, opened it, and turned to hand him the plastic card. "Jack at the hardware store knows you're working for me. Just run it through as a debit and you won't have to worry about a signature." She grinned, unable to help herself. "The PIN is 0866. Just don't go running off to San Francisco with it."

He grinned back, but his smile was full of promised pleasure. His voice lowered a notch—as if it could *get* any sexier—when he said, "Well, there are some pretty interesting shops in San Francisco. You sure you don't want me to pick up any…items?"

"Items" clearly meant "sex toys," and Angela bit her lip to keep from whimpering aloud.

Then something flickered through Tyler's expression, as if he realized he might have said too much. At the same time, Angela processed his teasing question in a different way.

They way they'd been flirting implied that there would definitely be sex again. They hadn't discussed that, although it was definitely likely. But investing in sex toys implied the potential of a longer-term relationship, and *that* was…

Was something Angela was *not* ready to think about.

"Keep it local," she said lightly. She was pretty sure Tyler hadn't meant to imply what his words could have implied. If he did, well, there was a discreet "pleasure boutique" in town. (San Sebastian got a lot of honeymooning couples, and the owner of All Things Romantic said business was brisk. Plus, she gave Angela and Kari a hefty discount thanks to their collaboration on a Valentine's Day promo.)

"You just want me close by in case of emergency," he said, one corner of his mouth crooking up.

"Of course," she said, all wide-eyed innocence. "You never know when we might need some work done."

Tyler growled something that sounded suspiciously like "Ah, fuck it," pulled her close, and gave her a searing kiss that melted her right down to her toes.

Things might have gone further if the phone hadn't chosen that moment to ring. Tyler stepped away, letting her slide back into her chair.

As she tucked the bud in her ear, he leaned down and murmured "See you later" into her other ear, his voice and the whisper of hot breath making her shiver.

Then he was gone, and she slipped herself back into professional mode, albeit an unusually perky version of it. (Well, she always tried to be cheerful when answering a call, because she believed a positive voice on the other end of the line led to more guest bookings.)

"Good morning, Angelika B&B and Spa, what can I do for you?"

"I'm looking for a Ms. Angela Georgenes." A male voice, rather officious sounding, and by the brief hesitation before he carefully pronounced her last name, someone who didn't know her.

"This is she," Angela said brightly, still not letting the officiousness worry her. Did she chirp? She hoped she hadn't chirped.

"Ah, hello, Ms. Georgenes. My name is Oliver DeNovo and I'm calling from the Humboldt County Department of Health and Human Services."

"Our restaurant inspection is current and up-to-date," Angela said, automatically reaching for the file that would give her the exact date of their last inspection, the account number of the business license allowing them to prepare and sell food and alcoholic beverages, and the amount they'd paid for those privileges.

"Yes, Ms. Georgenes, I can see here that it is," Officious Oliver agreed without a hint of enthusiasm. "I'm afraid that's not why I'm calling."

Something in his tone made her set down the file slowly and sit up straighter. As in, uh-oh.

"My office has received a report that vermin have been spotted in your kitchen."

"What?" Angela's voice shot up into a yelp.

So much for that good mood and positive outlook and "I can handle anything life throws at me" post-sex euphoria.

"Mr. DeNovo, I can assure you, we have an impeccably clean kitchen," she said. "May I ask where this report came from?"

"It was an anonymous tip called in to our office," he said. "I'm afraid I can't divulge any other information."

The hell he couldn't. Even if the tipster hadn't left his name, she was pretty sure she had a right to know when the call came in, and from where.

Thinkthinkthink. Even if the tip was unfounded—which is most assuredly had to be—they couldn't take any chances.

"I understand," she said, not wanting to antagonize him by arguing. When dealing with government officials, sounding like you agreed with them was half the battle to getting what you wanted out of them.

(The other half often included money changing hands, but Angelika didn't have any to spare at the moment. Plus, it raised her hackles to even consider bribery. Still, she couldn't help but wonder about Officious Oliver's opinion on the subject.)

"As I said, we pride ourselves in ensuring our establishment not only meets code but exceeds it," she said. "I'm sure this information is unfounded, but of course we'll do whatever is necessary to get this cleared up. What's the next step in the process? An inspection?"

"Yes," Oliver said. "We'd like to do it as soon as possible, of course."

"Absolutely." Angela was already pulling up the calendar program on her computer. "When can you come?"

Given San Sebastian's distance from the county seat, she feared it could take days, or even weeks. But Oliver had another inspection to do over in Bridgeville the next day, so it if was convenient…?

It was. It had to be.

Feeling like she was going to hurl, Angela hung up the phone and pinged Kari and Franklin for an emergency meeting.

They met in one of the spa rooms, because it was essentially sound-proofed so that outside noises didn't negatively affect the patron's treat-ment. It wasn't completely soundproofed, but as long as they didn't bellow and nobody had planted any listening devices, they'd be fine.

As expected, Franklin was beyond apoplectic. A fairer-skinned man would probably have turned beet red, but even though Angela couldn't see the flush, the popping vein on his forehead and his clenched fists gave a lot away. She managed to convince him that *she* didn't believe the report, that *she* knew he had the cleanest kitchen in California, if not the West Coast, before he messily exploded from sheer indignation.

It had been a close call there.

"Okay, so what do we do next?" Kari asked. Angela realized Kari had lit a couple of candles while she'd been calming Franklin down. Sandalwood and rose. Kari and her aromatherapy; those were calming scents.

But that was Kari's forte: nurturing. Even her voice had been pitched to a soothing tone, and on some level Angela realized her question was cleverly focused.

Because Angela's forte was organization.

"Okay," Angela said, pen and paper poised and ready. "We have to inform all the guests ASAP that the kitchen is closed until tomorrow afternoon. I don't know whether we'll be able to serve dinner tomorrow; it depends on how long the inspector's here."

"How are we going to explain why the kitchen's closed?" Kari asked.

Angela smiled. One small factor in their favor. "The dishwasher hose leak. It's not entirely a lie—the dishwasher *did* leak, and Barb may have mentioned it to Carole or any of the other guests. We'll say we want to double check everything else. We just need to put an optimistic spin on it, especially since Satya's going to be paying close attention."

This *would* have had to happen while someone was here to review the hotel. Argh!

"How will we feed them at *all*?" Franklin asked. "Breakfast is part of the B&B service we provide."

"Picnic on the veranda?" Kari suggested.

"It's not just that I can't cook—the kitchen's off limits. We can't serve food at all until we can prove it's free of contamination," Franklin said mournfully.

"We'll pick up some of those plastic plates—Chinettes or whatever—and plastic dinnerware," Angela said, scribbling and knowing she'd have to type up the list because her handwriting was appalling to the point of legendary. Kari once bought *gin* instead of *pens* in college thanks to Angela's scrawl, and never let her forget it.

Although the gin had been tasty.

"So, you're thinking about a cold buffet," Franklin said.

"Exactly," Angela said. "Call Sweet Treats and put in a pastry order. Let's see, what else?"

"We can hard boil eggs in the cottage," Kari suggested.

"Parma ham, cheese, fresh fruit, yogurt—stuff I can pick up at the grocery store early," Franklin threw in. His face was animated; Angela could see he was moving from concerned to excited again. It was a kitchen challenge, even if it didn't involve actual cooking.

Franklin and the rest of the hotel staff were a delight, and made the mayhem of running a hotel far more bearable.

She hid a smile. Tyler was making a nice addition to the staff, too, and making things much more than bearable.

"Tonight's dinner, though," Kari broke into Angela's thoughts, which had been sliding into decidedly racy territory. "Some of the guests might have been assuming they'd eat here—and we kind of have to make up for the limited breakfast tomorrow, too."

"The only think I can think of is that we send them all out to dinner in town—on our dime," Angela said, gulping on that last part because they really didn't have that dime to spare. "It'll show we're doing everything we can to make things better despite the circumstances."

"I hate to ask," Franklin said, "but what about the inspection tomorrow?"

Now she took a deep breath, wishing she had time to book herself in for a massage, because her shoulders were *that tense*. "We'll cross that bridge when we come to it."

Unfortunately, right now the bridge looked like one of those rickety rope-and-slat ones that invariable dangled over yawning jungle ravines in mediocre adventure movies.

*

Angela sat in front of the computer, chewed her lip, and tried to figure out a way to phrase the note she'd slip under each guests door and post outside the dining room so that it sounded perky and upbeat, not "We suck, this place is falling apart, and you'll never want to stay here again. Did I mention we suck?"

Yesterday we had an issue—no, no, "issue" could imply worse things.

Due to a minor problem with our industrial dishwasher, we're temporarily closing our kitchen—ugh, "kitchen closing" could lead people's minds in exactly the wrong direction.

To ensure everything is working in tip-top shape after we discovered a minor problem with our industrial dishwasher, we're offering you all a night on the town—on us!

Okay, that was better, wasn't it?

We have vouchers for a variety of local restaurants; choose where you want to go, and we'll make the reservation and arrange transportation if needed.

If you'd prefer to eat in, we'll place the order and bring it back to the hotel for you.

There. That sounded as least-threatening as possible, and focused on the positive.

Angela hoped everyone bought it.

She slid Victorian-esque decorated paper into the printer, set the flyer to print, and pulled up a website of San Sebastian restaurants. If she was promising vouchers, she had to make a million phone calls and call in every favor anyone had ever owed her.

She reached for the phone. If she got one call down, she'd have only nine hundred and ninety-nine thousand, nine hundred and ninety-nine to go....

Chapter 12

To her surprise, Angela slept hard that night.

Not hard as in "with Tyler's hard, hot body in her bed," but as in "asleep almost before her head hit the pillow."

Pity that it lasted for barely five hours.

Now it was midafternoon and she was trying to stop herself from chewing on her cuticle while she waited for Officious Oliver to make his appearance.

Deep breaths. In…out.

Kari had even burned some frankincense in the office to help her achieve a calm and positive state. Instead, it had made her sneeze.

Fact was, she shouldn't be nervous. She knew damn well Franklin was OCD when it came to a clean kitchen. None of the staff—kitchen crew or servers—confessed to having seen a rat. They'd all expressed horror at the very concept when she and Franklin had brought them up to speed (and given them the time off with pay).

Would any of them lie? Angela couldn't think of a reason for any of them. San Sebastian was a small town: you got to know your employees, either from them or from the local gossip mill. She and Kari had always done their best to be stellar employers.

Tyler would certainly think so.

Dammit. She shouldn't be thinking about him right now, either.

She knew why her nerves were on overdrive. She knew intellectually that businesses failed all the time, that successful businesspeople went through multiple projects, many which ended up unsuccessful. Angelika wasn't just a business to her, though; it was her home, the home she'd always yearned for.

And losing Angelika would be a personal failure.

She didn't want to let her childhood self down, and she didn't want to let Minerva down.

Her phone rang, startling her. Thankfully, it wasn't Oliver calling to cancel and delaying their reopening.

Still, it wasn't someone she felt thrilled to hear from. Cybelline was a dear, but Angela hadn't realized how tenacious her friend could be when she had a project.

Granted, Angela had been the one to threaten Cybelline if the medium didn't exorcise Minerva. But, somehow, exorcism had slid down on the crucial To Do list. You'd think it would stay primary. Ha.

After a moment of guilt, she hit the Decline button on her phone and let the call go to voice mail. She did listen to the message after it finished recording, just in case Cyb had come up with something new. But Cybelline's call was to ask again about rummaging through the house.

To assuage her guilt, Angela texted back, *Up 2 my eyeballs in meetings & stuff. Call u 2morrow?*

Then she pulled up iTunes on the computer, clicked on Enya, and closed her eyes.

Within thirty seconds, she hit Stop. There was only so much relaxing New Agey hoohah that one woman could take, no matter what Kari said. Instead, she went with her strength: work. Paying bills was *much* more relaxing right now.

Finally, the bell over the front door jingled, and unsurprisingly it was on the dot of Exactly When Oliver Said He'd Be There.

"Isabella, stay." She couldn't risk Oliver assuming a dog was allowed in the kitchen or dining room. Or him being afraid of dogs, even if the greyhound was the epitome of nonthreatening mellowness.

Isabella looked torn. On one hand, when she wasn't running, she found her bliss in sprawling on her bed. On the other hand, that bliss included being as near to Angela or Kari as possible. Her big, sad brown eyes held a universe of reproach before she sighed and closed them.

In a minute or so, Isabella would be asleep, snoring gently.

Angela had dressed with care for this meeting. Her slim skirt, eggplant-and-cream hound's-tooth-checked, was long enough to be professional while still sporting a discreet slit on one side. She'd paired the skirt with a sleeveless, high-necked cream sweater and black pumps that were just high enough to accent her bare legs; the weather had warmed to the degree that she could forego tights, and she'd smoothed lotion into her freshly waxed skin.

Her earrings were reproduction ancient Egyptian, large gold dangly heads of Nefertiti, a gift from her parents and an exotic touch to the otherwise businesslike outfit.

She wasn't above a little bit of flirting to help their case. It wasn't like she was going to prostitute herself. After all, she had standards.

Standards? A little nagging voice popped up. *What about this sleeping with the hired help thing?*

She imagined holding the little voice under the water until the bubbles stopped, pasted a welcoming smile on her face, and held out her hand.

"Mr. DeNovo, welcome to Angelika."

Officious Oliver was cute in a dark, Italianesque way, right down to the little wire-rimmed glasses he wore. If Angela hadn't currently been pleasantly sore from that most excellent romp with Tyler two nights ago, she might have been attracted to Oliver.

Well, it wasn't that she didn't find him attractive. She was just too distracted right now.

If Oliver found *her* attractive, he was very good at not letting it show. Oh well. So much for that strategy.

She politely enquired whether his trip out to the coast had been uneventful as she led him toward the kitchen, and he politely responded without giving much detail.

When they got to the entrance of the dining room, however, things started to head south. Rapidly.

Down the hall from the parlor, Satya was heading toward them, no doubt curious about the identity of the officious man with the clipboard.

Around the corner from the opposite direction came Tyler, looking mussed and smudged from his work on Bathhouse Five.

Thankfully, Tyler was closer.

"Tyler! Just the man I needed to see," Angela said brightly. She ushered Oliver into the dining room. "Mr. DeNovo, just go through those double doors back there. Franklin, our chef, is waiting for you. I'll be there in just a moment, after I have a quick discussion with our handyman."

She then dragged Tyler back around the corner. Her libido gave a little leap of joy at being in close proximity with him again.

"I need you to do something for me," she said quickly.

"Okay." He leaned in, nuzzled the sensitive spot behind her ear. "Mm, you smell nice."

She did? She hadn't put on any scent this morn— "It's that damned incense Kari's been burning. Stop it. Listen to me. This is serious."

"Yes, it is," he agreed, but the seductive tone of his voice made it clear he was referring to something else entirely.

Kari's words flashed into Angela's mind. Panic. If she pulled rank on him, would he sue her for sexual harassment or something?

She banked on the fact that she believed he truly did care for Angelika.

"The health inspector's here," she said.

It worked. Tyler snapped to attention. "What do you need?"

"Satya's coming. Keep her away from the kitchen!"

"How exactly am I supposed to do that?"

She hissed through her teeth, frustrated. "I don't *care*. Do whatever it takes."

A wicked smile spread lazily across his face. His eyes glinted as he said, "Why, Ms. Georgenes, you don't pay me enough to do *that*."

Even as she flushed at his misinterpretation of her words, a long, slow, sexual flush heated her body at the insinuation.

She matched his smile, cocked her head. "Are you sure about that? I suspect I'll be able to find a way to adequately…compensate you."

She reveled in the slight widening of his eyes, the sudden intake of his breath.

It was a game she loved. The verbal volley. The challenge to not just accept, but to throw something back—something even better.

Sadly, he didn't have the chance—even though she was sure he'd have risen to the challenge, in more ways than one.

"I'll hold you to that," he said, and they stepped back around the corner to waylay Satya just as she was about to enter the dining room.

"Well, hello there," Angela said. "Have you met Tyler, our handyman? I'm sorry I can't stay and chat—I'm late for a meeting with Franklin."

As she walked away, she heard Tyler go into action.

"Satya, isn't it? You're the reporter doing the story on the hotel, right? Have you had a chance to see the renovations we're working on? As you can imagine, older, historic buildings need constant upkeep, and…" His voice faded as he ushered Satya away.

Angela didn't have time to do more than blow out a breath of relief as she wove around the tables as fast as she could.

In the kitchen, Oliver was grilling Franklin, and Franklin looked about as unhappy as he could.

Angela didn't interfere, listening as Franklin, reining in his emotions, denied seeing any vermin droppings, chewed bags or boxes, nest detritus, etc. She made a mental note to give Franklin a big ol' bonus for this.

"Do you put out traps?" (Only in the basement and attic, and they haven't been touched for months.) "When was your last fumigation?" (Two months after they'd bought the hotel. Oliver may have looked ever so slightly impressed that she knew this off the top of her head.)

"Well," Oliver said, making a final tick on his clipboard "let me take a look around."

He proceeded to open every. single. cabinet. in the entire kitchen and pull out every. single. item. Occasionally he would make a humming or grunting noise, and Angela and Franklin would lean forward expectantly,

Angela with her heart in her throat, but then Oliver would fall silent again, and not pick up his clipboard.

She took it as a good sign that he never said "Ew!" or "Oh my God!" or "That's just not *right*!"

She was starting to relax, just a little—at least to the point where the cuticle on her right thumb had stopped looking as attractive as butter-drenched, sweet lobster—when Oliver, who had moved to peer underneath one of the heavy stainless-steel sinks, said, "How long has this hole been here?"

Both she and Franklin dropped to their knees. To her horror, Angela saw the hole in question, about the size of a fist, near the baseboard.

The sink was to the left of the dishwasher, an area Angela had become intimately acquainted with less than twenty-four hours ago.

"That was *not* there yesterday!"

Oliver raised an eyebrow, clearly indicating that he didn't believe her.

"The hose behind the dishwasher split last night, and our handyman fixed it," she explained. "I watched him do it—I would've noticed that hole then."

"She's right," Franklin said. Angela could tell from the tone of his voice that he was about to blow, and she put a calming hand on his broad shoulder.

"Well," Oliver said. "Well. It's certainly of a size that would allow rats through, so I suggest you get it patched as soon as possible."

From *his* tone, it was still apparent he didn't believe them, but a relatively small hole wasn't something they'd be written up for. Thank whatever deity might be listening. (Heritage-wise, Angela was partial to the Greek pantheon.)

"I'll have our handyman deal with it before the end of the day," Angela assured him.

Franklin twitched as if he wanted to add something, but he refrained. Angela mentally promised him a bigger bonus. She'd find the extra money somewhere.

Then, in the pantry, Oliver found rat poop.

*

Rat poop. *Rat poop.* If Angela ever got her hands on the…

No. Deep breath. Remember what Kari tries to teach you about stress reduction.

The fresh air helped, even across the short distance from the hotel to the bath houses through the garden. The scent of lavender and hyacinth hung in the air, and the slant of light heading toward sunset soothed her. Normally she would have been tempted to linger.

But she was checking on the progress in Bathhouse Five, because that was the next thing on her list. Then she'd grab dinner and get back to the pile of office work.

The fact that she hadn't seen Tyler for a few hours had nothing to do with the spring in her steps. Really.

She eased open the door to the bathhouse and took in the view.

Some Victorian bathhouses emphasized the therapeutic effect: plain white walls, cast-iron tubs stained by sulfur water and barely big enough for one. Minerva's original design, not surprisingly, emphasized the hedonistic, and they'd restored it lovingly. Turkish tiles and potted plants gave a colorful harem effect. The walls were painted a brilliant sky blue. A skylight gave the option of moon-gazing or cloud-studying while you bathed.

And the tubs were big enough for two, or in this bathhouse for three, four, or more. Maybe everyone used to soak in bathing suits, like in the communal Jacuzzi at a modern hotel, but Minerva's journals gave Angela no reason to think so.

Tyler added nicely to the sybaritic décor despite, or maybe because of, the tool belt wrapping his hips. It didn't hurt that he'd peeled off his shirt. She hadn't taken the time to appreciate the muscles of his back the other night, so she spent a few seconds quietly enjoying the view: the fine gleam of sweat on his skin and the play of muscle against muscle as he worked. He'd heard her come in—he'd said a distracted "hello, Boss Lady. I'll be right with you" without looking away from his work.

Was he that intent on what he was doing, or did he know how much she enjoyed the opportunity to stare? Probably a little of both. He focused like a laser on his work when something needed doing. On the other hand, he seemed the type who might like putting on a show.

She shook herself. She'd come out for a reason other than working-man eye candy and sexy daydreams. Although the eye-candy and sexiness factor might have played the tiniest part in her motivation. After the chaos of her day, she deserved some small pleasures. Not that Tyler was a *small* pleasure.

Tyler rocked back onto his heels and set down his hammer. He stood, wiped his hands on his jeans, and walked over to her. No, he swaggered.

And then he did something she didn't expect. He put an arm around her waist and hugged her. Just hugged her. Waves of pure, 100% Grade-A seductiveness poured off him, but for now, she wanted to relax against him and enjoy the simple human contact more than she wanted to jump his bones. Angela snuggled against his shoulder and let out a long sigh, feeling as if she'd been holding her breath all day. Which maybe she had.

"How did it go with the health inspector?" he asked, sounding serious for once.

"He found a hole in my wall!"

"Easy there, Boss Lady. You're shaking like you want to blow up and hurt someone." He stroked her hair soothingly.

"There was a hole. In my wall. It was right by the dishwasher. You didn't see anything last night, did you?"

"I'd have told you if I did. And then I'd have fixed it. That must be one ambitious rat."

"It wasn't a rat. That's the really weird part. Good, but weird. The inspector found a few droppings, but he said they looked months old. He figured a single rat must have checked the place out and been scared off by Franklin's aggressive cleaning."

"Or maybe just by Franklin. I'm surprised the *inspector* wasn't scared off by Franklin."

Angela chuckled. "Franklin was very polite. I could tell it was straining him."

"So we're okay?"

Angela's heart did something weird and fluttery at that *we*. Tyler had obviously succumbed to Angelika's magic and already felt part of the hotel's family. Even if he'd looked like the south end of a northbound camel (a familiar view from her youth), she'd like him for that. And since he didn't...

"We're okay. Kitchen's open for business, and thank God for that. But it's still bugging me. He found the droppings in with the baking pans. Franklin bakes daily; there's no way he wouldn't have noticed rat poop in with his precious bread pans. And then there's that hole."

Tyler shrugged—she could feel the muscles shifting under her, a pleasant momentary distraction from her worries. "Maybe Franklin and I damaged the wall when we moved the dishwasher. I'd think I'd have noticed—you distract me, but the crunch of wallboard gets my attention—but nothing else makes sense. Let me put on my list to patch tonight." He moved so he could pull a little pad out of his tool box and write it down.

It was ridiculous how much she missed being in contact with him.

"Speaking of fixing things, how's my favorite handyman's handiwork coming?" Damn, if that didn't come out as a loaded question. Even with all she had on her mind, the instinct to flirt was strong.

"The good news is the dry rot hadn't progressed too far." Tyler flashed a smile that suggested he was right with her in the gutter. "I just finished cleaning out the bad wood—" he pointed to a reassuringly small pile of debris "—and I'll be able to start patching tonight or tomorrow."

"About how long until it's ready for guests to use?" Bathhouse Five was the largest, and while they didn't have any large groups at the moment, the writers' group due to arrive next week might want to continue their brainstorming in comfort.

"Roughing in a patch will take an hour or so. Making it look good is fussier. But probably tomorrow night." He'd been using his all-business tone before, although it still had that something that sent butterflies dancing on her nipples, but now he changed its cadence to something with the smoky nuances of good single malt and the richness of Cabernet. "I'm told I'm quite good at filling holes. And I like to take my time on the finer details of…hole-filling."

If she'd had something small and harmless to throw at him, she would have for making such an outrageously cheesy remark.

And for making it in such an outrageously sexy voice that the butterflies were doing the fandango on her clit. It was one thing to jones for him whispering sweet, lustful nothings in her ear, but if he could turn her on with silly teasing, she was doomed.

Okay, she already knew that. Might as well enjoy the ride.

The only thing to do was to fight back with an equally cheesy suggestive remark. She thrust her chest out ridiculously, canted her hip, and purred in a really bad Bette Davis voice, "Why yes, that you are. Skilled, that is. And detail-oriented. And very hard working. Emphasis on *hard*."

That slow, easy smile again. *Game on.* She trusted he'd rise to the occasion—as it were—and he didn't disappoint.

"I don't think I've had enough opportunities show how detail-oriented I can be, Angela. Or how hard."

He stepped away from his big red tool box. There had to be a teasing line related to that box, but now Angela's brain went blank, at least on subjects other than how much she'd like to get Tyler out of his clothes and into her.

"Can I tempt you to stay for a while?" he went on.

A while? He tempted her to stay forever, or at least until they were exhausted with pleasure and badly in need of rare meat. And goodness knows she could use some fun after dealing with Oliver.

"I'd love to demonstrate some more of my work ethic." One step closer, not quite close enough to touch, but close enough that she could imagine his words caressing her across the slight distance. "But seriously, you need to relax. I wasn't kidding when I said you were shaking with tension, and what's the point of having all these bath houses if you don't ever take advantage of them?"

His voice snaked down Angela's body and found all her erogenous zones, including ones she didn't even know she possessed (and she'd thought he'd found them all in the laundry room).

Oh, what the hell. Maybe now wasn't the best time, but it was as good as any. When you literally lived at work, "free time" was a nebulous concept, but this was as close as she got before the middle of the night. The phones were covered. All the guests were at dinner, though tonight's meal was a simple affair since Franklin had to put it together quickly. Normally she took a short break around this time, though more to grab food than to grab hot handyman booty. "I can't stay too long. Not long enough to show you how detail-oriented I can be. But if we don't do something, we might spontaneously combust."

"That would be bad," he agreed solemnly. "And water prevents spontaneous combustion. Let's go next door."

Chapter 13

As soon as the door to Bathhouse Six closed, Angela put all of that pent-up sexual energy from flirting into savoring Tyler. He was tall enough she had to reach to kiss him even with moderate heels on, but that little stretch made it all the easier to sway into the gravitational pull of his body.

Maybe the joke about spontaneous combustion wasn't such a joke. When their lips touched, heat flared between them so fast and hard she swore flames licked at her skin. His mouth started out gentle but segued into demanding. He slid his hands up the length of her thighs, ruching up her skirt so she was effectively bare, except for panties, from the waist down. She opened to the kiss, ground against him, and threw caution to the four winds.

Zero to sixty in no time flat. She'd felt the undertone of lust, even through her tension, as soon as she'd seen Tyler, but the ramp-up speed was ridiculous.

"I'm on fire," she whispered when Tyler moved his lips from hers so he could turn his attention to her neck.

"Only cure for that is getting wet." He thrust against her to the rhythm of his words, increasing their already potent erotic charge.

"I'm plenty wet," she said, her voice husky. "It may take water to save me." Not that getting in the water would cool their ardor.

Excellent…idea, Minerva confirmed.

They were three great minds with one thought: to get naked as quickly as possible.

Well, she and Tyler were going to get naked. Ghost clothing was optional and, frankly, something she was too busy to think about.

Down the road, if all went well, there'd be time for slowly, luxuriously undressing each other and the kind of exploration that went with it. This time, by unspoken consent, Tyler and Angela dealt with their own clothes. Tyler's work boots took a little fumble-fingered effort, but once they were off, his jeans all but melted away. Once again, he was sans underwear. The view was just as good as she remembered. Cursing that she hadn't worn a simple jersey dress, Angela stripped out of her skirt and sweater and hung them on hooks, tucked her Nefertiti earrings in her skirt pocket.

Somehow, though, her bra ended up in the water. Tyler had just gotten his jeans off at that point and she'd been a trifle distracted.

She left her extremely unboyish red lace boyshorts on long enough for Tyler to take a long, appraising look. Sometimes almost naked was better than fully naked, and she knew that color suited her olive skin.

He smiled a slow, lazy smile and, equally slowly and lazily, she peeled the panties off.

"Yum" was his simple response. Amazing how he could imbue such a simple word with so much eroticism. She couldn't imagine how a long, lean dish of tasty naked man could say "yum" to her body and not have it sound sexy, but the way Tyler said it, half purr and half growl, was insanely erotic. Decadent, even, which was a good Minerva word.

She swore she heard Minerva make a similar purring growl.

"I could say the same." Her mouth felt curiously dry, as if to make up for the moisture that had found its way elsewhere.

A few brain cells that weren't entirely devoted to sex prompted her to put her hair into a rough knot at the back of her head.

Then he drew her closer, or she went to him, or maybe they met halfway. They'd closed the gap between them again, only this time they were touching naked skin to naked skin, and that was all that mattered.

They broke contact just long enough to slip into the warm water. Angela straddled Tyler's lap. Weightless in the water, she bobbed over him, teasing him with her pussy, grinding her clit against his cock to build both their arousal. Tyler's hands clasped her ass, but he wasn't steering her movements. He could have, easily, with those big, strong hands, and it would have been hot. Instead, he touched her for the joy of touching her and let her do what felt best for her, and that was maybe even hotter. (They'd have to try it the other way sometime, in the spirit of science.)

The bathhouse, warm and steamy to begin, heated up with their blood. They never stopped kissing. It was a shame he couldn't talk and kiss at the same time—she bet the soundtrack in his head was interesting at the moment and she loved the way he shared his naughty thoughts—but it wasn't enough of a shame to stop kissing him.

And when he paused the kissing, it was entirely worth it. "I want to be in you," he breathed, and she swore his voice entered her. As he said it, his grip tightened, became more demanding, and he started controlling movements more. Not more or less hot, but hot in a different way.

"Damn, yes. Just like we are now, not on the bench or something." She squirmed against him. Then she had one of those annoying sensible thoughts that never intruded on her fantasies about playing in the bath houses. "I'm not sure how well condoms and hot water mix in the long run, though. But I like feeling the water around us. "

"We can lean against the side. We're both tall enough. Not quite the same, but it'll work." Tyler grinned, but his grin looked strained. "I need to be in you. But I don't want to let go yet either. Want to feel you just like this for a little while longer."

The hint of desperation in his voice, the begging, was almost more than she could handle. She'd been horny before. Now she was as desperate as he was.

"Can you handle some teasing, if you know there will be pleasing afterward?"

"Only because I know you'll be in the same straits. You'll be tempted to put me inside you, won't you? To let your body overrule your brain and just fuck like there's no tomorrow and no risk." His voice was darker now, his hands more insistent, the way he moved her more demanding, and the combination was almost enough to send her over the edge. "We'll both be tempted. But we won't do it. And having to hold back will make it even hotter."

Her body clenched.

The familiar staticky radio clicked on in her head. Minerva's voice intruded. "…*risky…game…*" the ghost warned.

Tyler scrambled out of the tub, fumbled in his jeans pocket, and produced the needed foil packet. As he put it on, she circled her clit lightly, keeping herself warm for him.

The process took under a minute, but seemed like a lifetime before he was back in the tub. They positioned themselves so she leaned on the tiled side of the tub, standing on one of the low seats so her ass was out of the water. She missed the weightless feeling of bobbing in the water, wrapped around Tyler, but she stopped caring when Tyler reached between her legs.

"You're wet," he said, pleased wonder in his voice. "Wasn't sure if the water would wash it away."

"Too turned on," she acknowledged. This time she was amused rather than upset to realize Minerva was echoing it, dimly, in her head. Based on the journals, Minerva had a particular fondness for the bathhouses. If she wanted to enjoy them being put to good naughty use, Angela would let her, as long as she didn't talk *too* much.

Then Tyler entered her. At that point, Minerva could have offered a running commentary like a sportscaster and Angela would have just ignored it. After the long tease, Tyler's cock moving in and out of her felt like a touch of heaven. In the steamy air, she wasn't cold, but her damp nipples crinkled fiercely—all the more so when Tyler pinched one.

"This feels so good," Tyler sighed. "You're so tight around me, and the warm water splashing us and the air on our skin adds other sensations."

In response to his deep, sexy voice, she rolled her hips as he moved in her, sending the most amazing waves of pleasure through her body—and judging from his deep groan, through Tyler's as well. The static built up again, and she thought she heard Minerva trying to speak, but this time she ignored whatever the ghost had to say.

"I can't keep this up much longer," Tyler confessed in that sultry, deep voice. "All that teasing got to me. That's why I want you to come for me now." He snaked his hand down from her breast to circle her clit. His voice circled it too, drawing her higher. "Can you do that for me, Angela? Come for me now."

She bit her lip to keep from screaming as an orgasm ripped through her.

Tyler's hoarse cry burst out while she was still convulsing around him.

Tyler just managed to roll the condom off before he flopped back into the water. She resisted the urge to flop in after him, instead sinking down so she was mostly submerged, but her head was still above water. She knew the ends of her hair were already wet where they'd fallen from her hasty attempt at a bun, but she'd have absolutely no plausible deniability about what she'd been up to on break if her hair were soaked. Not that she'd have much if Kari asked her; Kari would read the truth from her body language in about half a second.

Though Kari would probably say something about her aura.

*

Angela peered in the steamed-over mirror. Impossible to see much of anything, between the haze of steam and the mirror's patina of age. She looked happy, that much was clear. How her hair looked was a bit harder to judge. Not good, certainly—she didn't need a mirror to figure that out!—but was it unspeakable or just disheveled?

"Don't worry," Tyler opined, creeping up behind her to plant a kiss on her collarbone. "You look good enough to eat. Matter of fact, that sounds like a great idea, although I guess I can't keep you here all evening."

She chuckled and reluctantly drew away, the memories of what his talented tongue could do reverberating through her body. *Down, girl!* "Another time."

"Tomorrow night, maybe? No, night after that. I have a commitment tomorrow night. Which I wish I could break, but I can't."

Angela's body screamed *yes! yes!* but it was probably wise to keep their plans loose. "Sounds great, but given how crazy things get around here sometimes, ask me again that day. Late in the day, when I have a feel for whether things are likely to explode." Keeping it loose would mean she'd be less disappointed if life in the hotel business got in the way of other plans, as it frequently did.

To her relief, he smiled, nodded, and drew her into a hug. "Being self-employed means you have the worst slave-driving boss ever, doesn't it?"

"Yeah, she's a real bitch. But I wouldn't've gotten as far as I have without her." Resigned that her hair looked as good as it was going to without a quick trip back to the cottage for some emergency mousse, she put on some lipstick, slipped on her shoes, and opened the door.

And nearly barreled right over Adelle Parsons.

Adelle's shrewd gaze ran from Angela's messed-up hair to a few droplets of water she only now realized clung to her ankle. "The nice young man at the desk said you might be out here. Only I swore he said you were checking on the repairs in number five. Don't tell me this one's having problems, too, dear."

Damn, she had said that, hadn't she? Of course, that was when she'd planned to pop her head in, see how the work was going, then head back. With luck the desk clerk hadn't told Adelle she'd been gone for forty-five minutes on a quick errand. If he had, she'd have to fire him.

As it was, he shouldn't have been telling just anyone about problems with the hotel. He was due for a stern talking-to already. But he was new.

"This one's fine. I was just showing him an older patch for comparison." Lame, but Adelle didn't know all that much about renovations, so maybe it would pass.

Trying to look casual and knowing she failed, Angela leaned back on the door to keep Tyler, his wet hair, and his shit-eating grin in there until she could steer Adelle away. Then she remembered the door opened inward and jumped forward. The situation was embarrassing enough without falling on her ass.

Adelle nodded. "I see, dear." The look in her eyes suggested she saw everything Angela was trying to hide and wasn't sure she approved. Which, frankly, was a surprise. Angela would have figured Adelle would pull a celebratory brass band and a bottle of champagne out of thin air—or out of her enormous orange patent tote bag—if she figured out Angela was getting laid.

Or maybe Adelle was peeved that Angela got to Tyler first.

The thought would've been funny if Tyler hadn't chosen that exact moment to emerge from the bathhouse.

He'd been a bit less careful about drying off than Angela had, so his T-shirt clung to damp skin. The shit-eating grin she'd predicted slid away, although he managed to school his features before he gave away too much more. As if there was anything left to give away.

He gamely plastered on a passably professional smile and said, "Oh, hi, Mrs. Parsons."

"Afternoon, Tyler." This time Adelle's assessing gaze seemed more approving, at least of the view. Still, her mouth had a stern set to it that Angela wouldn't have expected when she was getting a chance to gawk at one of her favorite "fine figures of a man" in clearly just-romped condition. "I see you've been hard at work."

Somehow, the old woman managed not to crack a smile when she said that, although Angela would bet good money she intended the double entendre.

"Definitely." Even more miraculously, Tyler didn't grin again, didn't even sound salacious. "But if you'll excuse me, ladies, I need to get a tool from my truck. Gotta run." He all but sprinted off.

Angela searched frantically for an excuse to do the same. Normally she got a kick out of Adelle's eccentricities, but her elderly friend looked like she was on the warpath about something and Angela didn't want her good mood spoiled.

On the other hand, in her extensive travels, Angela had learned one of the few universal constants was that old ladies shorter than five feet tall were forces of nature not to be trifled with.

"What can I do for you, Adelle?" With luck, it would be something simple. Maybe Adelle had heard rumors about the kitchen closing and, figuring it had to be a lie, was on the warpath on their behalf.

Yeah, that had to be it.

Instead, Adelle reached into her tote bag (Angela caught a glimpse of the lime green lining and wished she hadn't) and pulled out a large manila envelope. "Look this over as soon as you can."

Angela took the envelope. "What did you find for me? Ooh, could it be Minerva memorabilia?" Adelle knew all the other senior citizens in town. Maybe someone had found some interesting old articles or vintage photos stuffed in the back of a drawer.

Adelle glanced around as if she expected spies in the bushes. From Adelle, whose thick trifocals must prevent peripheral vision, it was funny. "I know you're busy and I don't want to hold you up. Just read it when you get a chance." She snatched Angela's hand and squeezed it between two wrinkled, bony ones. "Promise me. I'm concerned about this, Angela—I don't want to cause problems for you or the hotel, but I don't want to cause problems by not saying anything, either. Maybe I'm reading too much into it, so I want you to look it over, too.

"Meanwhile—" her voice dropped to a whisper "—you might want to think about doing something with your hair."

Chapter 14

To his utter dismay, Tyler felt as guilty as sin. Just not for the reasons that usually happened in the middle of the night.

He'd done any number of illegal things before—it was part of his job description, if you called what he did a "job"—without a twinge of regret. He believed in what he did, even if he had to bend societal and actual laws to do it.

But now…now there was this annoying nag of guilt poking at him as he slipped the slender metal rods into the lock and gently jimmied open Angela's office door.

The scent of the incense Angela had burned earlier today tickled his nose, and he muffled a sneeze in the crook of his arm.

He wasn't here to take anything—sort of.

He needed answers. He wasn't the only player here.

And while he might be weighing the idea of coming clean and giving up this job, at least one other person wasn't. Maybe two, if the blackmailer and the other person snooping around Angelika were different people.

And wouldn't that just be great?

Maybe if he could help Angela deal with the other crooks, she'd only dump him, not dump his dismembered body off the cliff.

Taking the penlight out from between his teeth, he went straight for the small safe in the corner. The few times he'd been in here talking with

Angela, he'd taken careful note of how she organized things, where she put things. He hadn't seen every nook and cranny, but he had a pretty good idea that the information he sought was in that safe.

He'd also paid careful attention when she'd opened the safe to get out petty cash. He wasn't sure of the combination—staring that intently would have been too obvious—but he knew enough to give his carefully practiced safe-cracking skills a boost.

On the third try, he opened the lock, eased the door open with a minimal amount of noise or drama, and nodded in satisfaction.

Every employee file, at his fingertips, arranged in a standing file.

Pushing her chair aside, he knelt beside the safe and pulled out the first manila folder. To his amusement, they had a silhouette of a fifties-style secretary and the words "I am SO organized!" printed on them.

They'd been a gift, he suspected, from someone who knew her all too well. Kari, maybe.

The problem was this: he was here for a reason, a reason beyond just being a handyman. He had a plan, almost a routine, and that included not causing any permanent damage or undue stress.

He also knew that everything *else* that had been going on couldn't be mere coincidences. Which meant they'd been caused by somebody else.

Somebody who was horning in on his territory. Probably the same person who was blackmailing him.

First step, look to the employees. They had the easiest access to all parts of the hotel, and had excuses for being there.

Angelika employed cleaning staff, receptionists, kitchen assistants, wait staff, massage therapists, cosmetologists, and a gardener. (What kind of a name was Greenwind?)

Most of them—including the interestingly monikered gardener—seemed perfectly harmless, at least so far as their résumés went. Tyler had a pretty good idea what had the potential to flag suspiciously on a résumé. His own was a work of art.

He didn't have an unlimited amount of time, nor did he dare to fire up the photocopier, so he was frustrated in his ability to do a real in-depth check on all these people. He took pictures of each document with his cell phone, though, hoping the photos would be clear enough to read later, if he decided to do a deeper investigation of anyone. On the surface, so far, the staff looked fine. Angela had done cursory background checks on them, a little more than most employers did, but still not deep enough to find someone who was really, truly hiding something.

She'd missed a whole lot about him, after all.

Then he got to a file that gave him pause.

Franklin, it seemed, had not always been called Franklin.

His original name wasn't in the file, but there was a certificate indicating that his name had been legally changed. Tyler rocked back on his heels and pondered that. There were lots of reasons to change your name, some perfectly legitimate—marriage and divorce, adoption—and it was relatively easy to do so.

But there were also many other reasons to obscure one's identity, and many of those were for not-so-legitimate motives.

He quickly took a photo of the information, then went back to perusing the rest of the files. Pull one out, carefully page through without disturbing anything, then slide in back exactly where it had come from. Lather, rinse, repeat.

His feet were starting to fall asleep by the time he finished. He had two more possible names, although neither seemed nearly as worrisome as Franklin. He considered glancing through the guest files, but he'd been here long enough for tonight. Most of the guests, except for that writer and her husband, were due to check out tomorrow, so if the incidents continued, that would rule them out.

He eased the safe shut and spun the dial.

The office door presented more of a problem, as it couldn't be relocked without a key. He could flip the lock from the inside, but then he'd have to climb out the narrow window that led to the reception desk, and the number of things he could conceivably knock over was daunting. The last thing he needed was that hanging potted fern upended on his head.

And the night clerk hadn't been there when he'd snuck in, but he didn't know whether she was off-duty since no one was due in or just in the rest room.

Hopefully Angela would just stick her key into the lock and not notice that she didn't really need to turn it.

Franklin. Tyler never would have expected the genial cook to have a suspicious background, something to hide. In the short time he'd known Franklin, Tyler had gotten the impression that Franklin was a stand-up sort of guy.

Just goes to show how easily people can be fooled. Franklin could also be an exceptional actor.

Pondering that, Tyler realized he wasn't on full alert only when he rounded the corner to the back door and saw a figure moving toward him.

Too late—nowhere to duck and hide. The main lights were off, but at night the refitted gas lamps on the walls gave off a soothing glow. No shadows for him to melt into.

That said, the other person was in full view, too.

"Oh my goodness!" She pressed a hand to her chest, gave a breathy laugh. "You startled me!"

"Ms. Swain, isn't it?" Tyler asked, wondering what the hell Barb was doing wandering around at three o'clock in the goddamn morning. "Is everything okay?"

"Oh yes, I'm just fine, now that I've caught my breath," she said with a smile.

The older woman sidled up close to him, seemed to analyze the situation and then decide not to make the effort. Good thing, because that would have been eighteen levels of awkward.

"I was having trouble sleeping, so I went ahead and started packing up," she continued. "We're leaving tomorrow. Anyway, I realized I must have left my reading glasses in the parlor, and I figured if I didn't come and get them now, I'd forget in the morning."

"I hope you enjoyed your stay with us here," he said, wondering why he sounded like a salesman. No matter what his underlying motives for being here, he supposed, he was still technically an employee and he wanted to represent Angelika in the best light.

Strange, that.

"I had a marvelous time!" Barb cooed. "And Carole did, too. And we got a lot done on the movie project—it's a great atmosphere for creativity. Even if, in my case, it's more creativity about financing." She shook her head. "Is everything all right with you? You're up rather late yourself."

"Caught a midnight movie in the next town. Animation festival." Which was really going on; there were brochures in the lobby, along with information on other local events. "When I drove past on the way home, I noticed one of the lights at the end of the driveway had blown a bulb. Just coming in to grab a new one." The light was fine, but Barb wasn't likely to wander to the end of the long driveway and check. For that matter, Angelika wouldn't have been on a direct route home from the film festival, but Barb didn't know where he lived.

She nodded. "Well, have a lovely evening—but I suppose it's morning now, isn't it?"

"And you have a safe trip back home," Tyler said. "Good night."

He didn't allow himself to breathe easy again until he was in his truck and halfway down the winding drive to the main road. Even then, he couldn't completely relax.

He had to find out who else had a hidden agenda when it came to Angelika.

*

Angela leaned back in her desk chair, enjoying the fact that for the first time in what seemed like hours, she wasn't on the phone.

Someone wanted to use Angelika for their wedding. The couple had gotten engaged after a weekend here and couldn't imagine being married anyplace else.

Angelika's first wedding!

You'd think that would be a good thing, but like all good things, it had its complications. On the bride's first choice of date, the place was already booked solid for an artists' gathering and a big antiques show in town.

Angela thought she'd convinced the bride-to-be that the gardens would look even better the following week, but it sounded like it would take a few more phone calls with a very frantic young woman—and her even more frantic mother—to get it settled.

Still, overpopularity was the kind of problem she wished she had more often.

If she hadn't been in a good mood to start with, it would be enough to make her smile. Since Tyler had left her in a very good mood indeed, she had to remind herself occasionally to wipe the cat-in-the-cream grin off her face.

Then again, why *not* grin? She had a date coming with a hot guy. A loosey-goosey unofficial kind of date, which is what you'd expect at this stage of…whatever they had. Friends with benefits? A proto-relationship? Great sex with no strings attached?

They'd figure that part out as they went along.

Meanwhile, she'd enjoy the bubbly feeling, the pleasant aches in odd places, the goofy but entertainingly adolescent way she mooned over not seeing him for a whole twenty-four hours. He'd left her a voice mail saying he was going out of town for his day off so any explosions would have to wait until he got back.

Predictably, he said *explosions* in a way designed to provoke lecherous thoughts, and never mind she got the voice mail at an hour when lechery was usually the last thing on her mind. (Unless she'd never gotten to sleep the night before, for the most interesting of reasons.)

She squirmed in her chair, feeling the sweet ache of having been well-fucked. She was still having plenty of those lecherous thoughts, but they made rote tasks more interesting.

Like finally checking out that envelope Adelle had pressed on her, although that wasn't a rote task, just one she hadn't gotten to yet. No time like the present, when things were fairly quiet. Adelle was forever unearthing interesting things for her: old photos of Minerva, a crumbling scrap of newspaper with a story about Angelika when it was Fenwick House, even a hair comb Adelle swore Theda Bara had worn while visiting the house.

Angela didn't entire believe that story, but it *was* a pretty enameled Art Deco comb, so she'd been happy to put it in a display case.

But Adelle had sounded strangely concerned about whatever she'd found this time. Maybe something that suggested a real scandal in the house's history. Illegitimate children? Murder?

Whatever it was, she could spin it as a positive.

What she pulled out of the envelope, though, was less exciting: a familiar copy of the *Northern California Living* that included the first article about Angelika. A nice thought, but she already had a half-dozen copies on file, and some of the photos from the article framed in the cottage she shared with Kari.

And why all the Nancy-Drew-hush-hush mysteriousness yesterday if it was only a magazine? Not even a great article, except that it was the first. The writer had gotten sidetracked by some offhand remarks Adelle and some of the other old-timers made about rumors of Minerva having a treasure, until you'd think that was the real story, not Minerva's history, or the process of restoration on a strict budget, or even the amenities Angelika offered.

Angela peered into the envelope again and saw another piece of paper.

She hadn't spent a lot of time thinking about it, but if someone had asked, she'd guess most of Adelle's contemporaries used notepaper decorated with flowers or seascapes or cute animals. Adelle's sported Michelangelo's David. So Adelle—arty, yet naked.

It took a few seconds to decipher Adelle's shaky handwriting. She might be young and randy at heart, but Adelle was well over seventy— how well over, she wouldn't admit—and her hands were arthritic. Angela finally made out, "I found this in Tyler's room when I was cleaning. Thought you should know."

Cleaning? More like snooping, Angela guessed. So he had a copy of an article about the hotel. He was a thorough guy, and the bookstore in San Sebastian had a few copies of the old issue on sale, along with any other publication that ever mentioned the town.

A receipt poked out the top of the magazine.

Had he picked up anything else at the same time? A thriller or mystery to pass the time, or maybe erotica with a revealing kinky title? Or maybe he was strictly a how-to kind of guy. Okay, it was blatantly nosy, but if Adelle could snoop, so could she.

It was an opportunity to get to know him a little better, she rationalized.

The receipt wasn't from the local bookstore. It was from Powell's in Portland, Oregon.

It was dated thirteen months ago, when the article first came out. And the magazine was the only thing on the receipt.

Strange that he hadn't mentioned it. Who knew what had prompted him to pick it up in the first place, but he must have made the connection long since.

Especially since the receipt had been bookmarking the article.

Then again, the male mind was a mysterious place. Maybe he didn't want to sound like a groupie, or admit he sometimes bought magazines that didn't have a macho hands-on focus. Or maybe it just hadn't occurred to him. Fodder for teasing him later, though.

Just then, Franklin buzzed her. "I just finished a trial batch of a new muffin recipe. Want to taste-test?"

She was about to ask him to set one aside for her to eat later, but her stomach rumbled, reminding her she'd put off lunch and it was now mid-afternoon. Besides, she was past due for a bathroom break. "Be right down," she confirmed.

She made it as far as the lobby, earpiece in place in case of still more calls, when Carole and Barb came in from the spa. They'd checked out earlier, but had opted to stay for lunch and a last massage before heading home. "Oh good," Carole said. "We caught you. I wanted to grab a few extra brochures. This place is such a great escape, and some of my friends could—"

Angela's phone rang. She held up her hand in the universal "just a minute" gesture and took the call.

"This is Pam Nestor from Coastal Mortgage and Trust. May I speak to Angela Georgenes?"

"Speaking." Angela's good-mood bubble burst. This couldn't be good. It never was when the mortgage company called.

"Ms. Georgenes, I'm sorry to inform you that you had insufficient funds to cover your mortgage payment this month."

"What?" She managed not to shout, but it was close. Too close. She'd double-checked the account balance yesterday. Even if all the outstanding checks cleared at once this morning, she should have been fine. Angela might not be perfect, but keeping the bank accounts under control was the kind of fussy work at which she excelled.

Carole and Barb still hovered. And Barb, at least, seemed a bit curious. In the frantic world of film, she probably heard a lot of carefully controlled but obviously outraged shrieks.

"It must be a mistake," she whispered.

At that moment, inevitably, Satya walked in carrying a bag from the local artisan cooperative.

And walked straight over to her. "Oh, great. I'm leaving later on, but I'd wanted to ask you…" the reporter started.

Angela pushed her hair back to show the earpiece, mouthed "later," and retreated for the safety of her office.

Thank goodness they banked in town, because in about two-point-five seconds, she'd grab Kari and heading over there to straighten this mess out and get her mortgage company paid.

With luck, it would turn out to be a bank error, or maybe a mistake on their end. Those were the most plausible scenarios. Or maybe a random hacking.

But if it wasn't a mistake, she was going to kill someone.

She wasn't completely sure who yet, but she had a pretty good idea.

And she didn't like it one bit.

Chapter 15

After the quiet charm of San Sebastian, the mayhem of San Francisco hit Tyler like a slap in the face.

He could never decide which he liked more, small towns or big cities. Small towns had the benefit that everyone felt secure; they didn't lock their doors or guard their wallets. On the other hand, everybody noticed the stranger in their midst, so it was hard to slip away undetected with something you'd liberated.

Nobody noticed a stranger in the city—or if they did, they weren't surprised, were unlikely to remember your face, and certainly didn't want to chat. But by the same token, people were paranoid, with alarm systems and security cameras and kung-fu moves.

Given the choice, Tyler would rather tackle the problem of a security camera than a nosy neighbor. Still, he'd learned how to deal with both.

The touristy dim sum restaurant in Chinatown was the perfect place to be unnoticed while you had a meeting. (Bars, especially in the middle of the day, were *so* cliché.) When Tyler entered, he was assaulted by the scents of soy sauce, shrimp, and onions. His stomach rumbled in response.

Food: another benefit to meeting in a touristy dim sum restaurant in Chinatown.

The small table in the middle of the room was perfect. Better there than by the bank of windows along the busy street, where people could glance in, or in the back, where you could look too obvious. Middle was neutral. Plus, the low ceiling bounced sound back down, and in the crowded room, conversations jumbled with the tinny music, making it harder to hear even the people at the next table.

He ordered a Tsingtao beer for himself and green tea for the person who'd be joining him, and the drinks arrived at the same time Ben did.

"Tyler, my man." They bumped fists as Ben slid into his seat.

Ben was wiry, and bald in a way that women seemed to find attractive, or maybe they were just charmed by his easy smile. He dealt in information, generally the kind that skimmed and skirted and then toppled right over the edge into illegal. But he knew how to cover his tracks, and he was discreet.

If there was anything Tyler knew, it was that you had to be discreet when you poked into the past of someone who didn't want to be poked at. Otherwise you ran the risk of spooking them or worse. Potentially much worse.

Ben's other specialty was fabricating new pasts, something he'd done for Tyler more than once. He was exceptional at that.

"I'm glad you had time to meet," Tyler said. "I know it was short notice."

"A man's gotta eat," Ben said. He glanced around at the red-and-gold lanterns and tassels strung on the ceiling, the smug Lucky Cat statues, and the ornate faux mahogany dragons. "Despite what you think, this place has some of the best dumplings in town."

The waitress returned, asked if they were ready to order. They both went for the sampler platter; special orders took longer, and neither of them had all day.

From her attention to and wider smile at Ben, it seemed she was taken with him. Typical. Sometimes Tyler would turn on his own charm out of sheer male competitiveness, but this time he just didn't feel the urge. She was pretty in a slender, graceful way, but she didn't have Angela's vibrancy. Her fire.

He noticed Ben looking at him funny.

"What?"

Ben shook his head. "Nothing. Now, what brings you back so soon? The job up on the coast fall through?"

"Still going," Tyler said. "It takes longer when I don't know what I'm looking for. Something's come up, though, that falls under your area of expertise."

"I figured as much."

Of course he had. Ben had to know Tyler wouldn't have come all the way here for a social chat. Or even for the best dim sum in Chinatown.

"Someone else on the staff has raised a red flag for me," Tyler went on. "Name change, new birth certificate."

"And you want me to check him or her out."

Tyler nodded. "Dig as deep as you need to, but unless this guy is another pro, you probably shouldn't have to do too much."

They didn't have to discuss a fee. Tyler knew Ben's rates. Ben knew Tyler would pay.

Their food arrived. Ben snagged a dumpling with his chopsticks, dunked it in scallion-laced sauce.

"If you don't mind my asking, why do you care about this guy?" he asked. "You're usual method is 'get in, get out'—you don't waste your time on this shit."

"I think someone else is trying to horn in on my action," Tyler said. "This guy seems a likely suspect. If it's him, maybe I can ride on his coattails. Let him do the work, then dive in and snatch the prize out from under him."

Like the blackmailer was hoping to do to him. It would be hilarious to turn the tables.

"Mm hm." Ben didn't seem convinced.

If it wasn't Franklin, then Tyler would be back to square one, at least in terms of the strange goings-on at the hotel. As it was, he wasn't much past square one when it came to his primary goal.

That frustrated him. If the thing was so obvious that someone would mention it in a magazine article, why wasn't it obvious to *him*? Why couldn't he find it?

"What if this guy's clean?" Ben wanted to know.

Tyler shrugged. "Then maybe I'm wrong about someone else being involved. Or maybe I'm just wrong about him. Nobody else raised a red flag for me. It could be somebody in town, or even one of the guests, although they're all on their way out soon."

"You'll let me know if there's anyone else you need looked at."

"You're my go-to guy." Tyler bit into another savory pork dumpling, looked up to find Ben staring at him. "What?" he demanded, exasperated.

"It's not just about someone trying to get a piece of your action," Ben said, shaking his head. "I've know you how long? You've gotten emotionally invested in something there."

"No, I haven't," Tyler said. "Don't be ridiculous. It's just that this job's important. Really important." He rubbed his fingers together, indicating big bucks. Damn. Ben was a professional at seeing through lies. Not that he was lying, of course. At this point, the job was important in order to get the blackmailer off his back.

And he wasn't emotionally invested in Angela. Not really.

Ben set down his chopsticks. "It's a woman, isn't it?"

"No."

Ben continued to stare at him. Tyler ate the rest of his dumpling, trying to ignore him.

He'd lost his appetite, though. The dumpling tasted like sawdust. He threw down his chopsticks.

He didn't throw them at Ben. That was good.

"Fine! There's a woman." Before Ben could say something along the lines of "I told you so," at which point Tyler would have to deck him, he added, "But it's nothing serious. She's sexy and we're having some fun. She doesn't want a relationship any more than I do."

"Oh, crap," Ben said. "It's the owner of the hotel, isn't it?"

"Another good reason why it's not serious," Tyler said. "If you say one more word about it, you're paying for lunch."

"I was planning to be magnanimous and offer to pay, but never mind now," Ben said.

Tyler glared at him and stabbed at another dumpling. He didn't want it, but the stabbing was cathartic.

When they were done, the waitress brought the bill on a plastic tray with a couple of fortune cookies. Although she tried to be surreptitious about it, Tyler was pretty sure he saw her slip her number to Ben.

Tyler cracked open his cookie, crunched down on the faintly lemony shards as he unfolded his fortune.

"The truth shall set you free."

Tyler laughed and tossed the strip of paper onto the table. Not hardly. The truth would more likely than not get him thrown in jail

And break the heart of a woman he hated to admit he was growing fond of.

Even so, it was still time to come clean and tell the truth

*

"What I don't understand is why Tyler would transfer money between accounts instead of just stealing it?" Angela resisted the urge to get up and pace along the beachfront.

"Hush," Kari said. "We agreed not to talk about that. Just sit here and breathe." Kari probably knew how likely *that* was, even if she'd managed to talk Angela into going to the beach instead of heading straight back to the hotel and trying to relax instead of making lists, at least not until they were clearer what she needed to make lists of.

Angela understood. Really she did. But her fingers itched for a pen or a keyboard.

Organizing her thoughts would keep them from spiraling downward into a morass of self-recrimination.

How could she have been so stupid?

She thought she was a good judge of character, but Tyler was a crook.

Or maybe he wasn't.

Still, she'd given him the debit card, their bank account had gotten screwed up, and then he'd left town.

The debit card wasn't linked to the mortgage account. But he was in and out of the office; he could have gotten his hands on the other account number somehow.

And when she was scrambling through paperwork, trying to find a deposit ticket with the wrong numbers on it or something to explain where the money had gone (and preferably to prove it was just a dumb mistake), she noticed that among Tyler's petty cash receipts was one for a hose clamp...dated the day the hose to the dishwasher broke. If nothing else was going on, she'd think it was a weird coincidence; Kari's first reaction, in fact, was that Tyler had somehow known he'd need a hose clamp, a psychic message from Minerva or the hotel itself or something. But under the circumstances, it seemed suspicious, in a nebulous way. Maybe the dishwasher fiasco had been a cover for the rat poop incident.

Although why he'd want to plant rat poop in the kitchen was beyond her.

Angela and Kari had taken over a bench at a waterfront park in town to watch the sun set over the ocean and, theoretically, to relax for a few minutes. So far, despite Nature's best efforts with a gloriously streaked sky, a fresh breeze that carried the scent of summer, and soothing wave music, they weren't doing so well on the relax-and-forget-their-troubles part.

Ice cream cones had distracted them briefly when they first got there, but all too quickly, the pleasures of raspberry chocolate chunk (Kari's choice) and green tea with ginger (Angela's) had been gobbled up, and they'd started thinking again. At least Angela had, and she couldn't seem to let Kari let it go, either.

"I just don't get it," she repeated.

Kari sighed. "Okay, okay, if it'll help you to think it through—my answer is: I have no clue. Maybe he had some more complicated scheme in mind. Maybe he wanted to harass us rather than rob us, although I can't imagine why. And maybe," she added in the voice she used to calm stressed-out executives who couldn't relax enough to appreciate a massage, "Tyler had nothing to do with it. Maybe it was a bank error. Some new employee hit the wrong key or something and bingo, money ended up in the wrong account."

Angela stared out at the water, willing the rhythmic pounding of the surf to pound some sense into her head.

She wanted to believe Kari's explanation. It was reasonable enough. The branch manager had even suggested it as a possibility, though he'd figured one of them had started the chain of mistakes by putting the wrong account number on a deposit slip.

Which was also a possibility, given they'd been moving at the speed of light the past few weeks. Probably more reasonable than imagining Tyler was running a complicated scam. He'd had the debit card. If he'd wanted to rob them, he could have simply withdrawn all their money, bought a ticket to Fiji, and bolted.

Okay, he couldn't have gotten as far as Fiji. Maybe Seattle. But the principle remained the same.

"At least it was easy to straighten out," Kari soothed as she rubbed Angela's stiff shoulders. "Our money's back where it belongs. And the mortgage company stopped screaming once the bank assured them the deposit would clear if they put it through again."

"Thank goodness for small mercies." She groaned as Kari's clever hands found a knot in her shoulder. Pity they couldn't get to the ones in her mind.

"I just wish I knew for sure Tyler wasn't involved." Angela sighed. "Or even that he was, because then I could do something about it. But the suspicion's going to drive me crazy. Now I'm seeing everything weird that's happened lately as being his fault: the rat poop, the hole in the wall, stuff getting moved around."

"That's your monkey mind talking, sweetie." Kari dug into the knot. It hurt, but in a good way. "You're letting your brain run so fast it's making more trouble for you. You need to do yoga with me tonight."

"I don't need yoga. I need answers. I feel like such an idiot. I trusted him, Kari." She closed her eyes against thoughts of Tyler's sexy voice, his fascination with history, the way he seemed to care about Angelika, and about her.

Unfortunately, closing her eyes made it easier to conjure up visuals to go with the thoughts, and that didn't help one bit. Her libido didn't give a damn whether Tyler was a thief.

Traitorous libido.

"My intuition says he's not your crook," Kari said. "My thinky brain says we need facts to back that up before we decide *anyone's* a crook. And my heart's sad that the first guy who's managed to get you to relax and play a little since we bought Angelika might be bad news—and not in a fun, black-leather-and-motorcycles way."

Angela managed a weak laugh. "The motorcycle thing is more you than me. But seriously—what am I supposed to do? If he's scamming us, I need to stop him before something worse happens. But maybe he's done nothing wrong." She hid her head in her hands. "All I have to go on are your intuition and my lists, once you let me make them. How can I be sure?"

Kari moved her hands up to work on Angela's scalp. It felt heavenly. "Too bad Minerva can't tell you. Seems like a ghost might be able to see things we can't."

Despite everything on her mind, the idea of asking a voyeuristic ghost for advice made Angela giggle. "Kari, that's the craziest…"

Then she remembered some of the strange things Minerva had said to her, things that seemed less like metaphors in light of recent events.

"No, it's not crazy. It's brilliant." She turned and hugged her friend. "Kari, have I told you how much I love you? And do you mind giving me a little alone time tonight?"

Chapter 16

*G*lass of Shiraz to relax her—check.

Vibrator—check.

Three volumes of erotica (backup was always good) because all her recent fantasies involved Tyler and she wanted some new fantasy fodder—check, check, and check.

Arousal? Maybe half a check. Angela felt a bit damp and, in the immortal words of Beetlejuice, "anxious," but miles away from orgasm.

Angela had set the erotic romance aside almost immediately. Hot vampires and the women who loved them usually turned her on, but tonight, she found herself distracted by thinking about whether it was brave or stupid to trust a bloodsucking fiend, even a really gorgeous one.

The second book she tried was a well-thumbed favorite, but the story she opened up to was from the point of view of a pair of criminals planning a big heist. The story was light-hearted and hot, but just seeing the word *thief* was a buzz-kill in her current mood.

The bondage erotica collection worked better. Normally Angela was more into the stories where an eager woman was tied up, maybe spanked a little, teased unmercifully, and then fucked senseless. (Hey, she worked hard for a living. She liked the idea of lying back and letting someone else do the work once in a while.)

Tonight, though, a different story caught her attention: one about punishing a boyfriend who'd screwed up. Of course, the punishment in the story was all in good fun, the bad behavior nothing near as bad as outright theft, but it did put some interesting images into her head.

If these images involved Tyler naked and bent over a chair so she could paddle his ass while she asked him a few pointed questions…well, she needed to get her anger out somehow, and fantasy was a safe way to do it.

And if he wasn't guilty, she was all for the idea of tying him to the bed and having her consensually wicked way with him.

No. Don't go there.

Don't go anywhere that implied a future, even a future as simple as a future kinky adventure.

The sooner she could let go of hopes she'd barely started admitting she had, the better.

She tried to focus on the story, then on another one that involved corsets and Victorian role-playing, but her brain wouldn't stop.

This must be what Kari called *monkey mind*. It certainly felt like she had unruly chimps at play in her skull, complete with the headache.

And it wasn't conducive to arousal.

Fine. Time to call in the big gun.

Angela didn't use her Hitachi too often. It had to live in her dresser drawer instead of on the steamer-trunk nightstand because it was so big and obvious, and out of sight meant out of mind in her busy life. Plus, it was loud, and while Kari slept better than the dead seemed to around here, Angela did feel a little self-conscious. It was one thing if your happy orgasm-noises woke your roomie up. It was another thing if your vibrator did.

But the damn thing worked like magic. And Kari was out. Probably at Mal's place in town, having a hot date with one actual living person, not a vibrator and a ghost. Lucky Kari.

She got up, plugged it in, sprawled on the bed, turned the buzzing monster on, and touched it to her clit.

Yeah, that was the ticket. Her brain might still be running a mile a minute, but her body couldn't resist the Hitachi's blatant charms for long.

After a few minutes with the Hitachi, she was closer than she'd gotten in half an hour with a less potent toy.

And thank goodness, the waves of sensation were drowning her less pleasant thoughts.

When Angela began to hear the by-now familiar buzzing in her head, she welcomed it instead of trying to shut it out. *Hi, Minerva. If you have something to tell me, now would be a good time.*

The crackling got louder, but she couldn't make out words.

Her hips began to buck. The little quivers that preceded orgasm started in her abs.

Damn this thing was fast. Too fast for her purposes. Had to give Minerva time to catch up. She pulled back, put her hand where the toy had been, trying to keep on that edge.

Angela flashed to the memory of Tyler's hand where her own was, doing all sorts of clever, wonderful things.

She tried not to think about it, but she swore her clit jumped at the image—and the crackling got louder, as if Minerva wanted to say something.

Come on, Minerva. Spit it out.

The crackling abruptly diminished, as if someone had tuned away from the fading radio station. Great, now she'd lost her ghost.

Half-panicking, Angela switched back to the Hitachi. *Sorry, Minerva. Didn't mean to sound cranky, but I need to know if I'm sleeping with the enemy.*

She waited for an answer as the tension grew in her body. The crackling in her head cut in again, but she couldn't make out words in it. It rose and fell like conversation, but despite her best efforts, she couldn't understand.

And pretty soon, at the rate her body was throbbing and pulsating, she wouldn't be able to pay attention much longer.

"Please," she begged out loud. "Minerva…if you know anything about Tyler, tell me. Please."

The last please came out almost as a scream, as her body let go, releasing some of the tensions of the day in a massive explosion of pleasure. Just before she lost control completely, Minerva answered.

But all Angela could make out was one word: *foolish.*

Great. What was *that* supposed to mean—that Angela had been foolish to trust him in the first place or that she was foolish to doubt him now?

Or maybe that she was foolish to ask a ghost for advice. Crashing down from the high of the orgasm, Angela certainly felt that way.

Something was poking her side: the bondage anthology.

She grabbed it to toss it aside.

Then stopped.

Wasn't there a story about an interrogation scene in there? Not a painful one, but one that was purely a mind-fuck, getting someone to let their guard down in bed?

Sure, it was fighting dirty, but desperate times called for desperate measures. And between that and the punishing a bad boyfriend scenario, she had all sorts of ideas for fighting dirty.

And whether Tyler fessed up or Minerva came through, she was bound to get answers somehow.

*

After meeting with Ben, Tyler had run some needed errands in San Francisco, then made the four-hour drive back to San Sebastian. By the time he'd arrived home, he'd been exhausted. Lack of sleep and too many conflicting details bouncing around in his head meant he actually pulled over in a secluded beachfront parking lot and napped for twenty minutes.

Better to face Angela with as clear a head as possible.

When he walked into Angelika and slipped behind the reception desk to Angela's office, he was gratified to find both Angela and Kari there. He'd planned to speak to both of them, because they were co-owners of the hotel, and being upfront with both of them would hopefully make him seem genuinely forthcoming.

Angela was in dark red again, a color that worked so well with her Mediterranean hair and skin. A simple knit dress with cap sleeves, but the way it hugged her curves and skimmed just above her knees made her look sexier than hell. Her curly black hair was pulled back, revealing large, dangly silver and lapis earrings, inlaid with brass, with tiny bells on the bottom. Central Asian tribal, he thought, maybe Turkmen or Kuchi. Nothing valuable, but exotic-looking, unusual.

Like Angela.

Although she was definitely valuable.

Kari wore black yoga pants and a soft blue T-shirt with subtly sparkly flowers on it, and her short, fair hair was damp. But she invested the casual outfit with an air of authority like a business suit, probably because it *was* her version of business attire. Her hazel eyes were serious and her posture was tense, which was new for the usually mellow spa manager.

Together, they made a surprisingly formidable presence

"Good morning," he said. "I'm glad you're both here. We need to talk."

Angela was doing an amazing job of not letting her emotions show, even though he could tell she was unhappy; the emotion radiated from her. Her face remained impassive as she said, "You can't quit until after Bathhouse Five is finished…unless I have to fire you first. Sit down, Tyler. You're right: we *do* need to talk."

Oh. Crap.

He sat. Isabella untangled her long limbs and stepped out of her dog bed. She padded over to him and leaned against his thigh. His hand automatically moved to scratch behind her ear. She sighed in contentment.

He watched Angela glance at Kari, and Kari nod. Even though the two of them co-owned Angelika, this was clearly Angela's responsibility.

"Tyler," she said. "A number of…unusual things have been going on, and we're starting to see a pattern: they all started just after you arrived."

He opened his mouth to explain, but she held up a hard to forestall him. The chunky turquoise ring on her middle finger distracted him for a millisecond as a certain part of his brain tried to calculate its provenance and value.

She ticked them off: a hose clamp receipt dated the day the dishwasher hose broke (obviously Angela was going to his head, because he certainly hadn't *meant* to turn that in), the obviously planted rat poop and subsequent call to the health department, the hole in the wall, things being moved around in the library—more than just a guest poking at the books—people skulking around at night, and, most damningly, the money missing out of one of their accounts.

"Here's the thing," Tyler said when Angela finished and they both watched him expectantly. "I think I know what might be going on. But to explain that, I have to explain who I am. Why I'm here. And I need you both to keep an open mind."

"Oh, this does *not* bode well," Kari murmured.

"Last year, Angelika had a write-up in *Northern California Living*," he said.

"We're aware of that," Angela said. "In fact, we're also aware that you've had a copy of that issue in your possession for nearly that long. When you arrived, you led us to believe that you hadn't heard of Angelika until you saw our ad for a handyman."

Her facial expression might have been neutral, but he heard the shift in her voice, in her unusually formal way of speaking.

"That article," he said, deliberately ignoring her pointed comment (and wondering, at the same time, how the hell she'd figured that out), "contained a comment that there was some valuable treasure here at Angelika."

It was his turn to hold up a hand to forestall both of them breaking in. "I believe someone is actively searching for that treasure, and that person has been responsible for the weird things that have been happening."

"And what makes you think that?" Angela asked.

Dammit. Now or never. "Because I came here to search for the same treasure."

Angela's nostrils flared as she sucked in air. He guessed she hadn't wanted to believe he was involved, even when the hard cold facts pointed in his direction. He hated disappointing her.

He'd never regretted his chosen profession until now.

"I want to make it clear: I haven't done anything to harm Angelika. Okay, I did cause the leaky hose in the dishwasher, so I had an excuse to poke around more in the kitchen. Which was bad, but I knew I could fix it again and knew it would be found before it did damage because Franklin's so on top of things in the kitchen. But none of the other things you're mentioning are my doing. I'll tell you the truth—I'll tell you why I'm here and what I do—but you have to believe me when I say someone else is involved. And I'm trying to find out who that person is."

"Go on," Kari said, sounding like she was grinding her teeth. She'd need a massage from the swarthy head therapist in the spa when this was over, Tyler suspected.

"You probably know this," he said, directing his words to Angela, "but all over the world, there are artifacts and works of art that nobody appreciates. That people don't realize they even have. It's not about the money; it's about access. Great-Aunt Bertha gave me this stupid vase, and I've shoved some clearly fake flowers in it and stuck it on the top of a bookshelf to gather dust…because I don't know it was smuggled out of China during the Opium Wars and is a rare Ming Dynasty antique"

Angela was just as sharp as he'd expected her to be. "If it's stuck on my bookshelf gathering dust and I don't appreciate it, much less know its value, then it's wasted. It should be in a museum where everyone can appreciate it."

He pointed a finger at her, like a kid's gun, and pretend-fired. In truth, he hated guns, never carried one. "Bingo."

"Like that ghastly statue, Kari." She turned to him and explained, "We found a bizarre statue in the attic. Kari figured out it was one Minerva mentioned it in her journal as a gift from a suitor. She didn't like either the piece or the man, she said, but she admired that someone had the courage to make something so utterly original, even if it was ugly, so she didn't have the heart to dispose of it. Turns out it was an early piece by one of the leaders of the Dadaist movement and was important to art history and rather valuable. But we still didn't want it in the house."

"Like that." He felt on slightly safer ground now. "Only you knew how to get more information about the weird art object. I liberate pieces no one's recognized."

"So you're a thief," Kari said flatly. "You came here to steal from us." Oddly, she didn't sound as judgmental or angry as the straightforward words implied. Just stating facts.

She wasn't wrong, even though he didn't think of it that way. He knew it came down to semantics.

His best bet was to be honest.

"Yes," he said. "I wanted to find whatever the treasure was. From the way it was phrased, it sounded like you two didn't know what it was or were even sure it existed. If it turned out you did know about it and appreciated it, then I would've walked away."

Okay, maybe not completely forthcoming. There was a much bigger problem, one he couldn't walk away from. If he didn't find this whatever-it-was and get it to the damn blackmailer, he was going to be hip-deep in shit-trouble.

And he didn't want to expose either of them to that danger.

"So what is this supposed treasure?" Angela asked.

He shook his head. "I have no idea. The article didn't say, and my follow-up research didn't tell me anything. I'd hoped to find something in plain sight, but…"

"I think," Angela said tightly, "that I'm experienced enough to know if something's valuable, or astute enough to get something appraised if I'm not sure."

"I figured that out pretty quickly once I got here," Tyler said. "I mean that. I realized there was no way you—either of you—would have something valuable and important here and not know about it, much less truly appreciate it."

Her shoulders relaxed, just a little. Then the phone rang, and she jumped, just a little. He wasn't surprised she was on edge.

She tucked the earbud in her ear and answered. Tyler tried not to listen, focusing instead on giving Isabella a good scratching, hard enough that her collar jangled.

But the relief in Angela's voice when she said, "Oh yes, thank you! Thank you so much!" caught his attention. Made him smile, even though he didn't know why she was happy.

Angela swiveled back to face him. "That was the bank," she said. "You're off the hook, and I'm a bonehead."

"No you're not," Tyler and Kari said simultaneously.

Angela rolled her shoulders. "Okay, you're right, I've just been so overwhelmed, it's not a surprise I screwed up. I accidentally deposited money to the wrong account, which is why the mortgage payment bounced.

They actually found the deposit slip on file, and the teller remembered me when they investigated. The bank is reversing the overdraft charges and late fees. Remind me to have Franklin bake a double batch of his killer chocolate-chip brownies to take over there."

"Back to the problem at hand," Kari said. She pointed at Tyler. "Okay, so you didn't drain one of our bank accounts, kudos to you. But you're still a thief by your own admission, and why should we believe you that someone else is also snooping around?"

"Because I'm coming clean."

Kari shrugged. "Could be a desperate attempt to throw us off the scent."

"Darlin'," Tyler said, "I never do anything out of desperation."

"Is he flirting with me?" Kari asked Angela. Then, to Tyler, "Stop flirting with me. That's inappropriate."

"I can't help it," Tyler said. "It's my natural rakish charm."

Angela looked sideways at Kari and raised one eyebrow, a look that seemed to convey a hell of a lot of information. Kari smiled tightly and nodded. A small motion, but Tyler picked up on it. The two women weren't an old married couple, but they'd known each other for years, and apparently had picked up the old-married-couple trick of saying a lot without speaking.

"The rakish charm is probably why no one's killed you yet," Angela said.

He forced himself to make a joke, to smile and flirt as if they weren't all in a hell of a mess. "Glad you still find me charming. I'd like to keep living." She did, didn't she? He hoped that a little too much for his own good.

"Charming and sexy and good company, which makes it hard to be objective. I want to believe you, or at least give you the benefit of the doubt…but I could be letting some not-so-smart bits do my thinking. Still, while all the suspicious incidents started after you arrived, I can't easily connect you to all of them. Things got moved around inside at times I'm pretty sure you were working outside. And Kari trusts you."

"More like, I think you're telling us the truth," Kari said. "Maybe not the whole truth, but the most important parts. I'm not sure I trust you, exactly, but I trust you're on our side at the moment." While Tyler was still processing that, Kari leaned forward and ran her hands, not over Tyler, but around him, as if she were petting the air. "Clear aura, good energy—for what it's worth."

She settled back in her chair, obviously having proven something to her own satisfaction.

Angela rolled her eyes, only a little bit. "For that matter, Isabella likes you."

"At least as reliable a sign of character as his aura," Kari agreed, smiling. Tyler felt curiously honored that he was catching a bit of a running joke between the two women.

"So we'll work with you to catch this would-be thief." Angela clenched her fists as if she were getting ready to punch the mystery thief. "But I'll be keeping a close watch on you. Not sure I should let you out of my sight at all."

From her tone of voice, she was being vehement, not suggestive. But Kari stifled a giggle. About two seconds later, Angela smacked her, laughing herself.

Tyler tried not to let himself get caught in the chuckling. It didn't seem appropriate, not with so much at stake and the accord between them still uneasy. But he couldn't help it. Even though things were still far from all right, coming clean lifted a great weight from his shoulders.

"Well, that was easier than I expected," Angela said when they all stopped laughing. "Although not as fun."

"What?" Tyler stared at her. Something flashed in her dark eyes, and the way the corners of her mouth curled up made his cock stir.

"My plan was to tie you up and sexually torture you until you confessed."

"You...*what?*" No, his cock was doing more than stirring. "Wait, maybe that's...maybe I still have things to confess."

Angela grinned. It was a sexy, confident, wicked grin, and it slammed straight into his groin.

"Hold on," Kari said. "I have a better idea."

They both turned to stare at her. "Better than sexual torture?" Angela asked. "Really?"

"You can hear Minerva only when you're on the verge of orgasm, right?" Kari said.

"*What?*" Tyler said. His brain felt like it had been whiplashed. His cock didn't know what to make of the hard left turn to Crazytown.

"It started the night of the séance," Angela said. "Apparently we *did* raise Minerva…and she ended up possessing me. Not full-time, thankfully," she added hastily. "Ninety-nine-point-nine percent of the time, I'm all me. Cybelline's been trying to get her out of me ever since."

They both seemed so earnest, so sincere.

Tyler imagined they sounded as credible as he did. Which was to say, on very shaky ground where believability was concerned. But he couldn't think why they'd make up such a crazy story (while he could list a dozen plausible reasons why he might have made a fake confession).

Then he remembered a truly unexplained occurrence. "So, Minerva's the one who goosed me that night?"

"Bingo," Kari said.

"Let's say I believe you," he said cautiously, glancing around for hidden cameras. "What happens the other point-one percent of the time? And what does this have to do with orgasms?"

"I can hear Minerva better the closer I get," Angela said. "And I think she's been trying to tell me something. She's been sounding like she's warning me. I thought she was warning me about you."

"We need to find out what Minerva's trying to say," Kari said. "She could give us the clues we need—or maybe she knows outright what's going on." She pointed at Tyler. "So you need to help her—" she pointed at Angela "—hear what Minerva's trying to tell her. By arousing her to the point of orgasm."

Angela actually blushed, a pretty pink tingeing her cheeks, which he found endearing.

Tyler's cock let him know exactly how enthusiastic it was about this plan.

"I think you both might be crazy," he said. "But for you I will fall on that grenade. So to speak."

Chapter 16

*B*eing alone in a bedroom with Tyler should have been impossibly awkward, given that Angela knew he was a crook (their crook, maybe, but still a crook) and that he knew she was occasionally possessed by a voyeuristic ghost.

And for a few minutes, it was. For a few minutes, they both perched on the side of the bed, fully dressed except for their shoes, a few feet apart, and just stared at each other.

Tyler looked as gorgeous as ever. But his blue eyes weren't as roguish and merry as they usually were, and he seemed subdued. Silent.

And neither of them seemed to be able to make the first move.

Which was ironic, considering he might have pulled off his scam and left with them none the wiser if they'd been able to keep their hands off each other in the first place.

Finally she begged, "Say something. Anything."

"I'm sorry, Angela. I'm really, really sorry."

"By anything I meant anything sexy. Or flirty. Or anything that doesn't pertain to crime or ghosts." She forced herself to move closer, put an arm around him. Okay, she didn't have to force herself too much. Tyler was one gorgeous, sexy hunk of maleness, and her body was still all happy and tingly about another chance to tangle up with him. But there was a big difference between a roll in the hay with a guy you trusted, just for the fun of it, and a roll in the hay with a guy you mostly trusted and probably shouldn't, with the explicit aim of luring out a ghost.

"I wanted you the first second I saw you," Tyler said unexpectedly. "Standing on that rickety ladder. Hadn't even seen your face yet and I wanted you."

"You'd said that before." She laughed uneasily. His voice was shredding her common sense and wetting her panties the way it always did. Only, at the moment, she supposed common sense (or at least a desperate and flaky plan that was somehow passing for common sense) told her it was all right to let go. It was her heart that wasn't so sure. "So you're an ass man."

"Yeah, and yours is spectacular, so that was a lot of it. Your ass and your whole body, really." He put his hand on her knee. It seemed casual, but he moved it a little higher, pushing up her skirt, and it felt elemental, like fire and ocean competing to take over her body. "But also that you were up there doing the work yourself. I liked that. You seemed relieved to find a professional to take it over, but meanwhile it needed to be done and you took matters into your own hands."

The way he said the last words made it clear he recognized the double-entendre. She realized she was biting her lip like a teenager and forced herself to stop.

"I wanted you, too," Angela admitted. "At first just because you're a hot guy, but the more we got to know each other, the more I liked you. Liked the way you looked at things. Liked your respect for history. Liked your sense of humor."

He opened his mouth. She thought he was going to apologize again. Something in his eyes, the way he was holding his body, the curve of his mouth.

And she couldn't stand to hear any more apologies or excuses. Not when she was going to use him—and it was using, although they'd both enjoy it—to get Minerva's attention. Not when she desperately wanted to forget, at least for a little while, that he had good reasons to apologize.

So she leaned in and kissed him.

For a second it felt stiff and strange. Then Tyler's lips softened and the kiss turned urgent. When he pulled her onto his lap so she was straddling him, she realized other things had hardened. Her dress hitched up around her hips and she rubbed her silky thong against rough denim. Tyler's hands skimmed down her back to cup her ass, moving her against him.

Blood rushed to Angela's pelvis. Her breath hitched. She'd gone from "I don't know if I can do this" to almost ready to fuck in about three-point-two seconds. Maybe it was because she'd been so shattered when she thought she couldn't trust Tyler and now she thought maybe she could, or because she still had doubts and wanted to snatch what pleasure she could before everything fell apart. Or maybe the insane chemistry between them didn't care whether it was a good idea or not.

She wasn't on the verge of orgasm yet, despite her growing arousal, but she swore she heard Minerva saying *yes*. Too bad she didn't know which option Minerva was affirming. But maybe she'd get clarification later.

She had to remember about Minerva. Had to remember that tonight wasn't just about hot sex—although she supposed it wouldn't work so well if it didn't involve hot sex.

Okay, Minerva, she sent the mental message. *This is your show. If you know who's behind all this, I need you to tell me…*

Tyler's deft hands tugged her dress up and over her head—she was glad she'd already slipped off the big, dangly Turkmen earrings before letting down her hair, because snagging wasn't sexy or romantic.

She wasn't wearing date underwear. Her thong was burgundy satin, but her bra was plain black, because it worked well under the dress. She had about a second to wish she'd found a nicer bra before Tyler unhooked it and she shrugged it away, so she supposed it didn't matter.

"My favorite lingerie is what's lying on the floor," he murmured in a husky voice as he tossed the bra aside. Then he turned his attention to doing absolutely devastating things to her nipples with his tongue and lips. He hadn't shaved, and the hint of five-o'clock rasp added another level of sensation. Angela gasped, arched her back to thrust her breasts forward for more attention as she rode his still-clothed cock. Her breasts ached and her nipples were so tight and swollen it was almost painful, but in a blissful way.

"So hot," Tyler said as he turned his attention from one needy nipple to the other. "You have such perfect nipples. Artwork too beautiful to neglect."

From someone else, it might have been too much, but it was Tyler, with his slightly cracked code about how art objects should be loved and shared with the world.

"You do appreciate art," she gasped.

"Wouldn't do to neglect such beauty." As Tyler spoke, he let his hands continue what his lips had started. She missed the heat of his mouth, but the heat of his voice made up for it. "Someone might steal it from under my nose."

Angela's brain crackled. Minerva tuning in. *Good man,* she heard dimly. *Wait, Minerva…is he a good man, or just good in bed?*

She distinctly heard *good,* but there were more words, ones she couldn't pick up amid the static in her brain.

Plenty of static in her body, too, the fun kind of static, but not enough to bring Minerva in clearly. She didn't want to tell Tyler what she'd heard, not until she was more certain Minerva had vetted him, but both her brain and her body urged more, more, more. Her brain wanted to tune in Minerva and ask questions. Her body just wanted.

On the other hand, it seemed important to let Tyler know the ghost was around. "Minerva's starting to talk."

"Anything of interest?"

"Nothing clear yet." Not a lie, and once she got an answer to her question, she'd fill in as appropriate. "Someone's overdressed for this party," she added, and her voice sounded as smoky and sexy as Minerva's did on the night of the séance when she'd heard the ghost so clearly. She reached for the hem of Tyler's shirt…

…and found herself flipped onto her back, Tyler's weight pinning her down. The hint of rough control made her moan. She wasn't submissive per se, but that didn't mean she couldn't enjoy playing the role sometimes.

"You said you heard Minerva best when you were on the verge of orgasm. So I'm going to keep you there. And that means I stay dressed for now or I might lose control." Tyler's beautiful voice was ragged with need in a way that amped her desire even higher. Somewhere in the distance, she heard or felt Minerva's approval. Or arousal. Or something.

She wanted to say something cocky like "do your worst," but all she could manage was a happy sigh. Her brain melted a little as Tyler kissed his way down her torso. Each kiss made her hotter. Each kiss made the noise in her head louder, but if Minerva was saying anything at the moment, it was just the moans and sighs of a woman enjoying the (indirect) attentions of a very talented man.

Tyler put his lips over her satin-covered clit and suckled. Suckled until her body strained with the need to come.

And then he backed off.

Lather, rinse, repeat, until Angela didn't care anymore about Minerva or mystery thieves or even clearing Tyler, just about release. She was begging and babbling nonsense and she needed, she needed…

She needed to get some information from Minerva, now, before her body decided to let go despite Tyler's best efforts or she developed super-strength and ripped Tyler's clothes so she could have her wicked way with him.

The static resolved into a throaty chuckle. *Good idea, darling. Doubt he'd fight much. Wants you…cares.*

Thanks for stating the obvious, Minerva.

Then she focused on one word. *He cares, Minerva? Does that mean he's telling the truth?*

It was hard to focus when Tyler was doing such delicious things to her. She wanted to let go. Wanted to come. She deserved an orgasm after the lousy couple of days she'd had, dammit.

And she'd get one…or more…soon, she reminded herself.

Yes. Came to steal…stole his heart.

Then who…?

Woman. Trusted. Not Kari, of course. Kari loves you like…better sister than mine. Which Angela thought was admirably clear, for Minerva. *False name…*

And then Tyler moved his lips just a little differently than he had before, and pinched her nipples just a little harder, and the voice in Angela's head changed to a blissful, wordless cry.

Which was pretty much what Angela was doing, too, so she could hardly fault Minerva for it.

When the room stopped spinning and shaking, Angela was alone in her head except for a quiet, contented presence, the mental equivalent of a purring cat.

"Minerva says you're telling us the truth!" she panted, drawing Tyler up into a kiss.

She didn't let him come up for breath for a bit, and when he did, he looked puzzled. "You're trusting me now on a ghost's say-so?" He screwed up his face thoughtfully, then added, "Then again, I guess a ghost would have no reason to lie and I have plenty of reason. Even I would wonder about my story if I didn't know I was telling the truth." It was a convoluted remark, but Angela had no trouble parsing it.

"Oh, and Minerva says the other would-be thief is a woman, but I came before she told me her name. Which is the first time in my life I've ever even thought about complaining about a really mind-blowing orgasm, or at least about the timing."

Tyler beamed a slow, sly smile. "Well then, I guess I just have to get you ramped up again and see if we can get her to tell us more."

He made it sound like a sweet, wicked threat. Angela shivered, her body reacting with heat once again to the sound of his voice.

He started to unzip his jeans.

She reached for a condom.

It didn't take much time for Tyler to undress and latex up, and almost no time for Angela to discard her now drenched thong, but it seemed like it took centuries. Partly Angela was eager to "hear" what else Minerva might know, but, despite a truly epic orgasm (there was a lot to be said for long, slow build-up), Angela wanted Tyler inside her, impure and simple. The ghost could show up or not.

And if Minerva didn't show, well, they'd have an excuse to try again later.

Tyler sank into her slowly. "Want to last…" he said huskily. "Don't know if I can."

His voice danced on her skin, and suddenly she was on fire again. She felt Minerva in her head, muttering *Oh yes… beautiful prick.*

Angela couldn't agree more. She wrapped her legs around Tyler's slim waist, grabbed his ass with both hands, and growled, "Fuck me hard. We'll take our time later."

As if she'd just let him off his leash, Tyler let go, pumping into her hard yet also somehow elegantly, murmuring wonderfully dirty things about how hot and tight and wet she was under his breath. Some of what he said didn't even make sense, but Angela didn't care. His voice worked with his cock, and his toned body, and the way his blue eyes had gone all smoky with lust, and the relief of feeling like she could trust him—or at least mostly trust him, and it was all right for a roguish bad boy to be just a little shady.

Pleasure was building again, hard and fast. She was going to come again and she knew she should hold back, but it was all too fierce and hot, and trying to think about quarterly taxes and that unpleasant incident with the health inspector didn't do much to slow her down.

But she had to try. *Minerva, the name…the name of the other treasure hunter.*

And Minerva answered, *Bugger that. Not the time.*

Which sounded remarkably like what the less sensible parts of Angela were thinking.

Still, this was important, important enough that she deliberately bit her lip to distract herself. It didn't work all that well, probably because she was so turned on she thought about Tyler biting her, which was counterproductive, but there was a second of clarity that let her ask again.

It's… Minerva started to say.

And then *Oh my. Your young man…impressive.*

Tyler's hips snapped faster. Angela instinctively raised her legs even more, thanking Kari for the yoga she'd insisted on teaching Angela. The slight shift in position meant Tyler was hitting her G-spot with every stroke, and it would have taken a stronger woman than Angela to resist that. She began to convulse, clutching Tyler's ass with her hands and Tyler's cock with her inner muscles.

Minerva said something else, or Angela thought she did, but it was lost in the roar of orgasm.

*

"Still no name?" Tyler toyed idly with Angela's dark curls.

She swatted his arm. "No, and it's all your fault. You're just too much fun. I got carried away. And so did Minerva, apparently."

Tyler couldn't help feeling a little smug. He believed in the ghost at this point, especially since Angela and Kari believed so strongly.

Neither of them seemed crazy and he couldn't see the point of his rival setting up a hoax-ghost who wanted to party with you, not make you run screaming from the premises. Therefore, the simplest explanation was that it was true. He'd never met a ghost, but he'd run into enough weird things in old houses that it didn't surprise him.

But what guy could resist knowing he'd managed to get two sensual, strong-willed women so hot and bothered they forgot serious business? Granted, it was freaky as hell if he let himself think too much about the fact that one of the women had been dead for decades. "At least we have more information than we did. And I'm kind of proud I'm that distracting."

Angela sat up abruptly. "Distraction! That's it!"

Tyler tried to think of something clever to say, but his brain was just coming back online after being thoroughly fucked out, so he ended up replying "What?"

"I know how to draw the other thief out. But I'll need your help."

"Of course." Especially if it involves more hot, sweet sex to get Minerva's attention. Or just for the sake of hot sweet sex.

"And Kari's." Angela grinned and added ominously. "And Adelle's."

*

Angela called Kari, who came to the cottage from the spa and gratefully accepted the cup of coffee Angela handed her.

Angela had thrown on a silky, bright red kimono, belted securely around her waist. Her hair was a flat-out mess and her mascara was smudged, and she was the sexiest damn thing Tyler had ever seen. It wasn't just that she had that glorious après-sex look about her. It was that she was utterly unselfconscious about it. He'd been with women who'd jumped right out of bed to fix their hair and makeup and, God forbid, perfume themselves in places that just shouldn't smell like flowers.

Granted, once they'd spent a little time in the afterglow, Angela had gone into efficiency mode, getting ahold of Kari and brewing coffee and pacing the few steps back and forth in the tiny outbuilding she and Kari called home. She'd found a notebook and pen, scribbled down what she could remember Minerva saying in case phrasing was important, muttering something about typing it up when they were done conferring. She wouldn't tell him anything until Kari got here.

And all that was sexy, too. He'd meant what he'd said about his first reaction to her—he had been impressed that the owner of a hotel would be up on a ladder because the work simply had to be done and there was no one else around to do it.

She and Kari had built this place from the ground up—not the house, obviously, but the business. She was smart, efficient, funny, gorgeous…

Kari interrupted his train of thought.

"So," she said with a waggle of her eyebrows, "how was the threesome?"

"I assume you're asking about whether we got info from Minerva, not positions and number of orgasms," Angela said. "No, don't sit on that end of the sofa—" she directed that last part at Tyler "—the arm's broken and you'll fall off and break something. I'm used to it."

Kari sank onto a floor pillow into a perfect lotus position, her back ramrod yet comfortably straight. "I always want the juicy deets," she said, "but in this case, yes, Minerva. Clues. Spill."

"We didn't get a name," Angela said, tucking her feet under her so she leaned away from the Sofa Arm of Doom, "although I got the sense Minerva knows. She got a little, um, distracted toward the end." She blushed a little, her cheeks turning the same color as her chest, visible in the vee of her robe.

He'd caused that orgasmic flush, and he felt damn smug about it.

Angela glanced at her notebook. "'Woman,'" she quoted. "'Trusted.' But not you, Kari, which made me laugh—on the inside, because I was pleasantly distracted. Then she said, and I think I have this right, 'Fake name.' Or maybe 'false name.'"

"A woman," Kari mused. "With a pseudonym. What does 'trusted' mean?"

"I'm thinking someone we know and trust," Angela said. "Since it's someone who has easy access to Angelika, there's Stella and the rest of the housekeeping staff, and everyone else, although I can't imagine any of them doing this. Even the guys, I suppose, if they're working with a woman. Or it could be someone we know and like in town." She sucked on the end of her pen as she thought, which was simultaneously silly-looking and oddly erotic because it drew attention to her full mouth and things she could do with it. While she could be an expert tease in the right mood, she was concentrating hard enough on the problem at hand she probably wasn't doing it deliberately.

He gulped some coffee to get his mind out of the gutter, then sputtered. Smooth move. His mind was still in the gutter because the pen was still absently moving in and out of her mouth, only now he had a burned tongue as well as a distraction issue.

"What about the reporter?" Tyler asked.

"Satya, looking for a bigger story?" Angela said. "Could be." She jotted down the name.

Thankfully she didn't put the pen back in her mouth, instead standing up to refill her coffee.

"But she has such a centered aura," Kari said. "Not to mention she checked out a couple of days ago."

"I don't know anything about auras," Tyler said, "but I know a fair number of people who routinely hide who or what they are. You're both very savvy and smart, and I don't think you'd be easily swindled. But there are professionals out there who can fool their own mothers."

"I'm not ruling out anyone except Kari at this point," Angela said. She sat back down, sipped some coffee, then set the cup on the floor within easy reach.

"What about Cybelline, in that case?" Kari asked. "I don't want to think so because she's our friend, but…"

Angela wrinkled up her face as she thought. "Not Cybelline," she finally concluded, "and not just because I like her. The timing's not right. She's been in town for six months, so why wouldn't she have moved before now if she was plotting something?"

Kari smiled over her coffee cup, visibly relieved. "There's also Margaret. Just because we haven't seen much of her doesn't mean she can't be involved."

"Her husband could be snooping around on her behalf," Angela said, jotting the name onto her list. "He does ask a lot of questions about Angelika. Just because Minerva said it's a woman doesn't mean she can't be working with someone."

"Margaret's pretty well known to also be a thief," Kari said. "But I suppose writing best-selling mysteries could teach you not to get caught."

"I'd wondered about Barb," Tyler said, "but she left before some of the stuff happened." He tugged his phone from the pocket of his jeans and began rapidly typing with his thumbs.

"Who are you texting?" Kari asked, leaning forward.

"I have a friend, Ben—I saw him yesterday in San Francisco—he…" Tyler paused, not looking up from his phone, but stilling his hands. "He's good at looking into people's backgrounds. I had some suspicions about someone, but now that's not an option, so I'm giving him these other names—"

"Suspicions about whom?" Angela asked, and he heard a tight note in her voice.

Crap.

Now he locked his gaze to hers, even though he didn't want to. "I looked through your employee records, and I noticed that Franklin had changed his name, and in my line of work, that's a red flag."

"You went through our employee records?" Angela, who'd seemed to be in motion since they'd gotten out of bed (which was exhausting to him, because as an admittedly typical guy, he really wanted a nap), was suddenly and completely still.

He dropped his head to the back of the sofa. It wasn't as cushioned as he'd expected. Ow. "I did. I wanted to figure out who was horning in on my job—and also to protect you if I could."

"How did you—never mind," Angela said. "You know, you could've just asked."

"Because, Franklin, of all people?" Kari almost sputtered.

"Besides, we know about the name change—he told us all about it," Angela said. "His mother loved Charlie Parker and so she named him Bird, and let's face it, 'Bird' fits a man who looks like Michael Clarke Duncan not at all. So he legally switched to his middle name, Franklin."

"Not 'Frank,'" Kari added. "Never 'Frank.'" She shuddered as if the very idea offended her.

"And not a woman—clearly not ever a woman—so he's not our perp," Tyler said. "That's partly why I'm contacting Ben. He can dig deeper on anyone. What's Stella's last name?"

After they finished giving him the details they needed, Angela shook her head. "I can't believe any of these people are involved. I know I should be more cynical and less trusting, but…"

Tyler captured her hand in his. "No," he said. "Don't ever let yourself get cynical. That's not who you are."

She managed a small smile. "Thanks."

"I'm glad you know someone who might be able to help," Kari said, "but I don't like the idea of it being our only option. What else can we do?"

"We need to be proactive," Angela agreed. "The first question is, what's the treasure? Tyler?"

He squeezed her hand as he shook his head. "I'm baffled. Before I got here, I figured it would be something obvious that you didn't know was worth anything. But not only haven't I found anything, I know you've got a good eye and would have recognized anything obvious, or even something that wasn't obvious. Could it be hidden somewhere?"

"We've never fully gone through the attic, and there are still boxes of stuff we took out of the bathhouses that we shoved in a storage room after we built the spa," Angela said. "We tried to do a cursory look through things, but we could easily have missed something small. Most of what we have found is Victoriana or later, and that doesn't bring in much. Even Minerva's collection of naughty things from around the world didn't have anything appreciably valuable in it, except as curiosities."

"I can't remember," Kari said, "who in the article said there was a treasure?"

"The source was described as 'multiple sources around town,'" Tyler said, "and before you ask, I tried to sweet-talk the writer with no success. I don't know if she was practicing in case she ever really needs to protect a source or she was flailing because she'd taken lousy notes."

"Adelle was one of those sources, but she says she doesn't know what it is, just that it's supposedly here, that Minerva dropped hints about it. And when the reporter asked me, I just laughed and said something about the place being full of treasures. As in bits of history. I don't think that sank in, though. Kari and I had a good laugh about it when the article came out, because she obviously wanted to make the story sound juicier. We hadn't even found the Dadaist sculpture yet, and that's the most valuable thing we've unearthed so far." Angela squinted her mascara-smudged eyes. "Do you think the other treasure-hunter knows what it is?"

"No idea," Tyler said, "but I would guess not, because if they did, they'd either have already taken it or would be making a more concise attempt. Right now, we both seem to be flailing."

"Then why don't we give the other person something to come after?" Angela asked.

"You mean, bait the trap?" Tyler was impressed.

"I like it!" Kari said.

"Exactly," Angela answered Tyler as she leaned over to return Kari's fist-bump. She flashed her breast when she did, and Tyler found himself thinking about round two of Ask Minerva.

She continued. "We put out some object on display and announce that we found something interesting in the attic. The local weekly would probably run a couple of paragraphs about it—that's the joy of small-town newspapers."

"And once Adelle gets wind of it, she'll tell anyone within earshot," Kari added.

"And then," Tyler said, smiling, "we sit back and wait for the perp to pop."

Chapter 18

She was just too irresistible.

Tyler let himself out of the cottage, pulling the door shut slowly behind him because he'd already learned if you moved it too fast, it let out a squeal that prompted Isabella to howl. He made a mental note to hit the hinges with WD-40 when he got back to the hotel.

Right now, though, it was 6 a.m. and the sun was pinkening the sky. Looked like it would be another clear day, and he shivered in the chill. "Summer" on the Northern California coast….

He hadn't wanted to leave Angela's warm bed—or, more precisely, Angela's warm body. When she'd asked him to spend the night, he hadn't been able to resist her charms. But now he wanted to swing back to Adelle's, shower, and change into fresh clothes before starting another day of work. He still had Bathhouse Five to finish up.

Honest work. Huh. He'd never expected it to come to this.

How things might shake out after they figured out who was after the treasure was anyone's guess. He refused to think about it right now.

Except he was going to leave a change of clothes in his truck and see if it was okay to use the shower room in the spa occasionally.

He entered the building just as stealthily as he'd left the cottage, even remembering to skip the squeaky stair on the way up to his room, but apparently Adelle had bionic hearing, because he was just easing his key into the lock when her voice came from right behind him: "Well, well, well, had a late night, did we?"

A lesser man might have screamed like a teenage girl at a pop concert. He managed to keep his reaction to just jumping and dropping his key.

"Good morning, Adelle," he said, turning to face her. "I hope I didn't wake you."

"Pfff." She waved a hand dismissively. She was already dressed in one of her many matching track suits, this one with a sparkly rose over her left breast, and she wore lipstick that matched the hot pink of the rose. And, in fact, she reeked like she'd been hit with a rose-scented fire hose. How had he not smelled her sneaking up behind him?

"I suspect I got more sleep than you did," she went on, just as he crouched to pick up his key. He banged his head on the doorknob, bit back a curse, and stood to unlock the door. She'd said it in such a way that made it clear she knew what he'd been up to, and probably with whom.

Which meant that rumor would start floating around town pretty damn quickly.

He wasn't sure how Angela would feel about that, so he dove right into the story they'd been planning to tell Adelle anyway.

"We had a lot of excitement at the hotel yesterday, so it was easier to catch a few hours' sleep there," he said, opening the door.

"Oh?" If Adelle had dog ears, they would have just pricked up.

"Did you ever hear about there being a treasure at Angelika?" he asked, pretending he didn't already know.

"Oh, yes." The tiny woman nodded. "Everyone in town knows about that. I remember Minerva talking about it when I was younger. She never said what it was, though." Her sketched-in eyebrows arched. "Did you find it?" she breathed.

"We're pretty sure we did," Tyler said. "You know Minerva was a world traveler, right? Well, we were going through things in the attic, and we found an Egyptian urn wrapped up in a box of 1970s sheets. We need to have an expert confirm it, but Angela's parents are archeologists and they spent a few years in Egypt when she was growing up, and she's pretty sure it's Eighteenth Dynasty—from around 1500 BCE."

In fact, it was a replica urn that Angela herself had bought with her allowance years ago. It had been in her bedroom; she'd had a bunch of ostrich feathers in it.

They'd put one of those feathers to good use last night....

"Goodness," Adelle breathed, her hand fluttering over the sparkly rose on her breast. "That's just astonishing."

"Isn't it, though?" Tyler said, finally unlocking his door "Sorry, but I need to shower and change and get back to the hotel."

"Of course," Adelle said. As he closed the door, she called, "Tell Angela I hope she's having a good time! Lord knows with how hard that woman works, she needs a good fucking once in a while."

*

That night, Angela and Kari met Cybelline at MacGowan's again, to try and make up for their last aborted girls' night.

"By the way," Cybelline said, tilting her half-full pint glass of beer at Angela, "I've noticed that you've stopped bugging me about exorcising Minerva. What gives, girl?"

Angela gave a valiant effort but was unable to stop the grin that insisted on spreading across her face. Because thoughts of Minerva now immediately led to thoughts of Tyler helping her channel Minerva...

"Well, Tyler and I are finding her kinda useful..."

Cybelline had been sitting sideways on the booth bench, her legs, clad in Kelly green and black striped tights under a short denim skirt, stretched out in front of her. (Tonight's wig matched the green in the tights and was styled in a Louise Brooks bob. It wasn't her best look.) Now she swung her feet down and faced them. "You and...*what*? I mean, Angela, you sly dog! Schtupping the help!" She tapped Angela's martini glass with her pint glass. "Spill. Tell all. I'm not getting any right now so I have to live vicariously through you."

"But you don't bat for our team," Kari protested. "Wait. Is that the metaphor I want?" She frowned at her nearly empty wine glass.

"No, I don't, but that doesn't mean I don't want juicy details," Cybelline said. "You don't have to tell me about his penis," she added to Angela.

"Gosh, thanks," Angela retorted, feeling the heat in her cheeks. But she'd had two martinis and Cybelline was a friend, and they still needed to keep spreading the treasure rumor, so why not?

"It started after the last time we had drinks," she said. "Remember when we got called back because the dishwasher exploded? Tyler's clothes got all wet when he was cleaning up, so I offered to dry them, and well, the dryer puts out some really nice vibrations."

Kari hid her face in her hands. "I'm going to have that mental picture in my head every single time I do laundry now, dammit."

"What does this have to do with Minerva?" Cybelline asked.

"Right, well, let me back up for a sec," Angela said. "Some weird stuff has been going on at the hotel, and we figured out that someone's trying to find a fabled treasure that Minerva hid somewhere. Minerva seems to know who it is, but she can only talk to me when I'm, uh—" She leaned in and lowered her voice, even though the ambient music and conversation in the bar meant nobody else would hear her unless she shouted "—on the verge of orgasm. So Tyler's been helping with that."

Cybelline blinked behind her green cat's-eye glasses, several shades darker than the brilliant wig. "That's…quite a story. Hidden treasure? I've heard rumors about that. Have you found it? What is it?"

Angela, Kari, and Tyler had agreed to keep the detail that the urn was fake between the three of them. Not that they didn't trust Franklin or Cyb or any number of other people, but the more people who knew, the more chances someone would accidentally let it slip.

"We actually did, last night!" Kari said excitedly. "We started looking for it because of everything that's been going on, and we found it! It's an Egyptian urn that Minerva brought back from her travels there." She went on to relay the story of the hideous 1970s sheets.

"Thank God we didn't take the whole box to Goodwill without looking through it," Angela added. "Can you imagine? I never would have forgiven myself."

Cybelline took a sip of her beer, set the glass down. "Are you sure it's authentic?"

"Pretty sure," Angela said. "My parents will be in San Francisco soon, so I'm going to have them look at it. If they agree it looks legit, I'll have it formally appraised."

"That's tremendous," Cybelline said. "I'm so happy for you. And it's Egyptian, and you've spent time there, so that might explain why Minerva attached herself to you. When can I see it?"

Angela thought fast. The fewer people who saw the "treasure," the fewer the chances someone would spot it as a fake. "We won't be displaying it or anything until my parents have a look. But I'm sure we can arrange a time for you to see it."

"Is it a funerary urn?" Cybelline asked eagerly. "Because maybe I could do another séance and…"

"No!" Angela and Kari exclaimed simultaneously.

"You've seen *The Mummy*, right?" Kari added. "Bad enough Angela has a Victorian free-love advocate in her head. She's not getting an amorous ancient Egyptian priest after her, too."

*

Tyler spooned around Angela, enjoying the warmth of her body. She'd been adorably tipsy when she and Kari had arrived back at Angelika after an evening out, so he'd stayed out of her way as she stumbled around the cottage readying herself for bed, then slipped into bed with her.

He wasn't surprised that she fell asleep almost immediately. He didn't begrudge her that, and lying in the dark listening to her breathe was pretty awesome.

Shit. He had it bad, didn't he?

So it was with great reluctance that he eased away from Angela—who responded by rolling onto her stomach, one arm flopping off the edge of the bed—and picked up his phone, shielding it with his body so the light wouldn't disturb her (although he suspected nothing short of a major earthquake would do that).

Earlier that night, he'd received an e-mail, sent to one of his many private accounts…the one the blackmailer knew. The one that, by the very fact that the blackmailer knew it, meant the guy almost definitely had enough dirt on Tyler to make life very difficult for him…. Or he could be a she, if the thief and the blackmailer were one and the same. And they probably were, since the blackmailer also seemed to be after the so-called treasure.

I know the urn is in the house, the e-mail read. *Get it and deliver it tonight. San Sebastian H.S., locker 142, combo 18-26-3.*

On the plus side, it meant they'd smoked out the thief.

On the negative side, the thief had involved Tyler rather than coming for the treasure him- or herself.

Tyler lay on his back in the dark, listening to Angela's breathing and running through the options in his mind—again.

He'd told her as much of the truth as he'd dared to—and it really was most of the truth. Even now, he still didn't want to tell her about the black-mailer, didn't want to potentially expose her to the blackmailer's threats.

Bad enough for him to be exposed, but at least he'd actually done the crimes. He'd hate for Angela's reputation to be blackened just because she was sleeping with him.

He had to deliver the urn, obviously. Then stake out the school and wait to see who opened locker number 142.

What was the worst that could happen? The urn had no value. The thief would have to give up—clearly if Angela and Kari couldn't find the treasure, then the treasure wasn't easy to find…if it existed at all. Tyler knew from experience that there was a point where you gave up on a job, when the time and effort cost more than the reward.

He would've given up on this job long ago if it hadn't been for the threats to rat him out. But he had to at least play along.

He hadn't wanted to take the urn while Angela and Kari were out with Cybelline, because one of them might have gone into the hotel after they came home and discovered the urn already gone. He'd had to wait until now.

He suppressed a sigh and eased out of the bed. Dressing in the dark was second nature for him.

He'd get a backpack out of his truck, get the urn, deliver it, and be back before Angela woke up. And then he'd figure out about staking out the area if he didn't see the guilty party before he had to leave.

It was as solid a plan as he could come up with under the circumstances.

*

Angela woke from a bizarre dream involving buying mint chocolate chip ice cream to appease the Egyptian lion goddess Sekhmet. As she rolled from her stomach to her right side, she made two mental notes.

One: Tell Tyler about the dream when he woke up; he was one of the few people she knew who weren't her parents or their colleagues who'd appreciate the full absurdity. Two: Jump Tyler after telling him about the wacky dream, since they hadn't had a chance when she got home.

In the morning, though. Technically, 4:32 a.m. *was* morning, but it was a little early to wake Tyler up for romping.

She blinked sleepily. Her view of the clock should have been obstructed by a sleeping hunk, and it wasn't. Must have gone to the bathroom.

Which come to think of it, sounded like a good idea. She swung out of bed and padded toward the bathroom in the dark; maybe she could steal a quick kiss as he exited and she entered.

Only Tyler wasn't in the bathroom. Angela succumbed to the need to pee, wondering where he was. Certainly there was no need for concern, but there were only so many places a guy could hide in the cottage and after she finished, a quick glance told her he wasn't in the tiny common room that served as living room, dining room, and kitchen.

And while it was remotely possible he'd stumbled into Kari's room by mistake after using the bathroom, she was the one who'd been drinking, not Tyler, so it didn't seem likely. Plus she hadn't heard Kari scream.

Maybe he'd heard a noise and stepped outside to play hero—hopefully with more success or at least less mud and low comedy than she'd met with on her attempt. Yeah, that was probably it. He was checking out something on the grounds even now.

It peeved her slightly that he'd decided to check things out on his own rather than wake her. It was, after all, *her* hotel, and she was no shrinking violet. They should do it as a team.

The window in the bedroom, the one that didn't open because the frame was warped, faced the hotel. Angela glanced out, not that she expected to see much in the dark.

And saw Tyler sneaking into the back door of Angelika, carrying a backpack.

Chapter 19

Angela fumbled on a pair of yoga pants and the nearest T-shirt within reach, then eased open the cottage door. She narrowed her eyes. Tyler had hit the hinges with WD-40 earlier that day to deal with the squeak she and Kari had thought was permanent.

At the time, she'd though the gesture sweet. Now, it fell into the realm of suspicious.

There had to be a good explanation. Maybe he couldn't sleep and was just getting a head start on some work, or was hungry and wanted to snag some leftover brownies (ye gods, Franklin's double-dark-chocolate brownies were phenomenal…damn, now *she* was hungry).

She sucked in a breath as her bare feet hit the cold, dewy grass of the garden. Her skin goosepimpled and her nipples perked up, just as they had the last time she'd done this late-night excursion.

Except this time, she didn't feel the need to channel a Navy Seal. This time, she stomped right up to the door.

Thankfully it wasn't locked. It would've been embarrassing (even if nobody else knew) to have to go back to the cottage to get the key she'd forgotten.

She walked down the back hall in the multicolored, faceted glow of a few Tiffany-style table lamps—they always left a few on throughout the lower floor on the off chance an insomniac guest came down to snag a book out of the library or whatever—and continued to try and convince herself she was overreacting, that it was all innocent and she and Tyler would have a good laugh about it when…

Then she reached the parlor entrance and nearly ran into Tyler, and the backpack in his hand now bulged, and over his shoulder she saw the urn was gone, and her stomach plummeted past her knees to hit the lovingly polished hardwood floor.

Anger, disappointment, betrayal all gathered in her voice as she hissed, "Tyler, what the hell? I *trusted* you."

She hoped the quaver in her voice would pass as fury. It *was* mostly fury, but hurt was definitely a component—hurt and a desperate hope that it wasn't what it appeared: that after spinning a wild yarn about a rival treasure-hunter to win her trust and Kari's (and Minerva's, for that matter), he was making off with the urn because…

Because why? He knew it was fake. Did he figure if it disappeared, it would make the story about the other thief more believable?

Didn't matter. If he was making off with the urn, she'd expect him to either turn on the charm or try to get away once he was caught. Instead, he gently tugged her into the parlor, then slid the pocket doors shut. He set the backpack on an Eastlake chair (one she'd rescued from a garage sale and recovered), turned on a lamp, and faced her.

"I probably should have told you before now, but I wanted to keep you out of harm's way." His husky whisper didn't play music on her nerve endings the way it usually did, and that made her feel a little better. If he wasn't trying to distract her with lust, he might just be telling the truth.

"What the hell?" seemed like an appropriate response. He sounded sincere and earnest while making no actual sense. "Start talking."

"I can do you one better: I have visual aids."

Any other time, Angela would have made a joke about visual aids. Even without any specific erotic images attached to it, it sounded suggestive, at least coming from Tyler. But there was no playfulness in his voice now and a tight hint of anxiousness she hadn't heard even when he was confessing his dubious profession to her and Kari.

Which could just mean he was really good at deception, even better than she already figured he'd have to be in his line of "work." But he knew perfectly well the "ancient Egyptian treasure" was a good reproduction and while there were nice pieces in the hotel, she couldn't think of any that would be worth the risk of stealing when it would be so obvious who perpetrated the theft.

That practical note, more than her desire to trust him—and face it, she did want to trust him, even standing in the parlor in ratty clothes staring at him obviously filching something from her beloved hotel—kept her from going postal on his thieving ass and let her say, "Sure, let's see these visual aids. They'd better be good. Start with the backpack; I want to see just how much you were making off with."

She even sounded calm when she said it. She was proud of that.

Tyler unzipped the backpack and pulled out a single object wrapped in towels. Not her towels, at least, she noted, and wondered why that mattered to her. Carefully, he unwrapped the towel-mummy and revealed the urn. She could see there was nothing else in the backpack.

"You were stealing something you already knew was a fake? Did I actually and truly fuck your brains out?"

He smiled, though she couldn't help noticing it didn't reach his eyes. "We only cuddled last night, remember. Which was sweet, but unfortunately, I don't even have brain-melting sex as an explanation."

While she was still fuming silently and trying to figure out what questions to ask next, he extricated his phone from his pocket, pulled something up on the screen, and handed it to her.

When she read the e-mail, things began to make more sense, though she hesitated to say anything until her still sleepy thought processes caught up and she was sure of what she'd just read. "You're a genius. A warped genius, but a genius. How did you manage to make contact with the other thief? Did you figure out who it was but didn't want to tell me until you got confirmation?"

Tyler shook his head. "That's the part I should have told you before. She or he found *me*. At least I assume it's the same person. Angela, someone's been blackmailing me, starting the night of the séance, making some pretty dire threats about exposing me, getting the police involved. It's someone who knows a lot about my past, what I've done, right down to what pieces I've liberated and where I did it."

He ran a hand through his hair. "It almost has to be the other thief or someone collaborating with her. If only because otherwise, we have two unknown criminals involved, and that's just too unlikely to handle. I have to make this drop…but hopefully I'll be able to spot our bad guy—girl—whatever—in the process."

Angela stopped in her tracks. She caught herself wringing her hands like a character in one of the Victorian thrillers in Minerva's library. Since she was doing so because it was preferable to wringing someone's neck, either Tyler's or ideally the real villain's, she might have to rethink those simpering Victorian heroines. "What else have you been keeping from me?"

Tyler sighed. "Nothing, I swear. I had selfish motives for not telling you about my treasure-hunting business at first, but I was only keeping this from you for your own good."

"Right." She added a few extra syllables to the word. He might even be telling the truth from his point of view, but it sounded fishy.

"No, I mean it. I'm serious, Angela. You've worked your ass off to make Angelika a success, and you're liked and respected in this community. And it's your home and I know that means everything to you. I wanted to keep you as far from the blackmailer as possible, because I didn't want to give her any reason to drag your name through the mud along with mine.

"I didn't want to give her any ammunition to destroy everything you've built here. It's too important. *You're* too important."

Oh. When he said it like that…

She pulled herself together and insisted, "You still should have told me."

"Remember, the first time I saw you was on that ladder," Tyler said, and it seemed nonsensical until she saw where he was going. She didn't especially like it, but from a protective-male point of view, it made sense. "When you see something that needs doing, you do it," he elaborated. "I love that about you when it's a home improvement project or figuring out new software, but when it comes to fixing your reputation—or Angelika's—it's dicier."

"You're the one she's after, not me," Angela argued. "There's nothing the blackmailer could tell the police about me that couldn't be covered by 'I checked Tyler's references; when was the last time you did that much for someone you boinked?' And I'd have figured out a way to help." It sounded logical.

"You're right, but I just didn't want to take the chance. I didn't want someone like that to get anywhere you." He managed to smile, but it was clearly forced. "Hell, I don't want someone like that anywhere near *me*, but I've accepted certain risks thanks to choosing to live partly outside the law. You didn't. For what it's worth, I wish I could have told you sooner. Having a Greek goddess on my side is bound to come in handy."

He'd been sounding serious, befitting the occasion, but with the last sentence, his voice slid over her skin like the silk of her favorite bathrobe.

She couldn't maintain the distance between them anymore and took the few steps necessary to close the distance between them. She wrapped her arms around his neck, realizing she no longer had any desire to wring it.

He ran his hands down her back, caressing her through the cotton shirt, giving her butt a playful squeeze. "Unfortunately I need to get my ass—and that piece of pretty junk—over to the high school before the staff starts showing up."

It felt good touching and being touched, but after a second Angela slipped away. "Just give me time to get really dressed and grab shoes. Especially shoes."

"I don't think that's a good idea." Tyler stood. "Coming along, that is, not getting dressed. Though I'm biased toward you naked."

"Nice try." She put a hand on his chest, allowed herself to be briefly distracted by the play of hard muscles. "Tyler, I have to ask," she said, and felt the mood in the room grow serious again. "Is there anything—*anything*—else you're keeping from me?"

He took her hand, brought it to his lips, pressed a kiss on her fingers. "I swear to you, no. That was it. The last secret."

She curled her fingers around his. "Then we're a team now. This affects both of us, so we're doing it together. You can argue with me all you want, but I'm still going with you."

Tyler opened his mouth, then laughed under his breath. "All right. Another pair of eyes won't hurt. And I always wanted a getaway driver. Just never wanted to be in a situation where I needed one."

"Then I'll see if I can find my Bonnie and Clyde beret."

*

At that hour, the high school was deserted, not even a lone car in the lot to hint at the presence of a janitor.

Though it would just be Tyler's luck if the janitor lived nearby and walked to work.

Neither Tyler nor Angela had ever had reason to visit San Sebastian High School, although at various times they'd both driven by it. In the dim, pre-dawn light, it showed itself as expected: a fairly standard campus for a small-town Northern California school with a scattering of red-roofed, one-story cement buildings surrounding an inner courtyard, and playing fields out to the back.

"Most California schools have the lockers on the outside of the buildings," Angela had told him on the way over. "Think covered walkways, and you enter the classrooms from the outside doors between the lockers."

"It's a good thing I don't have to go into a building, because I'm sure they have an alarm system."

"The outside gate's locked." Angela's voice now held a note of well-controlled concern as they pulled up across the street and looked at the high, white-painted wrought-iron fence. The larger gate for vehicles had a code system, although it probably stayed open during the day—or so it looked when they first cruised by—but there was also a pedestrian gate with a standard deadbolt.

"Professional acquirer of forgotten antiquities, remember?" Tyler opened the glove box and grabbed a small, innocuous-looking hard plastic case, which had originally held a first-aid kit. Now he opened it to reveal a set of lock picks and other handy tools of his trade.

Which, to his astonishment and delight, Angela recognized. "Occasionally my parents had to get somewhere other people didn't want them to be," was her only explanation.

He made a mental note to ask more questions later. Weren't her parents archeologists? Indiana Jones and Lara Croft to the contrary, most archeologists didn't use lock picks as standard tools.

But right now he didn't want to take the time to ask. He slipped out of the truck and headed across the street. He picked the lock and opened the gate with a little flourish and a bow in Angela's direction. (Hey, he wasn't above showing off for a pretty woman.)

Once she got his signal, Angela, who'd left the truck running, moved it down the street a bit, between streetlights. The world was quiet at this hour, but no point in making it obvious someone was loitering outside the school.

Emergency lights dimly illuminated the school grounds, and judging by the smell, the grass had been cut recently. Tyler slipped from shadow to shadow, looking for banks of lockers.

Which were located in the middle of the cluster of buildings, where they'd be invisible from the street. And locker 142 was way, way in the back.

Damn blackmailer had thought it through way too well. Unless he could come up with an excuse to skulk around school grounds without looking like a pervert or a potential mad gunman, he'd be hard pressed to spot who was carrying off the ersatz prize from locker 142. Even Angela or Kari would have to have a good excuse to be there.

And if the blackmailer had hired some kid to deliver it from there, they were royally screwed. How could they pick out one teenager with a backpack among several hundred?

With a shrug, he unlocked the locker, opened his backpack, and transferred the towel-swathed urn into the locker. He eased the metal door shut, twirled the combination lock, and made his way back to the gate.

Then he was down the street and back in the truck with Angela, breathing in the sweet, warm scent of her.

"Everything go okay?" she asked. When he nodded, she grabbed the front of his shirt and pulled him in for a kiss. "Good," she said when she released him. "Because the kids will start arriving at seven, and I need to get back to Angelika, wake Kari up—which is never easy—and set up a schedule for keeping an eye on the school. Today and tomorrow we're getting new guests in, so it's going to be craaaazy."

That was Angela, he mused. Even in the face of blackmail and thievery, she was organized and efficient.

*

Angela had trouble sitting still. She jiggled one leg, then the other; she tapped her pen on the blotter; she stood and paced through the tiny office. Isabella looked up hopefully the first time—walkies?—but had finally given up and now just sighed every time Angela rose.

First, they'd spent a day staking out the school with whatever excuse they could come up with: jogging, walking Isabella (no wonder she was so hopeful), driving by in their various vehicles.

They'd known it would be an exercise in futility, but at least they'd been doing *something*, unlike yesterday and today.

Oh, she still had a lot of *something* to do, what with the guest changeovers and the fact that she'd been so distracted with Tyler and Minerva and urn-napping and everything that she'd gotten behind on work.

But she was antsy and on edge. They all were. Yesterday they'd been anxious, waiting for some contact from the blackmailing thief chick. The silence meant…what? That she'd left town with the faux urn? That she'd figured out it was a fake and given up? That she was contacting Interpol? (Was that who she'd contact about Tyler? Angela had no earthly idea.)

And today was no different. Okay, maybe they were marginally more relaxed—although Angela could also ascribe that to the fact that she'd had an almost normal night's sleep last night. Tyler had offered to stay away, commenting that she needed to recharge, and she'd appreciated that, because he was right.

She felt rested, and she felt grateful that he'd not only understood, but suggested it.

Which meant that now, when he walked into the office, sexy and gorgeous in his usual work attire of tight faded jeans and fitted T-shirt, and propped his hip on the desk and said "Afternoon, Boss Lady," her body responded.

She stood and stepped into his arms, pressed her body against his and kissed him. Threaded her fingers through his hair and drew him into that kiss, making it as clear as possible what her intentions were.

When they drew apart, they were both panting.

"Wow," Tyler said, "if that's what I get just for walking in the door, I can't wait to see how you react to some good news."

Angela froze. "The thief?"

He shook his head, grinning. "Better. You now have a fully functional Bathhouse Five."

Okay, that *was* better, given that Bathhouse Five was the only really big one and some guests really liked the group atmosphere.

"You win," she said, returning his grin with a coy smile. She walked her fingers down his chest. "I promise to reward you in full…but later, when we have more privacy and horizontal surfaces."

"The door locks and the floor is horizontal," he pointed out, taking her hand and doing something amazing with his tongue on the inside of her wrist, so amazing that her clit was already clamoring to join in the fun. She couldn't stop the soft moan from escaping her lips.

…man's…got a point…

"Yes, yes he does," she said.

That made Tyler stop. "What?"

"Minerva putting in her two cents—sorry," she said.

"Did she say anything interesting?" He threaded his fingers with hers, but slid his other hand slowly down her back to rest on the curve of her ass.

"No, but I didn't ask her anything, either. I was… distracted. But we probably should ask her if she'll give us any more info about the thief. Even if she doesn't have a name, she might be able to give us a description."

"So maybe you should ask her…" Tyler eased her hair back and nuzzled her neck.

She was seriously considering taking him up on the suggestion, because dammit, she wanted to be naked against his nakedness, when the phone rang.

Of course.

She eased away from him as she tapped the button on her earpiece. "Angelika Boutique Hotel and Spa, what can I do for you?"

Tyler looked rueful, but nodded in understanding. "Tonight," he mouthed, and left.

Twenty minutes later he returned, set something on her desk, kissed the top of her head, and left again.

A sandwich—looked to be her favorite, veggies and Swiss and avocado on a yummy locally made multigrain—and a note scribbled on the napkin: *Franklin said you skipped lunch. You need to keep your strength up for tonight…*

Angela smiled, took a big bite, and wondered if she'd ever be able to eat this kind of sandwich again without getting horny.

*

Naked, desperate, and teased. Angela thought she might go mad, if it hadn't been her idea in the first place. Or maybe that made it worse.

Kari was doing paperwork at the spa to give them alone time. She and Tyler had taken their time undressing each other, playing. But now…now she lay helplessly prone on her bed, her wrists pinned above her head in one of Tyler's capable hands.

His other hand had done a delightful, if frustratingly languid, exploration of her body. Now he wielded a vibrator with wicked efficiency, letting it hum against her mound but not touching her clit, so the vibrations were too muted to send her over the edge.

And because he knelt between her spread legs, she couldn't close her thighs, rub against anything…

"You're so beautiful when you get close," Tyler murmured in that sex god voice of his. "Your whole body tenses up like it's bracing for impact, and your eyes…you get this amazed expression like you've just seen the most glorious thing in the world…"

Angela's abs fluttered, a first sign of impending orgasm. Tyler's voice was so arousing to her that she imagined he could just talk to her until she came, no touching needed.

Now *that* would be glorious. Glorious torture…

He sensed her need, pulled the vibrator away. She whimpered, but remembered what she needed to do.

Dammit, Minerva, where are you? I can't take much more of this.

She heard the sizzle that always preceded Minerva's entrance. Then, *Oh dear…close…*

Yes, I know I'm close! Angela didn't know whether to laugh or cry.

"I wonder how long I could keep you on edge like this," Tyler continued, touching her again with the vibrator. "Get you to the point of begging. That would be so hot, because it would mean then I could make you come so hard, because I love watching you come, feeling you come. God, it gets me so hard…"

…not much time… Minerva said.

So tell me what you can about the thief, please? If you don't know her name, what does she look like? Where did she come from? Anything!

…so many colors. Blue, green, red.

Great. Minerva had discovered Skittles. *Skip tasting the rainbow and—*

Disguise. Minerva sounded peeved. *Master of disguise…*

And that's when Angela knew.

She felt like she'd just been dumped naked into the frigid Pacific. She stiffened. "Oh my God, Tyler, stop—I never thought I'd tell you to stop but crap, I mean it—I think it's—"

The cottage door banged open, and she heard Kari say "Sorry to interrupt, but, uh, we have a big problem here."

As long as she'd known Kari, she'd never heard that shaky tone in Kari's voice.

Kari, usually so cheerful, so grounded and centered even in the face of adversity, sounded terrified.

Chapter Twenty

"Be right out," Angela called to Kari, pulling herself to a sitting position. Tyler started to speak, but she put a finger to his lips and whispered, "Something's really wrong, I can tell. We have to go out there."

Tyler grabbed his jeans and pulled them on. He patted his pocket for his phone, intending to have 911 dialed in and ready to hit *send*, but then he remembered that it, along with Angela's phone, was charging in the main room. Her shoebox-sized bedroom didn't have enough outlets, and the power strip she used was already overloaded to the point that he worried about electrical fire.

He'd already been thinking about checking the wiring.

He shouldn't be thinking about it now.

He yanked his T-shirt on. Beside him, Angela was already dressed in jeans and a shirt. She looked grim.

"I'm going out first," he said quietly, and before she could protest, he reached for the door handle.

*

"I'm going out first," he said, and as much as Angela wanted to protest her equality, she appreciated his willingness to take the bullet. So to speak. There wouldn't be bullets, would there?

But likely, given his dodgy profession, he'd been in tight spots before. As a child she'd learned to be aware of locals who might be unhappy with foreigners digging up their history, but she'd never encountered anyone truly dangerous.

She'd never even been mugged.

Still, she was as close behind him as she could manage, because Kari sounded terrified, and Kari was her best friend, and by gods she was going to drop-kick anyone who made Kari sound that way.

Thanks to Minerva, she wasn't completely shocked by what she saw.

Cybelline. With a small but no doubt deadly gun currently digging into Kari's midsection.

Kari's face was white.

"Dammit, Cybelline," Angela said. "We *trusted* you."

"That's nice," Cybelline said, in a tone of voice that indicated pretty much the exact opposite. "I was *trying* to gain your trust, you dumbass. Pity you don't—how did Kari put it?—bat for my team, because I could've had you seduced, had the treasure, and been gone before Tyler ever showed up. That's your usual method, isn't it?" She directed that question at Tyler. "Swan in and be all charming, and they never know what hit them. Every single time."

"Every…" Angela said. "Tyler? Do you two *know* each other?"

Again with the feeling of being dunked in the Pacific, only this time from a very long height, because her stomach plummeted like a roller-coaster ride. Fuck, was this some sort of convoluted long con that Tyler and Cybelline did together?

Had she really been that naïve?

Now she wasn't sure who she wanted to drop-kick first. Starting with herself.

*

Tyler stared at Cybelline, whose accent was slowly changing from middle-America bland to British.

"Oh *please*," Cybelline said. "I nearly shat myself when you walked into the séance, but then you told me—*again*—that I reminded you of your sister. Seriously? Wigs and colored contacts threw you off that much?"

And then Tyler saw a woman with blue eyes and light brown hair and a chip in her tooth, superimposed over a woman wearing green contact lenses and a tousled blond wig, who'd obviously gotten that tooth fixed.

Well, obvious *now*.

And not a British accent. Australian.

"Cyndi Langerhans," he said. "Son of a bitch."

"You *know* her?" Angela asked again in a strangled voice.

"We crossed paths once, because we're in the same line of work," he said, not taking his eyes off the woman currently known as Cybelline, small-town psychic. "She looked a bit different then. She reminded me a little of my sister. Still does, which is weird, because my sister isn't a *psychotic nutjob*."

Cyndi's reputation was that she often bled her marks dry—but only in the financial sense. She was an expert grifter and thief, adept at the long con and probably willing to sell her mother if the price were right, but not violent.

Until now.

Great time for her to turn psycho.

Tyler canvassed the room, looking for options. Cybelline and the gun and Kari blocked the door. There were no obvious weapons in the room; certainly nothing as deadly as a gun. And the damn cottage was so tiny that neither he nor Angela could go far in either direction, which, if they could, would make it hard for Cybelline (he couldn't stop thinking of her by that name) to keep them all within easy gunshot.

And he couldn't make any sudden moves for fear of Cybelline shooting Kari.

The tiny place felt positively claustrophobic and hot, and smelled of nervous sweat and stale coffee and an incense he'd come to recognize as Kari's favorite.

"Now, now," Cybelline said, "this isn't a time for name calling. I'm just doing my job, same as you. We both came here for the treasure, and in our profession, it's finders keepers, right?" She scowled. "Unless you try to fuck me over with a fake artifact. Nice try, but please, it was insulting. Now, where's the *real* treasure?"

Angela sucked in a breath, trying to ground and center herself like Kari had taught her, and failing miserably. The heightened sensations of her hearing and the sense that time was moving a little slowly made her guess adrenaline was yelling at her to fight or flee.

She just had no idea which one was even possible.

Okay, so Tyler hadn't betrayed them, and she wasn't a complete idiot for trusting him. At least that problem seemed to be a non-issue.

But there was still the very crucial issue of the gun jammed into Kari's side, by a slightly deranged-sounding Australian treasure hunter who she thought had been their friend for the past six months.

Today is brought to you by the word surreal *and the letters* W, T, and F.

"Cybelline—Cyndi," she said. "There is no treasure…or if there is, we honestly don't know what it is. That rumor has been floating around San Sebastian since before we ever bought Angelika."

"I don't believe you," Cybelline said. "If that were true, why would *he* be here?"

"I'm guessing you read the same article I did," Tyler said. "The treasure rumor was boosted when they bought the hotel and started getting reviews."

"If you knew what the treasure was, you'd be gone already," Cybelline said. "Which means you're expendable. So stop yabbering before I shoot you."

"I've never heard of you waving a gun around before now," Tyler said in his most soothing voice.

"Never was tempted to before now. I've spent six months cultivating these two and you swanned in and just…smiled and cropped trou. I paid good money for that useless Barb to snoop and sabotage. Damn woman couldn't even plant rat poop convincingly. I blackmailed you and you just went ahead and told them who you really are! I stuck with Jill—who is really, really boring out of the sack—because she works with the troubled kids at the high school and troubled kids are great accomplices. They work cheap and don't ask many questions, and I knew those outside lockers might come in handy. And now you…you…I'm having a hard time thinking why I shouldn't just kill you all to pay for my aggravation."

"Listen to her." Kari spoke for the first time since she'd asked them to come out of the bedroom. Her voice shook. "She's already poisoned Isabella."

"*You killed my dog?!*" Angela had already been pissed off by Cybelline's betrayal and the fact that the woman was threatening to shoot her best friend, but now she felt real anger—no, *rage*—surge through her.

What kind of cold-hearted bitch thief poisoned a defenseless, pacifist greyhound?

Angela understood the concept of seeing red, because a crimson film seemed to wash over her vision.

Then she heard that familiar radio-tuning static that heralded the arrival of Minerva.

"Just give me the damn treasure!" Cybelline said. "What is it, jewelry? Those earrings Minerva's wearing in the portrait in the library would be worth something. Or, you said she went to India—is it a sapphire? Or maybe a golden idol?"

Angela had heard of the phrase "the top of my head blew off," but she'd never really understood it…until now.

The room temperature plummeted, from stuffy hot to who-left-the-damn-window-open-in-winter. Angela felt something like a tornado swirling in her torso, and then it was mirrored by a breeze in the room, clockwise, fluttering papers and curtains and hair.

And then *boom*, there was a pressure in her skull that suddenly shot upward, and the voice that came out of her mouth was absolutely not her own.

"It's my bloody journal, you coopered gonoph!" Minerva shouted, her cigarette-and-whisky rasp fraught with anger of her own. "It's not about money, and you'll never understand that. How dare you harm a defenseless animal for your base thievery?"

Cybelline's faux green eyes had widened when the cold breeze started. By the end of Minerva's rant, she'd taken a shaky step back, the gun no longer jammed into Kari's side but dangling from Cybelline's hand.

Kari, lithe from years of yoga, did some groovy Tai Chi move to twist away from Cybelline while at the same time knocking her off-balance.

It took Tyler only two steps to get to Cybelline. The gun clattered to the floor and Tyler kicked it aside and had Cybelline down on the floor, hands pinned behind her back, before she could react.

Angela/Minerva walked over to and nudged Cybelline with her foot. Not a kick—she wasn't a violent person—just a dismissive tap.

"And by the way," Minerva said with a sniff, "that wig makes you look like a cheap toffer."

*

Angela burst in the door carrying Isabella's limp body in her arms. "She's not dead. Thank God she's not dead!" Angela exclaimed, and as she did, Isabella opened one bleary eye, fixed it on Tyler, then closed it again. Kari squealed with delight. Taking the dog from Angela's arms, Kari settled her on a large green corduroy floor pillow, and, as best as Tyler could tell, started doing Reiki on her.

Angela crouched down next to the sofa and turned on Cybelline/Cyndi, whom Tyler had tied up using his belt on her ankles and the cord from a pair of Angela's sweatpants on her wrists. "What the *hell* did you do to my dog? I'll need to tell the emergency vet."

The would-be thief snarled something rude under her breath. Tyler leaned in, doing his best to pull off a menacing snarl—he certainly felt angry enough to menace, but he didn't have either practice or natural inclination. "Tell her, you crazy bitch."

"Or what? You're a pussy, Tyler. Everyone knows that. You're not going to hurt me."

She had a point. For one, Tyler didn't approve of violence, tempting though it was in this instance; it was such a crass solution compared to outsmarting your opponent. Plus, he was already going to be getting an uncomfortable amount of attention once the cops arrived unless they could figure a way to get rid of Cyndi without getting the cops involved. Damaging the suspect might make the cops more likely to listen to the accusations she was sure to make against him.

But before he could come up with a clever answer, Angela did it for him. "Or else Minerva will have another little talk with you."

Cybelline/Cyndi slumped deeper into the sofa, as if in surrender, before she said, "Alprazolam mixed into ground lamb. It's a sedative. Did you wankers really think I'd kill a dog?"

"You had a gun poking into my liver," Kari said, amazingly calm under the circumstances. "So, yeah, we did."

"The dog wasn't trying to cheat me. I had no reason to hurt her." She managed to sound self-righteous and full of injured dignity. Tyler wasn't sure if that was her scamming talents in action or if she was so far gone she actually believed that not wanting to hurt a dog made up for intending to hurt humans.

"What a rank cesspool your mind must be if that passes for virtue." The words came out of Angela's mouth, but not in Angela's voice, and the temperature in the room plummeted again.

Cyndi turned her face toward the back of the couch, as if that would help her hide from an irate ghost, and whimpered.

"So the psychic fears ghosts? You're as much a fraud in that as you are in the rest of your life." This time, it sounded like Minerva and Angela talking at once, which was really freaky.

"I really am a bit psychic," Cyndi insisted. "I mostly use it to impress marks, but it's real. That's *why* I'm scared of ghosts." She curled up into as tight a ball as her bonds would allow.

Tyler took Angela by the elbow and guided her up and as far away from the sofa as he could, which wasn't very far in the tiny cottage, but it was enough that it seemed to knock the Minerva-possession out of her again. He sat her in one of the two tall metal chairs at the small square café table tucked in a corner next to the kitchenette wall.

The chair rocked a little, its cheap design meaning the legs weren't quite right. He made a mental note to fix that, too.

Given everything that needed to be fixed in the cottage, where Angela and Kari clearly scrimped to have more money for the hotel, his brain was going to be full of mental notes very, very soon.

Angela's back relaxed out of the Victorian ramrod straightness as Minerva left her. "Is everything okay?" she asked.

"It's going to be fine," he said, tucking a spiral of black hair behind her cheek. Over his shoulder, he added, "Kari, why don't you call the vet?"

Kari did, while Tyler started a pot of coffee and got everyone a glass of water. (Well, except for Cyndi; she didn't deserve one. Although if she asked, he'd help her drink, because as angry as he was, he still wasn't into making people suffer.)

He was also thinking furiously, trying to figure out how to keep the bad situation from getting much, much worse.

Kari came over to them. "The vet says if she's awake and moving around, it's already working out of her system and we don't need to bring her in. But we should keep an eye on her. If she pukes, we'll need to get her in right away in case she aspirates."

"As long as she doesn't do it on any carpets in Angelika, we're golden," Angela said. The color had come back into her cheeks and Tyler felt a warmth that she was able to make a gentle joke.

"Listen," Tyler said. "We need to talk about something: what to do with her." He nodded to indicate Cyndi.

"My next call was going to be to the cops," Kari said.

"That's what we need to talk about," he said. "Hear me out, please, before you say anything." He watched Kari glance at Angela, and Angela give a small nod, just like before when he'd prepared to tell them about his wicked, thieving ways.

That had been only three days ago, but it seemed like ancient history.

"The bottom line is this: I can't testify against Cyndi," he said, pitching his voice low so the woman in question wouldn't hear. "It'll bring up too much about my past, and probably piss her off enough to tell the cops and her attorney all about me."

"We were here, too, and she had a gun on me," Kari said. "I think we can testify pretty well without you."

"But you'd have to lie about me even being here in order to keep me out of things," Tyler said, "and I can't ask either of you to do that. Plus it would be a hard story to stick to; the likelihood of it falling apart is high."

The coffee maker burbled, and the aroma was heavenly. He looked forward to it.

"So what *do* we do?" Angela, his ever-practical Angela, asked.

"I think we should let her go," he said.

"*What?*" Angela didn't manage to keep quiet, but she winced at the level of her own voice and bit her lip.

Kari, meanwhile, looked thoughtful. Tyler had suspected she might warm to the plan. She believed in people, believed in forgiveness and the good catching up and second chances.

"Threatening someone with a gun is a felony, and probably drugging the dog is, too, but in the end she didn't hurt you or Isabella," he said. "Unless she has a record—and if she's any good, she's covered her tracks well—she probably won't get a harsh sentence. On the other hand, if we let her go, it's in her best interests to get the hell out of Dodge so we *don't* call the cops on her. Or send a ghost after her."

Angela gnawed on her lower lip. "You're making a lot of sense, but I'm still pissed off." She reached across the glass-topped table to take Kari's hand. "She had a gun on you, Kari. She drugged Isabella."

"But she didn't hurt me or the dog." Kari repeated Tyler's words while covering both their hands with her free one and squeezing. "And this makes things a lot less complicated."

"I like less complicated," Angela admitted slowly. To Tyler, she said, "Can you promise she'll never come back?"

He smiled, and by their expressions, he guessed that his smile looked a little dangerous. "I think I can do that," he said.

Chapter 21

*A*ngela didn't know what Tyler had said to Cyndi—he'd taken her outside, her wrists still bound, and Angela and Kari had chosen to wait inside. A little while later, they heard the spray of gravel as a vehicle sped away, and then Tyler came back inside.

They'd indulged in a three-way comforting hug, and if Angela had been feeling cheekier she might have made a crack about threesomes, but she didn't.

Instead, when they'd all stepped back and she'd handed Tyler a cup of coffee, she said, "What about the gun?"

The gun was still on the floor where Tyler had kicked it, half-under the pressboard bookcase on which their small, mostly unwatched TV sat. Neither she nor Kari had wanted to touch it. Angela had handled antique weapons and knew how to fire a gun safely, but she still didn't like them. Kari loathed them and wouldn't go anywhere near the one on the floor, as if it were a tarantula.

Except that Kari loved all creatures, so that was a bad metaphor. Okay, Kari avoided it as if it were a jar of high fructose corn syrup.

"We need to get rid of it," Tyler said.

Angela nodded, a flash of inspiration making her grin. "Agreed. Let's chuck it in the fucking ocean," she said.

Kari stayed behind to keep an eye on Isabella; they'd take shifts for the rest of the night and through tomorrow.

It was probably in the 50s, but the wind off the ocean made it feel colder. Angela was grateful for the burgundy-and-gold spiral scarf Adelle had knitted for her. The coffee they'd ingested also helped, and she looked forward to more when they returned. But most of all, she felt warmed by the feel of Tyler's hand in hers.

It was near to a full moon. Kari would know the exact phase. The glow gave them enough light to pick their way to the cliff, find their way back.

If any of the guests who had rooms on that side of the hotel happened to be awake and looking out the window, they'd see two lovers taking a moonlit walk across the long expanse of lawn to the edge of the cliff.

When they got there, Angela closed her eyes and took a deep breath, filling her senses with the salty scent and rhythmic growl of the surf below.

This was the right thing to do.

Tyler let go of her hand, and she opened her eyes again to watch him reach into his pocket and draw out the small pistol. He had a good arm, strong, and the gun arced through the night, slowly spinning, catching in the moonlight, until it plummeted and finally splashed, far below and far out, into the ever-churning Pacific.

He dug into his other pocket, pulled out the bullets he'd taken out of the gun immediately after they'd restrained Cyndi, and tossed those, too.

His hand found hers again, and they stood for a long moment in silence. Acknowledging the end, preparing for whatever came next.

"Now that this is all over," Angela said finally, "I know…I know you're not a handyman. I mean, you're the best handyman we've had, but I know this isn't your job, it's not what you do."

"Trying to get rid of me so soon?" Tyler said, his voice light, but she sensed there was an undercurrent of something else.

"Not trying," she said. "Just understanding. Acknowledging." She swallowed against the lump in her throat. "Accepting."

"I'm not leaving just yet," he said, and she hated the way her heart leapt, gave her hope, just like it had when her parents would say they were all going to a new place and she'd believed, because she'd wanted to believe, that it would be a permanent home. "Fact is, I don't have another job lined up after this. That's the name of the game: I hear about something, I do the research, I investigate and maybe liberate. For that, it doesn't matter where my home base is." He shrugged. "I have potential home bases all over the US, and a few outside the US. But none I'd call *home*."

Angela's breath caught, making it hard to ask the question. "Are you saying you want to make Angelika—San Sebastian—a home base?"

"I'm saying that right now, I can't imagine making anywhere else a home base," he said. "I'm okay with closing down some of the other bases, even."

He turned to her, and even in the dark she saw the sensual, cocky curve of his mouth. "Not the one in Paris, though," he said. "I like the idea of you and me in Paris."

"Not because you want to steal something there, I hope."

"Just steal your breath away, at the top of the Eiffel Tower, looking down at the camera flashes that look like fireflies," he said. "On the banks of the Seine. In the shadow of Notre Dame. On the secret roof of Ste. Chappelle, because I know a tour guide who knows the entrance…"

"You know, I've been a lot of places—Egypt, the Middle East, Skara Brae—but I've never been to Paris," Angela mused. She tried to ignore the pitter-pat of her heart, but the thumping was pretty insistent. "I think I'd like that."

She caught herself as she said it, weighed the words.

No, it wasn't just an automatic response to romantic words uttered in a devastatingly seductive voice.

For the first time in far too many years, Angela liked the idea of traveling.

And not just because Tyler made a tempting traveling companion. He would make exotic nights in some foreign land even more exciting, and he'd be able to geek out about history and architecture with her, but it wasn't just Tyler.

It was that she—and maybe Tyler, too, if he was serious about staying in the area—could see the world and then come home again.

She had a home now. And since Angelika had weathered its recent storms, she figured the home wasn't going anywhere. After all, she had Minerva on her side, as well as her best friend, her very own Robin-Hood-of-the-arts, and a faithful hound.

Although she hoped the faithful hound wouldn't take any more candy from strangers or, rather, lamb from criminals.

"Yeah," she repeated, "I'd love to go to Paris with you. But I have to come back here to tell Minerva how it's changed since her day."

She meeped in surprise when he swung her around and gathered her up for a kiss. Then she let herself be drawn in to the feel of his lips on hers, his arms holding her close. For the first time in weeks, she felt like she could relax.

When they pulled apart, she grinned and said, "Hey, I've got an idea: let's go have wild monkey sex for the hell of it; not because we need information from Minerva."

He laughed and kissed her again. "As much as I love that idea, I think we'll have to table it for tonight. You and Kari need to keep an eye on Isabella, and I want to drive over and sit in front of Cyndi's place until she's packed and gone."

*

So it wasn't until the next night that Angela found herself tangled together with Tyler on her bed, cuddling and kissing, blissfully naked. They kind of had to be tangled together—not that they had any objections. The cramped bedroom could hold only a double bed and since they were both tall, long-legged people, they didn't have room to sprawl.

"Now we can focus on…well, everything else we need to focus on so this place can run smoothly." She ran her hand over Tyler's muscular chest. "And having some fun together when it's not an involuntary threesome."

"Are you sure Minerva's gone?" He winked.

Angela thought for a second and conceded, "I bet she's still around. She doesn't seem like the type to go into the light or whatever when the world is so interesting. I hope she's not in my head anymore, but I also hope she'll say hello in some ghostly way now and then. As long as she's not commenting about how yummy you are while you and I are playing." She kissed his chest, where his heart beat. "She can think it all she wants, because it's true, but I don't want to hear it."

Tyler laughed, then rolled both of them over so he was on top. They'd gotten pretty good at that maneuver despite the cramped space.

"I'm still boggled," Tyler said, "that after all that fuss, the treasure was a diary, not an art object or jewels or something."

"But it's so cool," Angela insisted. "Anyone could bring something valuable back from their world tour. Instead she invented sex-positive feminism long before anyone had thought of the phrase." Angela cupped Tyler's truly fine ass with both hands, appreciating the muscles and the velvety texture of his skin. "And I heartily approve."

"Doesn't have the resale value of a golden idol." Tyler twisted his hips, grinding himself enticingly against her most sensitive areas. "But it's certainly more fun." Tyler's voice dropped to that sexy pitch she loved so much. "And she indirectly gave us another treasure. I've gotten addicted to teasing you." One of his hands slipped to her breast, cupping it while two fingers tweaked her nipple with just the right force. Not too hard, not tickly-soft, just perfect.

Tyler's words and his touch, the tone of his voice and his smoldering eyes, worked together to push Angela to a point where she could have stopped only if the cottage were on fire.

And once they got to safety, she might want to take up where they left off.

"Do you have scarves?" Tyler whispered, the words and his warm breath caressing her ear.

"One sec." She squirmed away from Tyler, for the definition of *away* applicable to the small bed. (She added extra wiggle to her hips because it felt good.) With only a little stretching, she reached her small, battered dresser and pulled two hand-painted silk scarves, one in predominantly teal and green tones, the other burgundy and gold. "Kari's always telling me it's important to see the positive in every situation," she said as she brushed the scarves along Tyler's torso. "I think I just found the positive in having a bedroom so small I have to go outside to change my mind."

Tyler squirmed as the cool silk brushed his skin. They'd ended up in a position where she could tease his nipples, so she did. He let out a soft huff of breath. "Hadn't thought of you using them on me," he admitted. "But I should have." He grabbed at the end of the teal-and-green scarf. She grinned and jerked it just out of reach like she was playing with a kitten.

A tall, flexible kitten who didn't have to work hard to snatch it out of her hand.

Then again, she'd wanted him to end up with it eventually, so she didn't exactly fight.

Though she did flick the other one at him a few times before that, too, ended up in his possession.

She didn't have handy-dandy bedposts as anchor-points for the scarves, but between the two of them, they figured out the scarves could just barely make it around the edges of the cheap futon frame. Another positive-thinking moment: if she had a sturdier frame instead of a chintzy one, it probably wouldn't have worked. He tied the scarves off, then positioned her stretched out to reach them. As he spread her arms, she spread her legs, and the cool air brushed over a pussy made wet and hot by anticipation.

First one wrist, and it worked like magic, feeling the silk and Tyler's sure hands and that sexy voice muttering a simple "there you go. All secure."

By the time he got her other hand tied down, her brain was fluffy as cotton candy. "Gotta try this in the hotel in the off-season," she said in a breathy voice.

For about half a second, she wondered if she'd assumed too much. She and Tyler had obviously moved beyond a fling and into budding-relationship territory, but they hadn't had a chance to even think about what that might mean down the road.

But either Tyler was fine with her unthinking assumption or, like she had been (and with luck would be again in oh-point-five seconds), utterly focused on the moment. "Good old Victorian four-posters. From what you've said about Minerva and her friends, it wouldn't be the first time."

"If those beds could talk…"

"They'd have great stories. But right now, I'd rather tell this one." His mouth closed on her nipple.

Her nipples were especially sensitive today and somehow he knew it. He scraped his teeth over them without biting, a shivery sensation. He suckled with just the right pressure. He licked and nibbled with gusto, but moved on to her other nipple when it bordered on too much.

And he stayed focused on them long after the point where a guy would normally turn his attentions elsewhere.

The prolonged breast-worship was beautiful and squirm-inducing at the same time. Angela moved her legs restlessly, canted her hips upward against his cock. She couldn't quite reach it anyway, and he shifted away as best he could in the narrow bed. But still he sucked and licked and teased.

The sensations he evoked, the sensations rolling through her body from her nipples, were so lush and sensual she didn't want them to stop.

Her body ached to feel his cock inside her, to grip it with her pussy. But at the same time, she wasn't in a hurry. The silk scarves and the weight of Tyler's body restrained her in the sweetest way and, within the mild restraints, she felt freer than ever. Not frustrated, though her position could have been frustrating, the long tease with no movement toward release. Instead, she was soaring, riding the sensations like a hawk gliding on a thermal. She circled over orgasm, looking down at it lazily from a height, knowing she'd get there eventually but enjoying the journey too much to rush it.

"Like you said," she said, although it was difficult to string words together sensibly, "teasing's addictive."

Tyler raised his head. His eyes were smoky with desire and his voice was smoked velvet as he whispered, "Good. I could do this all night." The words made her clench and moan. "Oh yeah," he murmured, and returned his avid mouth to her nipples.

And then it occurred to her that something was missing.

Not from what Tyler was doing, although when he either added his cock to the game or moved his talented mouth between her legs, it would be wonderful in a different way.

No, what was missing was itching and pressure and a sense she wasn't alone in her own skull, and cryptic remarks and explicit commentary in a sultry voice coming from beyond the grave.

Minerva seemed to be well and truly gone, at least as an uninvited participant in their lovemaking.

Angela, delighted to be alone with Tyler, giggled as he swirled his tongue in her navel. Then, since they no longer had to worry about contacting Minerva, she slipped one hand out of the loose bondage and pushed gently on Tyler's head, urging him between her legs. Teasing was grand, but she was ready for pleasing.

And since Tyler didn't fight her attempts at direction, she figured he was, too.

Tyler's lips and tongue began to work their magic on her clit. *Too bad you're missing this, Minerva,* she thought affectionately. *But it's good to have Tyler to myself now. Nothing personal, you know.*

For a second, Angela swore she glimpsed a woman's transparent form hovering near the ceiling. Shadowy though the figure was, she thought the ghost (if it was a ghost and not her imagination) winked at her before vanishing.

*

Tyler licked his lips in the dark, replaying the details of the night with Angela. The woman was a feast in every sense.

After a wild, wet, sumptuous session of teasing, licking, and fucking, they'd dozed off, or at least he had. He'd woken a little while later to Angela's scarves securing *his* wrists and her hot mouth on his cock.

What a woman.

In the dark, his eyes closed, Angela breathing softly by his side (well, half on top of him, but he wasn't complaining), he could admit to himself that he didn't just have it bad for her, or any of those other words you used to describe a crush. And he was way more than just turned on, although Angela was enough to give him a semipermanent hard-on that threatened to become permanent without fun like blackmailers to distract him from the all-sex-twenty-four/seven channel.

Face it, he was in love with Angela and wanted to figure out some way to…if not settle down with her, then at least spend a lot of time with her.

Assuming she felt the same way about him. She liked and respected him, she'd said, and her actions confirmed it. She trusted him, even though he hadn't exactly made it easy. She'd had his back when he was in trouble, and wouldn't let him go it alone even though it would have been safer for her.

Looked like it might be love, or the start of it.

Now all they had to do was actually say the words and then figure out the next step.

Which sounded way easier than it actually was.

While Tyler was pondering imponderables, Angela stirred and swung herself out of bed. Bathroom, he figured, since she was sneaking like she didn't want to wake him.

Well, he was already awake and if she was, too, his cock was presenting him with all sorts of lovely, deviant ideas about Round Three. They'd both regret the lack of sleep as they faced whatever crises Angelika threw at them tomorrow. (Mini-crises. As long as no irate, gun-toting, dog-poisoning criminals were involved, anything else counted as a mini-crisis.) But they'd both go through the day smiling between stifled yawns, and that was all good.

But then he heard the front door's familiar squeak, which had been defeated only briefly by WD-40, and that shocked him into wakefulness faster than an irate, gun-toting, dog-poisoning criminal.

He fumbled for his clothes, tugged them on, not happily being reminded of doing so in order to confront Crazy Cyndi. He didn't bother trying to keep quiet as he banged around, having already learned Kari could sleep through noise akin to a Megadeath concert.

In the living room, Isabella swung her head around from staring at the door to look at him with an expression that clearly asked why the fuck people kept tromping through her sleep space in the middle of the god-damn night. He gave her a quick scritch behind the ears before he headed out the door.

Angela hadn't bothered to close the door behind her, which concerned him even more.

She left the back door to Angelika open, too—he saw a glimpse of her scarlet kimono as she stepped inside. She was barefoot, and he couldn't imagine how she wasn't shivering. He jogged to the entrance, took the time to close the door just in case a guest wandered.

He caught up to Angela in the library. It housed older volumes in a locked case (guests were invited to peruse under supervision) and a variety of modern novels for pleasure reading.

It also had a portrait of Minerva, a book in hand, although she gazed at the painter with a small smile and an expression that Tyler could interpret only to mean the text she read was salacious.

And the room also had an antique writing desk that Angela and Kari were convinced was Minerva's own.

That's where Tyler found Angela, sitting at that desk.

She sat ramrod straight, which did great things for her tits, but the posture was simultaneously dignified and normal, like she always wrote memos or notes to herself in her favorite silk robe in the middle of the night. Maybe she did, for all he knew.

Except he doubted she came into the hotel in the middle of the night just to jot down some passing thoughts.

He moved a little closer and realized she was staring straight ahead, looking in his direction but not seeming to see him. Her hand was flying across the page, but he'd never seen anyone write that much, that fast, without looking down.

Let alone without seeming to know she was doing it.

He knew about walking in your sleep and talking in your sleep, but writing? That was a new one. Should he wake her or let her be?

Let her be for now, he decided. Freaky though this was, she was safe and he could make sure she didn't give up on writing and wander farther into the night.

For all he knew, she *did* do this regularly. They'd spent the night together only a few times and none of those nights had involved much actual sleep.

She turned to a blank page and kept on writing, still staring straight ahead of her.

This might take a while. Tyler eased into a wingback chair and set his feet gently on the coffee table.

He hoped he was doing the right thing by not waking her.

Chapter 22

*A*ngela woke with a start. How the hell had she ended up in the library? And why did her hand ache?

The library question was more worrisome, but the hand question was easier to explain: maybe because she was clutching a green rollerball pen in a death grip and the notepad on her hand was covered with writing.

Writing that didn't look anything like her own.

Thanks to her erratic education, she'd never learned cursive properly—her parents didn't care and most of her classroom education took places in countries where the teacher had grown up using a completely different alphabet and hadn't mastered cursive either. She tended to print when she couldn't use a computer.

Which is why she almost always used a computer, or her phone.

The page was covered with perfect Victorian copperplate, or as close as you could get to it using a modern pen.

She wasn't a handwriting expert, but that copperplate looked familiar. She'd seen it on letters and ledgers and all sorts of other paperwork from the hotel's history—not to mention a risqué tell-all diary.

Angela threw the pen and notebook aside (the pen rolled away toward the door, the notebook skidded under a cane-backed chair) and jumped to her feet with a little shriek. This was too weird, even though her weirdness bar had been reset pretty high lately.

She'd been too bewildered to even register Tyler's presence in the room, but suddenly his arms were around her, pulling her toward his side. Once she got over her overall confused terror, she was happy he was solid and warm and not remotely paranormal.

"Hey, you all right?" His voice was a soothing balm.

"The writer's cramp won't kill me, but the brain cramp's pretty bad." She forced a smile and then realized it wasn't entirely forced. This might be the most bizarre Minerva episode yet, but it wasn't terrifying, just weird as hell, and could even end up being funny once she wrapped her head around it.

"You're shaking."

"I'm a little chilled and a lot freaked out. Minerva was dictating to me or something."

Tyler kissed the top of her head and squeezed her closer. "Okay, that's even weirder than what I thought, which was that you sleepwork instead of sleepwalk."

She snorted. "I'm sure I've done that. But this was different. Check this out." She grabbed the now-rumpled notebook from under the chair.

Tyler's eyebrows went up. "I bet your normal writing doesn't look like a wedding invitation."

"More like a chicken scratch." A silly thought brought a smile to her lips. "Maybe she's using me to write the next bestselling erotic novel. That wouldn't be so bad. We could use the money."

She flipped back to the first page of Minerva's dictation and the smile faded. "Uh, no. It's more bizarre than that, even." She read a little further. "But I think it's good."

She and Tyler squeezed together on the antique fainting couch, which was a great piece of furniture for solo reading but not quite as comfy for two. Still, an excuse to squirm against Tyler never sucked.

Together they set to work reading what Minerva had written. Deciphering, more like. The beautiful handwriting wasn't always the easiest to read, but after a few lines, they both got the trick of it.

Dear Angela, forgive me for taking this liberty, but with your heart as open as it is now, allowing me to move your body, it seems easier to communicate this way than to attempt to speak when you are in the throes of passion, when you are open to etheric influences but understandably distracted.

First, let me promise that now the danger to our home is past, I will no longer intrude on your lovemaking. Unless another threat to our home or its inhabitants arises, I shall remain a quiet observer at Angelika, doing no worse than perhaps providing fodder for stories of an atmospheric, benevolently haunted place.

You may still wonder why I called my journal a treasure. In my day there were no frank accounts of a woman's sensual and sexual life, lived with gusto and freedom on her own terms. I hoped someday my journal might inspire other women to seize the joys of their own bodies, just as the published accounts of my travels inspired some to more adventurous pilgrimages.

Alas, I could not make the account of my amorous adventures public at the time. Published anonymously and without names and details, it would appear to be erotic fiction, and few would believe a woman had written it. Published under my own name, it could ruin my friends. Even if I concealed names, the circle in which I moved was not so large that identities could not be guessed. I already had a reputation for being fast, but since I had money of my own, no children or husband, and relatives who mostly ignored my foibles, I needn't worry if Mrs. Grundy thought me a hussy. Some of my friends were not so fortunate.

So I hid the journal in hopes that someday it could see the light of day. I think the time has come. Share my treasure with the world, my friends—and may it set the world on fire with passion.

There is one more treasure I would share with you. You may have noticed my erotic journal stopped rather abruptly. That is because, to my astonishment, I fell in love.

Oh, I had loved many men and women before that as friends and dear companions, but I never deliberately sought romantic love. I did not speak of love in my journal because I did not wish for women to set it as a goal, any more than I had for myself. The need for a grand romance, it seemed to me, could push a woman (or a man, for that matter) inch by inch into a narrow life, bounded by wedding vows and wearisome social conventions. Let love happen if it would, I believed, but make pleasure and self-discovery the goals of one's erotic life.

Then in the gloaming of my years I was blessed to meet Samuel—who looked a bit like that handsome devil, Tyler. With him, I found a love that encouraged pleasure and self-discovery, a love that encouraged us both to be braver and better than we were alone. Living my life, at that point, became far more interesting than keeping a record of it to inspire others!

Samuel and I never married, for the marriage laws of the time were not to our taste, and sometimes our lives sent us in different directions. But we always came back to this house, and to each other's arms.

I still think romance is not the ultimate goal of a life well lived. But when you encounter the right person, it will enhance your life immeasurably and give you the freedom in which to pursue your dreams. Angela, Tyler, you sought a treasure. I think you've found one in each other.

Angela set down the notebook and looked at Tyler. "I…uh…damn her for putting it better than I could."

Tyler actually flushed, which won any tiny corners of her heart that might have been holding out against loving her adorable thief. "That's one perceptive ghost. How did she know I was trying to find the words to tell you I love you?"

"Those words work," Angela said. "I'll even echo them: I love you. Now what?"

Chapter 23

They were already snuggled close, but Tyler put his arm around Angela's waist and snuggled closer, his strong thigh pressing against hers. "I was serious about making this my home base. I can't promise I'll be here every day, but I'll always come back to San Sebastian. And I'll be here more often than not."

Tyler's voice shivered on Angela's skin and teased her clit, as usual, but his words touched her heart. Miraculously, she was able to think of that cliché and not flash to Aztec sacrifices and Roman priests reading entrails.

Okay, those images still popped into her head, but for the first time ever, she didn't break into inappropriate laughter when she thought of touching a heart.

Instead, she focused on what the cliché meant: Tyler's commitment to stick around made her feel he was caressing places in her soul that she'd never known needed soothing.

"Tyler, I…" She fought an urge to simultaneously cry and dance around the room, but she didn't try to keep the foolish grin off her face or the catch out of her voice. "I'd love that. And I'll try to remember to come up for air more often. Take a few days off now and then to travel with you. I think you'll be good company for exploring new places." She kissed his cheek quickly. "As long as you're just exploring, not casing the joint. That you do on your own time."

"Promise. Hell, I might even look into more legit restoration work," Tyler added thoughtfully. "It's not as exciting as liberating art, but it's satisfying and I'm good at it. And it's legal."

"Tyler, you're not thinking giving up your work!" Angela surprised herself with the vehemence in her voice. And the volume. Must remember they were in Angelika, not the cottage, and she needed to keep it down. "I guess I should be thrilled you'd think about abandoning your life of crime, but I don't want you to change who you are."

Tyler squeezed her hand. His eyes were serious, his voice intent as he assured her. "I'm not giving anything up, just expanding my options. Even before we met, I was pondering making the artifact liberation more of a sideline. Face it, crime doesn't pay much in my case. The most satisfying jobs seem to be the ones where I don't make a lot of money—where I get a small fee to retrieve something that someone else stole, or I donate the object to a museum. But I don't want to stop, because there's so much hidden knowledge and beauty out there, waiting to be found and shared with the world."

Angela smiled to herself. This sounded so familiar, like stuff she'd overheard from her parents and their colleagues, but with a larcenous twist. "You should have been an archeologist. Lousy pay, but high job satisfaction, and you don't risk arrest. Well, not often, although the police in some countries really like their bribes and get nasty if you don't pay."

"Thought about it as a kid, but I was disappointed when I realized that a whip and a cool hat aren't standard issue."

Angela's smile grew to a grin that she suspected looked a bit demented. "You have to meet my parents!"

"If you tell me you're actually related to Indiana Jones and Lara Croft, I won't believe you." Suddenly what she'd said seemed to sink in, because Tyler's eyes grew wide and nervous, and he looked twitchy as a cat in a room full of rocking chairs. "Wait, did you say something about meeting your parents?"

Angela couldn't help laughing at his gobsmacked expression. "You look almost as panicked as you did when you saw Cyndi with the gun.

I think you'd like my parents, that's all. It wasn't always easy being their kid due to the whole Exotic-Country-of-the-Month thing, but they're fascinating people, and I really do love them. And my father owns a whip, although that's either part of a joke along with the Indiana Jones hat he wears sometimes, or I really don't want to know because I support everyone's right to be kinky, but they're my *parents*."

Tyler snorted. "You're right. I would like them." Then his expression softened. "And not just because they're your parents and I'm grateful to them."

"That is so corny. Good thing I love you." Angela had to laugh or she'd tear up. "Oh shit, I almost forgot! They'll be in San Francisco soon and want to get together. Want to come with me?"

Tyler gulped theatrically, then said, "Why not? Less stressful than waiting for Thanksgiving, right?"

"Don't worry about the holidays. I'll be busy here and they'll probably be someplace I can't pronounce."

"I'm not worried about the holidays. But I hope even a busy hotel owner can take a few hours for turkey and stuffing—and by stuffing, I mean sex. And by the way, I was serious about taking you to Paris," Tyler whispered. "That wasn't just moonlight and adrenaline."

"I'd love to, if we can make it work. It'll have to be in winter. Quieter then." It had seemed like a pipe dream the other night, but at the moment Paris seemed closer than the next room.

"Paris is still beautiful in winter. I've never seen Notre Dame in snow. And you'll be with me, so even Cleveland would be beautiful, let alone Paris. " Tyler kissed her. At first it was light, a sealing-the-deal gesture, but there was no way it could stay that way on this charged night. His tongue teased at her lips in a way that inevitably made her think of him licking elsewhere…down below. She groaned, opened her mouth, let their tongues dance together.

So good. Tyler's kisses were always hot and delicious, but this was dizzying.

His arms tightened around her and helped her onto his lap. As she straddled him, her robe partly opened and slipped off her shoulders. Tyler's kisses moved from her lips down the sensitive side of her neck and from there across her collarbone. Each kiss sent a frisson of delight through her body. Tyler's sure hands caused the silk to glide sensuously on her skin as it slipped lower. Angela forgot where she was.

Or rather, she pretended to forget she was in the hotel, that she in fact was one of the owners of the hotel, and let the beautiful room with its lush and deceptively proper portrait of Minerva weave a fantasy in which she simply opened Tyler's jeans and slipped his cock inside her. She'd ride him that way until they were both crazy, and then they'd move so she could lean on the arm of the fainting couch, facing the glass-fronted bookcase (not as good as a mirror, but it would do) and he could take her from behind. She reached between their bodies, fumbling for his zipper…

Someone moved on the second floor, a faint sound of footsteps cutting through the quiet that previously had been disturbed only by soft sighs of lust. It was just a few steps, so it was probably someone heading for their bathroom, but it was enough to break the spell. Angela jumped and drew her robe around her.

"Oops. Got carried away there." Tyler sounded cocky—he almost always sounded cocky—but Angela heard a tender note in his voice, one she didn't think she'd heard before, and in the dark, she smiled.

She slipped off his lap and stood, making sure her robe was wrapped and tied securely. "Guess that's our cue to head back to the cottage." She offered Tyler her hand—not that he needed it—and tugged him to his feet.

"Not the same atmosphere."

Holding his hand, she led him out of the library. "We'll have our chance this winter. If the weather's nasty, we can be almost empty for a few days running. Not good, but at least this year I can see potential for a lot of Minerva-approved fun while it's slow."

*

A few days of distraction had left Angela with paperwork galore piled up—but as a pleasant change, none of it was dire and some of it was downright good, including a letter from the health inspector certifying that the little Cybelline-created problem with the rat poop was completely resolved. More bookings, not too many bills…it was all good.

Someone knocked on the door of the little office, even though it was open. Isabella lazily raised her head to check out the visitors, then stretched, play bowed, and stood. When Angela saw it was Margaret Blum and David Strauss, she rose and so did the dog, who trotted over to get scritches from David.

While David occupied himself with the dog, Margaret said, "David is dragging me out for some sightseeing, so I wanted to take the opportunity to thank you for helping me have a wonderful, productive stay. I expected to make progress on my book here, but Angelika must be inspirational, because I already finished the draft and got a few chapters of a new book sketched out. And David hasn't been as bored as he often gets on these retreats, between the local history and the beautiful coastline and your delightful dog…" She lowered her voice. "…and, well, this is a romantic setting."

"That's exactly what we like to hear." Minerva would be proud, Angela thought, about the finished book and the happy couple.

"I told a number of my writer friends about this place," Margaret added, "and we've decided we want to do a formal retreat here this winter, maybe hold some workshops." Margaret then mentioned a few names of the friends she'd recruited and Angela's eyebrows went up. Margaret had famous friends.

"That would be wonderful!" If it came together. She hated to be cynical, but Angela knew how many great ideas never got out of the talking stage.

And then Margaret handed her a check. A large check. "Would this do as a down payment? We were looking at the second week of January if that's good for you. We'd need most of the hotel."

Angela pretended to check the dates, but she already knew the answer. January was dismal for business.

Usually. Not this coming January.

And with guaranteed income, she could relax enough to make plans for that winter vacation.

Once she'd gotten Margaret's retreat blocked out on the hotel calendar and accepted a hug from the writer, Angela waved the couple on their way.

Then she called Tyler's cell. Without any lead-in, she said, "If we go to Paris the first weekend of February, can we pretend it's really Valentine's Day?"

"You. Paris. Who needs to pretend? Valentine's Day is more a state of mind anyway."

Yeah, there was a reason she loved him. "Fine. It's too early to book flights, and something could conceivably come up…but I'm putting it on the calendar."

"Mmm," Tyler said. His voice was low and sexy and made her feel all shivery in the parts where it counted. "That'll give us enough time, then."

"Time for what?" Angela wondered if she'd had a tiny little erotic fugue and missed something.

"Time for us to…practice our French."

The way he said it make it clear he wasn't talking about the language.

Angela moaned and sank into her chair.

Chapter 24

Although there were a number of elegant, upscale restaurants in San Francisco, Angela's parents opted for their version of homey: comfort food from a culture exotic to most Americans. They'd ended up at an excellent, unpretentious Ethiopian place, eating on plates of injera flatbread and sitting close to the floor.

A variety of delicious dishes was spread before them, including raw beef in hot butter, spicy chicken and egg stew, and a preparation of collards that would make vegetable-haters change their minds, all to be washed down with honey wine.

Tyler's staid Midwestern parents would have fled screaming. The Georgeneses seemed right at home, and Lea had addressed the waiter in his native language. (Amharic. Tyler had had to ask. Now he was going to have to read up on Ethiopia because he realized he knew almost nothing about the country.)

All in all, meeting the parents was going well. Right now, Angela was catching them up on the latest developments in her world. "And then I got a call from Carole van Horn, a movie producer who'd stayed at Angelika earlier in the spring. She found an investor—a real one this time, Tyler, not Barb the assistant con artist—who's also fascinated by Minerva's travels and unconventional lifestyle, and they're developing a movie that would be filmed at least partly on site."

Tyler had heard the story several times, so he allowed himself to tune out and study Angela's parents. Dr. Georgenes ("call me Peter") was the source of Angela's coloring and height; dramatic grey streaks accented his wavy black hair and he had a killer smile. Dr. Simons-Georgenes, aka Lea, had a striking figure similar to her daughter's, and the laugh lines on her attractive face suggested what Angela might look like in a few decades. And from their interactions so far, both seemed to be sources of Angela's intelligence and spirit.

"Minerva's surviving family would get a larger share of the proceeds," Angela continued, "but we stand to make money from the use of the hotel as a location, and we'll certainly get media attention. Of course it's all down the road, but it's still exciting."

Peter beamed at his daughter. "What fun. I admit we've been concerned about you and this hotel of yours."

Angela didn't sigh or roll her eyes, but Tyler suspected she wanted to. "It takes a new business time to gain momentum, but we're doing fine, Dad."

Lea laughed, a rich, hearty laugh very much like Angela's. "Not that, silly. We were afraid you'd be bored in one place, running a business, and when you couldn't make it out to Turkey last year, it seemed you'd gotten stuck in a rut. But between conniving mediums and famous writers and a movie deal, not to mention hiring a new handyman and finding a kindred spirit, running a hotel sounds more exciting than we imagined. Although you seem pretty relaxed despite all the excitement. More so than you have in a while. Tyler must be good for you."

Angela and Tyler smiled at each other. The parents didn't know quite how exciting the past few weeks had really been; Angela left out the parts about being possessed by a horny ghost, Cyndi threatening Kari with a gun, and his own extralegal activities.

"Anyway, enough about me. You said you two were involved in a new project?" Angela tore off a piece of injera, made a mini-wrap with the chicken, and settled in to eat as if she expected a long story.

Tyler refilled Peter's wine. It never hurt to be polite, especially to your partner's parents. (Partner. He'd never had one of those before, not in the life-partner sense. It still boggled him, but in a good way.) Then he refilled his own glass and sipped as he listened. Honey wine would never be his first choice, but it was growing on him.

Lea leaned forward, her chunky silver and lapis necklace—Middle Eastern or Central Asian, Tyler guessed—venturing perilously close to the food. She glanced from side to side as if she was about to impart a great secret. Tyler didn't grin, but he thought about it. Lea was just a little overdramatic, but he could picture her daughter doing the same thing when she had exciting news.

Apparently satisfied that no one from another table was listening, Lea said in a quiet voice, "The UN has approached us about heading up a commission for recovering antiquities lost or stolen during times of war or civil unrest."

Peter put his hand on Lea's shoulder. "Not so much a commission as putting together a *team*. Commissions study problems. Teams act."

Tyler backpedaled on several counts.

Lea wasn't being jokingly dramatic. This was big.

And maybe Angela's parents were closer to his favorite fictional archeologists than he'd imagined.

Angela gasped. "That's amazing. A little scary, but amazing. Is this because of that incident in Iraq a few years ago?"

The older couple nodded. "Partly," Peter confirmed. "But we're not going to be confronting the looters personally this time."

"Peter keeps telling me we're too old for that shit, that this is a good way to keep involved in archeology without so much travel and physical work and risk. I'll believe that part when I see it. Desk jobs aren't exactly him, or me, for that matter." Lea smiled, and Tyler decided that he definitely needed to stay on her good side, because a woman who smiled like that was not someone to annoy.

"Right now we're putting together a team," Peter added. "Researchers, country experts, art historians, archeologists…meeting with a few people at Berkeley tomorrow, in fact. But we're getting stymied finding recovery experts."

Angela raised her elegant eyebrows.

Tyler held his breath. He saw where this was going.

"Thieves, basically, but on the side of good," Lea confirmed his suspicion. "Officially, we're getting national treasures back where they belong through negotiation or purchase. Unofficially, several of the involved governments have asked us to be more…proactive. But how in the world do you go about looking for a thief who's an expert on antiquities and is willing to take on risky, challenging jobs?"

"For a flat fee, no less." Peter grinned. "It's not like I can just ask people, 'Hey, can you recommend a cat burglar with a conscience?'"

Angela's parents were holding out his dream job.

Tyler glanced at Angela and found her smiling. He reached across and took her hand, giving it a squeeze to let her know it was all right to talk.

Angela leaned over and kissed him, a kiss that stirred desire but also, wonderfully, spoke of intimacy and love.

Then she imitated her mother, leaning forward and looking around for eavesdroppers before whispering, "Funny you should say that, Dad. I actually can. But you and the UN can only have him part-time."

sophie mouette

author of *Possessed, Undressed, and in a Mess*

OUT OF THE
frying pan

a hollywood spice novel

Fancy a madcap, steamy romance set in the wacky world of Hollywood?
Turn the page for a sneak preview of *Out of the Frying Pan*,
available now from your favorite retailers in print and eboo< formats.

Chapter 1

That morning, Chloe's horoscope had said "avoid false turns."

If only she'd heeded that advice. It was just that she'd never put much stock in astrology, and only started reading the horoscope page when she'd moved to Los Angeles a month ago, adrift and starting a new life across the country with nothing much to do in the morning but read every inch of the *LA Times*, starting with the food section and ending with the horoscopes.

She hadn't expected it to be so hard, the move and all. In Boston, she'd had a fabulous job as the sous-chef at an acclaimed restaurant.

What she hadn't known until she'd gotten here was that acclaimed restaurants in Boston were sneered at by acclaimed restaurants in LA. Who knew that LA restaurants looked down their long noses and sniffed at Boston restaurants, then turned dismissively away, making snide comments under their breaths?

Which is why she'd taken this temp job helping cater for the American Action Movie Awards, or AAMies. It was beneath her talent and skill, but it would help pay the rent—and rent in LA was outlandish.

But everything was going horribly wrong.

First of all, she'd been late. Very late. Boston traffic was bad, but it didn't hold a candle to the southern California freeways.

She'd had to show her ID and pass to five different security checkpoint guards, and then she'd gotten turned around and almost missed the door to the kitchen.

Only to learn that she'd been hired as a waitress.

There had to be a mistake. She was a *chef*, dammit. Trained at Culinary Institute of America. Paid her dues at Printemps and Harvest before working for Maurice.

She was not, by any stretch of the imagination, a goddamn waitress.

Chloe wanted to storm out. She *almost* stormed out.

Almost.

But she had no money, and no real job.

And Luanna was counting on her to pay her half of the rent. Because if she didn't, they'd be out on the street. That meant Evenrude, Luanna's Welsh corgi wouldn't get fed, or even have a home. When Chloe imagined those big, liquid brown eyes staring up at her, she caved. She pushed aside her pride (it pushed back, but in the end, she muscled it into submission), grabbed hold of her responsibilities with both hands, gritted her teeth, and said,

"Right. Waitress. Where do I change?"

She repeated the directions under her breath. "Down the hall, past the dining room, across the lobby, behind the staging area, the door's on your left. No, on the right. It's not marked, but it's just past the Steven Seagal display."

Getting across the lobby entailed going through two more security checkpoints, one at either end, and at the first one she'd forgotten where she'd shoved her ID once she thought she was free and clear, and in the lobby she thought she'd spotted The Rock, so she was admittedly flustered.

And she didn't even *like* The Rock that much.

So where was the staging area?

"Excuse me," a voice said. "Do you need any help?"

"I'm looking for the staging area," she said as she turned.

If she hadn't been so frazzled and late and miffed, she would've taken more time than just *Huh, he's really cute!* But all she processed was a killer pair of bedroom eyes behind a cute pair of little wire-rimmed glasses as he said, "I think it's that way, but I'm not sure—let me ask."

He headed back towards the lobby, and Chloe felt bad but she just didn't have time to wait. She went in the direction he suggested, and hallelujah! found the Steven Seagal cardboard cutout surrounded by posters from *Marked for Death* and *Out of Reach* and *Under Siege* (*1, 2,* and *3*). She pushed open the first door on her left. It was heavier than she expected, and she stumbled in.

No, she stumbled *out*. She was outside.

On the freaking red carpet.

Red was all she saw before the flashbulbs started going off, at which point just about all she could see was yellow and white glowing blobs. She'd been blinded. She'd never see again.

Chloe whirled. The door, swinging shut on its well-oiled hinges, was almost closed. She lunged.

There was no handle. It was an out-only door.

Her fingers scrabbled for a handhold, to just catch the very crack of space before the door—

—shut with an utter, resounding finality.

Shit. Oh holy shit on a stick.

Surely there was another door. She scanned the wall, left and right, back and forth. Nothing. Nada.

She turned back around, frantically seeking an exit. Running right along in front of her like the damn Yellow Brick Road was the red carpet. There were stars on it—not The Rock, or even Vin Diesel, although that woman there could have been Angelina Jolie's stunt double—as well as the press—she was sure that lady there was from VH-1's *Hottest Entertainment News.*

Just beyond the carpet was a rope barrier and a buttload of paparazzi, all with cameras and booms and mics and equipment she couldn't recognize and didn't want to, and where the hell was she going to go?

Okay. She couldn't go left, in the direction the stars were headed. That would send her through the front door, and she didn't have the creds to get through the front door. So she'd go right, and find the street where they were all coming from, and then she'd get her bearings...

Who was she kidding? She didn't know the damn Hollywood streets without a Thomas Guide or a cheap GPS.

Still, it was better than no plan at all.

She took a step forwards, and lights exploded in her face.

"Wait, no, I'm not famous—"

They couldn't hear her. She was on the red carpet, and thus they had to capture her for tonight's television recap and tomorrow's website and next week's *US Weekly*.

And that's when she saw the security team advancing, looking as menacing as rent-a-cops could.

Rent-a-cops with tazers, she saw, and gulped.

"Hey," a deep voice said. It didn't sound menacing, thank goodness.

She turned.

He was tall, broad-shouldered, and his tuxedo jacket had obviously been tailor-made for him because nothing off the rack would have contained those bulging biceps and sculpted pecs.

He looked a little familiar.

"Who are you?" he asked.

His brown eyes were kind, and somehow they reminded Chloe of Evenrude, and something broke inside of her and she started to babble.

"I'm one of the caterers." Okay, technically not true, but she *ought* to be one of the caterers, dammit. "I got lost, and I came out the wrong door, and it closed behind me and doesn't open from the outside. I'm really, really lost."

He laughed, a rumbling chuckle that triggered some memory for her. "Yes, you really, really are." He glanced over his shoulder. "They don't look too happy," he said of the guards.

"Please don't let them arrest me," she said in a teeny-tiny voice that made her cringe, but she couldn't help it. That was the way it came out when she was in a panic.

"Okay, Miss Pretty Caterer," he said. He held out his arm. When she didn't respond—she was still gaping in dread—he gently took her hand and tucked it into the crook of his arm, and started back down the red carpet at a leisurely pace, smiling and waving at the photographers.

Out of the corner of her eye, Chloe saw the guards stop, confer quickly, and then turn away.

She wilted, relieved. It was all going to be okay.

"Ray!" a reporter cooed. "Where's Sandrine? Who's the lovely lady you're escorting tonight?"

Ray. Suddenly it all crashed down, complete with a roaring in her ears. She was on the arm of Ray Stark, who was expected to win the Best Action Actor AAMie for his role in *Rode Hard and Put Away Wet* (although Jackie Chan was considered a close contender for his latest kung-fu flick).

Of course he looked familiar. He looked just a little bit like Brad Pitt (if Brad Pitt were bald and three inches taller and beefier), which all the media capitalized on.

And *Rode Hard had* been an awfully fun movie.

"Just a new friend," Ray told the reporter. "Sandrine's still resting her foot—the temporary cast doesn't go with any of her evening gowns."

"Ray!" another reporter called. "What's her name?"

Ray glanced down at Chloe.

"Chloe Montiero," she whispered.

"Chloe Montiero," he told the reporter.

"And where did you meet her?"

"It's a long story," he said, flashing that twinkling grin that made the ladies swoon and had put him in *People* magazine's Most Beautiful People issue (although he hadn't made the cover, sadly). "Let's just say we sort of ran into each other."

A microphone was shoved into Chloe's face, a very bright light hovering over it. She could feel the heat pouring out of bulb. Dizzied, she tried to step back, but the crowd had gotten too thick.

"Chloe, that's an unusual choice for the red carpet," the interviewer said. "Who are you wearing?"

"I—uh—" She was wearing a strappy little turquoise dress, one of Luanna's creations. It had been so hot today that she hadn't wanted to put on more. The little sandals were off-brand, although she'd been vain enough to go with spiky heels to add to her height, figuring she'd change into flat shoes right before she got to work.

Thank the gods she wasn't wearing her chef's whites already. Nobody would have believed she belonged there. The tote bag—thank goodness a cute bohemian-chic one embroidered with shisha mirrors—containing her comfy shoes was bad enough.

"Luanna Devenaux," she said to fill the silence.

"So how did you and Ray…"

Inexplicably, Ray saved the day again. "I'm sorry we don't have more time to talk, but I need to get inside. Don't want to miss those exquisite hors d'oeuvres they always serve." He smiled that dazzling smile again, and steered Chloe in the direction they needed to go. It was all she could do to keep herself from stumbling, the after-effects of the flashbulbs still causing spots in front of her eyes.

Inside it was just as cacophonous as outside, but in a different way. Whereas outside there had been a lot of shouting to get the stars' attention, inside it was just crowded and busy, the normal sounds trapped and bounced back off the walls and ceiling. Harried PAs tried to direct the flow of people, but everyone seemed to have their own agenda of where to go and what they wanted.

"Well, this is where I get off the train," Ray said. "I gotta go in and make sure I haven't forgotten anybody in my acceptance speech, just in case." He patted his chest, where he had apparently tucked the speech.

"Good luck," Chloe said. "I mean, break a leg. Is that what I'm supposed to say? I hope you win. I loved *Rode Hard*."

Jesus, could she *ever* stop babbling?

"Good luck to you, too, Miss Pretty Caterer," he said, a smile crossing his face and making him look far less menacing than he did on screen when he was beating the bad guys all the way to hell and back. "Go make some of those fabulous hors d'oeuvres."

He put an arm around her, leaned down, and kissed her cheek. Just barely brushed against her skin, a touch that was obviously brotherly as opposed to flirtatious or sexual. (Brotherly she knew, having an abundance of big brothers.)

Then he was gone, lost in the crowd of people except for the fact that he was one of the tallest among them. Chloe watched him go, still reeling, until someone bumped into her. She opened her mouth to bitch, but thankfully no words came out before she realized that the offender was Kit Harding, star of the *Amazon* series of films.

You don't piss off a six-foot-tall woman with gladiator arms who could wipe the floor with Jennifer Garner's Elektra. You just don't.

"Sorry, my fault," she mumbled and squeezed her way through the crowd until she found a wall to press herself against.

Right. She just had to find her way back to the Steven Seagal exhibit and figure out where she'd gone wrong. They wouldn't've needed any servers yet, and even if they did, she could slip in and grab a tray from some overworked waiter and everything would be fine.

Taking a deep breath, she pushed away from the wall.

"Hey, aren't you Ray Stark's date?" A reporter shoved a microphone in her face.

Shit. There was no way she could go out there in a waitress uniform and not get attacked by a camera.

Self-preservation won over rent money. Chloe ducked under the man's outstretched arm and fled, right out the door she'd first entered not half an hour before.

*

Chloe woke when a violent shaking nearly tumbled her out of bed.

Earthquake!?

Her heart thudding as hard and painfully as her head, she ripped the sleep mask off her eyes. She squinted in the bright sunlight pouring in her window that made her head throb worse.

Luanna had been out when she'd gotten home last night, and she'd fixed a miserable (but creative) dinner while sipping Trader Joe's Two-buck Chuck, and she didn't remember much more than that.

Well, okay, she remembered being concerned that Eventude had split into three corgis, and she'd wondered whether she needed glasses, which she couldn't afford anyway.

Now there was a blurry blob blocking some of the light. Was their apartment haunted? Did those crumbling Art Deco features and once-fancy molding mask a sordid and horrifying tale of murder and revenge?

At least the shaking had stopped. If it had been an earthquake, it was over now. She braced herself in case there was an aftershock and she'd have to fling herself at the nearest doorway. (She wasn't sure why you were supposed to do that—the doorframe was just as creaky as the rest of the place—but that's what everybody said.)

The blurry blob in front of her shifted into semi-focus of a dark outline of Luanna.

Oh good. She didn't need glasses.

Then her morning took a sudden downturn as her best friend demanded, "What the hell have you done?"

Chapter 2

$\mathcal{E}$venrude put a paw over her eyes when Luanna showed Chloe the online gossip page.

"I swear, nothing happened," Chloe repeated for the millionth time, or at least the nth time in the span it took her to get out of bed, escape to the bathroom to pee, splash cold water on her face, pop some much-needed Advil, and pull her hair up with a tortoiseshell butterfly clip because the feel of anything on her neck right now made her want to scream, and never mind that her hair was barely chin-length.

During all that, she'd carefully explained to Luanna how the evening had gone. Late arrival, wrong turn, red carpet, saved by a polite Ray, and retreat. The end.

"That's not what everybody else is saying," Luanna said.

Everybody else?

Which is when Luanna showed her the website.

Her stomach churned, but not from the effects of last night's wine.

> RAY DUMPS SANDRINE FOR MYSTERY DATE?
> Ray Stark showed up at the AAMies—where he went on to win Best Action Actor for his role in *Rode Hard*—with Chloe Montero, whom he introduced deliberately vaguely as "a new friend."

Montero.

"*Filho da puta*. Can't they even spell it right?" she muttered.

> The two were seen in an intimate embrace just inside the Shrine Auditorium, but Ms. Montero appears to have left soon thereafter and was not seen in the audience when Stark collected his Best Action Actor statue.
>
> Stark's long-time girlfriend, Sandrine Moss, was not present at the ceremony. When asked, Stark said she was resting.
>
> Ms. Moss has been recovering from a foot injury, which she suffered on the set of her last movie, the soon-to-be-released *Soul's Road*.
>
> Stark and Ms. Moss's relationship seemed rocky in its early years, but Stark recently moved into Ms. Moss's Bel Air estate and the couple seemed to be content. Stark's mystery date may be a sign that cracks are beginning to show.
>
> Ms. Moss's agent said her client had no comment at this time.

Accompanying the article was a picture of them on the red carpet, her hand tucked protectively in the crook of his arm.

Then, worse—far, far worse—a picture of him kissing her.

"Ray Stark kissed you!" Luanna's voice went up to a register that made the gorgeous but very old stained glass in the window rattle in its loose lead panes.

"Just on the cheek."

"It doesn't look that way to me."

And it didn't. The angle the photographer had found made the innocent, brotherly peck look steamy. Ray's head blocked hers just enough that it looked as though he was meeting her head-on, lip-to-lip. The casual arm he had around her had mutated into a groping hug that seemed to be pulling her against him.

"What are you going to do?" Luanna whispered.

"First, I'm going to sit down and put my head between my knees." Chloe did exactly that. Evenrude jumped up on the sofa next to her and lay down with a sigh.

"Here." Luanna reappeared with a tumbler of cold orange juice.

Chloe grabbed the glass with both hands and guzzled the juice like it was the first thing she'd had to drink after being trapped on *Survivor*. It felt like that, anyway.

It didn't ease the pounding in her skull, but it was still good.

That was when the phone started to ring. And ring. And ring…

*

Her horoscope that morning read, "Remember: The truth shall set you free."

That wouldn't be so hard. She already intended to tell nothing but the truth. Her mama had raised her to be an honest girl (with a healthy dollop of politeness—white lies were okay if they were employed to keep someone's feelings from getting hurt).

So when Luanna politely began to dissuade the third reporter who called, Chloe reached out for the phone. "Let me clear this up," she told her friend. "Once and for all. I'll get it over with, and then everybody will go away and it'll all be a bad memory, like that recipe I tried with catfish, molé sauce, and brie."

"Chloe Montiero," she said into the phone. "How may I help you?"

Her mama had also taught her that politeness, even feigned, was a virtue.

"Chloe, this is Grace Templeton with VH-1's *Hottest Entertainment News*. I'd like to ask you a few questions about your relationship with Ray Stark."

"Oh, we don't have a relationship."

"So it was a first date?"

"No, no, you've got it all wrong. It wasn't a date. I was there to cater—"

Okay, she'd accidentally been sent there to be a waitress. Which reminded her, she had to call MerryTemps and complain. Yes, she'd checked the box that said "food service experience," but she'd written right next to it that she meant cooking. Couldn't they read?

"To cater to Ray's needs?" Grace Templeton, girl reporter, asked.

"Good lord, no! I'm a *chef*."

"And that's how you know Ray?"

How much did she want to say? Getting locked outside the venue was pretty embarrassing. It shouldn't affect her ability to get a job or anything…but then again, if a potential employer heard about this, maybe they'd think she was flaky or something.

So much for falling off anybody's radar.

"In a manner of speaking, yes," she said. It wasn't a lie. She'd been there to cook, and that's how she'd run into Ray. No need to tell them about the getting-lost part, or the getting-locked-out part, and certainly not about the waitressing part. That was to keep her own feelings from getting hurt.

The cell phone buzzed in her hand, and she checked the display. Crap, it was her mother. It wasn't that she didn't want to talk to her mother; it was just that her mother would panic if Chloe didn't answer the phone. Because Chloe lived in Los Angeles now, and everyone knew Los Angeles was full of kooky people who would kidnap you and get you hooked on drugs and the next thing you knew you were a dried-up former porn star and current junkie starting the cycle all over again by preying on innocent newcomers.

She wasn't sure which part her mother was most concerned about, and she didn't dare ask. The bottom line was, if she didn't answer her phone, the downward spiral must already have begun.

"I'm sorry, Grace, but I have another call coming in," she said. "I hope I've cleared everything up. Thank you."

"Thank *you*." Grace sounded burblingly happy.

Chloe hung up and answered her mother's call. "Morning, Mama."

"Sweetie! Pumpkin! Chloe-pie! What's all this about you marrying some actor?"

Luanna handed her a fresh glass of orange juice and mouthed that she was going out for Krispy Kremes.

It was going to be a long morning.

*

Brand's phone sang the original *Star Trek* theme. Without taking his eyes from the thirty-inch flat-panel monitor that displayed the CGI magic he was creating, he answered.

"Brand? It's Olive."

His sister's personal assistant. Uh oh. She never called unless there was a problem with Sandrine that only he could handle. He sat up, dropping his feet to the floor, and glanced around. It was lunchtime, so half of his team members were gone and the other half were at their work stations in the open floor plan, slices of celebratory pizza in their left hands while with their rights they continued clicking and typing.

Joe had stopped in mid-chew to zoom in on some detail. Brand hoped he wouldn't drip cheese on his track pad.

He probably wouldn't be disturbed. He reached out and eased his office door closed.

"What's wrong?" he asked.

"Did you hear what happened last night?"

Last night his team had won a Best Special Effects AAMie for *Jane Austen in Space*, and there had been much carousing. His sister's beau, Ray Stark, had won the coveted Best Actor award, but by the time Brand had stumbled home, it had been too late for congratulations.

"I'm afraid to ask."

"Apparently some woman got lost and ended up on the red carpet, and Ray took pity on her. Next thing you know, there's a pap shot that makes it look like he's kissing her, and then Perez Hilton reported his usual half-correct info, and now VH-1…oh, it's probably already on YouTube."

Brand had already been accessing the gossip site, so he opened a new window and did the keyword search Olive suggested.

The boringly pretty VH-1 reporter said, "The mystery woman spotted with Ray Stark has identified herself as his personal chef. Given that Ray has taken up housekeeping with his girlfriend, starlet Sandrine Moss, it stands to reason that Chloe Montiero is cooking for both of them. It's still not clear what she was doing on the red carpet with Ray, but we can only guess that Sandrine's notoriously fussy eating habits have rubbed off on the action star."

Brand groaned. Sands had fired her latest in a long string of chefs last week, and thanks to the stories in the cooking community about her notoriously picky tastes, she hadn't found a replacement. That some woman was claiming to be the replacement was very, very bad.

Then the woman in question's face flashed up on the screen, a shot from the red carpet, and Brand's stomach dropped faster than Gandalf tumbling after the Balrog.

He knew that woman. She'd asked him for directions at the AAMies, and—it appeared now—he'd sent her the wrong way.

The camera pulled back. Her hand was tucked in Ray's arm, and Ray looked his usual easy-going self. The woman looked terrified and vaguely ill, but her chin was up, as if she were telling herself that she would get through this somehow, probably by sheer force of will.

He respected that, even as he wanted to reach through the computer screen and pluck her out of there and Make It All Go Away.

(And, he had to admit, he also wanted to pluck her out of there to find out if her curves really were as luscious as that flirty little green sundress indicated. He was, after all, a guy. And she was tempting and adorable and spunky.)

The new view was accompanied by voice-over of another conversation with her. She said, "…to cater—I'm a chef."

"And that's how you know Ray?" the VH-1 reporter's voice asked.

"—yes."

He cradled his forehead in his hand, shaking his head. Typical press and their soundbites. It was clear there had been much more to the conversation. Clear to anyone with half a brain, that was. The rest of the tabloid media, and a good portion of America, would take it at face value.

"Has Sands seen this?" he asked Olive.

"Not yet, but—"

In the background came a furious shriek. It almost sounded like one of the peacocks on the estate, but Brand knew better.

"She's seen it now," Olive said. "I'd better go. Ray and I will handle her. If not, I'll call you if you need to come home."

Brand opened his organization software and stared at the long list of things he had to do: mockups for the new movie, two employee reviews, check some dailies, and, oh, follow up on a slew of phone calls thanks to their AAMie. By all rights, he couldn't—as much as he wanted to—leave to go take care of his sister.

Responsibility tugged him in both directions.

He had to stay. But he was unable to resist doing a quick search for more clips and photos of the hapless but striking Chloe Montiero.

*

Chloe ignored the incessant ringing of her phone for several hours, through various relatives, Boston and Culinary Institute friends, and a couple of members of the press (including one fashion writer trying to find out more about Luanna).

She ignored them long enough to take Evenrude for a long walk to the farmer's market on the other side of town, where she looked longingly at beautiful produce and instead splurged on one 75-cent bunch of epa-zote to dress up tonight's Cheap Dinner Special of rice and black beans.

She ignored them long enough to get the already-cooked beans reheating with epazote and chilies.

She ignored them long enough to decide that a dollop of Trader Joe's Two-buck Chuck red would make the mixture taste better, and that since it was open, a drink was a reasonable investment in her obvious future career as an unemployed alcoholic.

Just as the first sips of the rough-but-fruity red were hitting—the alcohol hadn't taken effect but the idea of alcohol was already starting to relax her—the phone rang again.

"Go away!" she yelled, startling the drowsing Evenrude into a barking frenzy. "Just go away."

A crisp, professional voice came through the answering machine. "Hello. This is Olive Welsh, Sandrine Moss's personal assistant, calling for Chloe Montiero."

At least Chloe figured it had to be "Olive." The woman pronounced it Ah-*leave*, accent on the last syllable, so it took a few seconds to process.

At any other moment, Chloe would have been inclined to giggle. This was not one of those moments. This was one of those moments that made her inclined to throw up….

Acknowledgements

Just as a boutique hotel can't run without a staff, neither can a writer publish a book without the assistance of many magical folks.

Beta readers KJ Montgomery, Lisa Silverthorne, and Thea Hutchinson slipped between the pages to check out my technique. As always, my enthusiastic copyeditor, Colleen Kuehne, saved me from potential embarrassment while claiming to love every minute of it. Finally, a shout-out to Karen Purcell, DVM, for information on how to safely knock out a greyhound. Any errors still in the book are my own damn fault, probably because I was distracted by the voices in my head.

About the Author

Author of the 4-star (*Romantic Times*) novel *Cat Scratch Fever*, *Out of the Frying Pan*, and many short stories, Sophie Mouette is the brain-child of two widely published authors of erotica, romance, and speculative fiction.

The two halves of Sophie—Dayle A. Dermatis (aka Andrea Dale) and Teresa Noelle Roberts—met more than two decades ago at a writers' conference. Talking nonstop, they closed down the hotel bar and went somewhere else to keep on talking. Although they've always lived on opposite sides of the country (and for a few years, on opposite sides of the Atlantic), they've remained very close friends, and it was only natural that they should start writing together as well.

Sophie's latest novel, *Love, in Stitches*, is the second in the popular Hollywood Spice series.

Visit SophieMouette.com for more information.

www.ingramcontent.com/pod-product-compliance
Lightning Source LLC
Chambersburg PA
CBHW052045240626

47153CB00006B/2219